DRUNK SLUTTY ELF
And Other Stories

Funny Fantasy and Science Fiction

By

D. G. Valdron

FOSSIL COVE PRESS

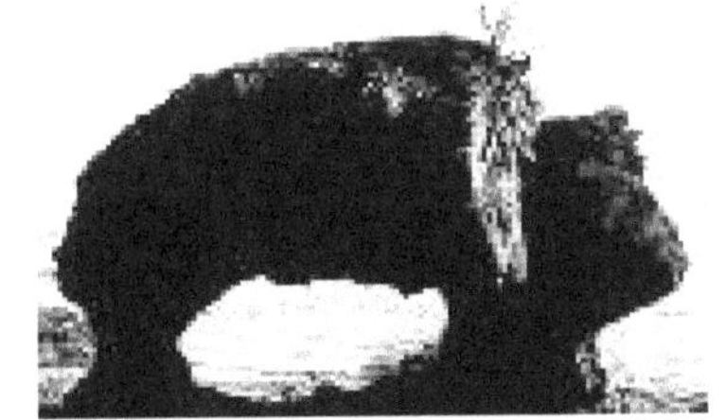

Winnipeg, Manitoba

DRUNK SLUTTY ELF
Table of Contents

Drunk Slutty Elf...1

Waiting For Gorgo.............................24

The Romance of the Undead...............36

Alice in the Mirror 48

Armageddon When? 60

Simulaw...73

Courtesy Call....................................84

Silver Giant Sexy 90

A Hard Day's Blight 100

The Furry Tentacles of Menace........... 113

Duty 130

The Revolution Begins With a Pause .. 144

The Monkey Sea.............................. 150

The Stone Blockage.......................... 158

The Princess So Sweet and Fair........... 166

The Voice from the Mantlepiece 180

The Djewel and the Djinn.................... 191

A Note and More Books by the
Author 230

Drunk Slutty Elf

Salvra, half-Elf, three-fifth's-Halfling, foursixteenth's Dwarf, exiled Princess and sixth level thief sidled up to the bar, where she tried to catch the eye of the one-third Orc, but otherwise pretty human bartender, Logo Longlegs.

The bartender gave her a baleful glare, his eyebrow furrowing in disgust.

"Here to clear up your tab?"

"I'm good for it," Salvra replied nonchalantly.

Longlegs grunted.

"Give me a mug of your best Aelvish Ale," she said confidently. "I'm a bit hung over, and I need a pick-me-up. On the tab."

"No."

"Dwarf Mead then," she said, "the good stuff!"

"No."

"Regular Dwarf Mead," she said.

"No."

"Beer?"

"No."

She sighed and gave him a cold look. Something that tried to convey 'If I weren't so hung over, I'd pick this place clean.'

It didn't work.

She sighed and felt through her purse. She thought she'd had more in there. Someone must have picked her pocket while she'd been drunk. She found a lone bent coin. She looked at it in disgust and slapped it on the bar. Longlegs eyed it doubtfully.

"What will this buy me?" she asked.

"A flagon of drunken Orc's piss," he said.

She wasn't sure if he was being sarcastic, but she decided to give it a try.

"I'll take it."

Longlegs grunted once. Using tongs, he tossed the coin into a small register, then he grabbed a mug and turned his back to her, fiddling with his trousers.

"Is this going to take long?" she said.

"No more than a minute," he called back to her. Then he sighed deeply, and she heard the hissing sound of the mug being filled. A second later, he turned back to her slapped the mug on the bar in front of her, careful not to spill any of the thick green liquid in it.

She eyed the mug critically. There was a good head of foam on it, which meant it was fresh. And there were things swimming in it. That was a good sign. She grabbed the handle, threw her head back, and quaffed a deep draught, gasping as the foul liquid slid down her throat. There was a moment when the rest of her stomach contents, appalled at this new visitor, tried to escape. But she'd been down this road before, and held her nostrils closed and lips sealed until everything, including her liver, had resigned itself to fate.

"I'm starting to like the taste," she said conversationally.

Longlegs gave her a long baleful look.

"There's work for you," he said.

She made a face.

"I'm a ninth level thief," she said, "and an exiled princess. I don't clean outhouses."

"Not what I meant."

Drunk Slutty Elf, Page 2

"Not that either!" she said indignantly.

"No," Longlegs said. "That guy."

He pointed.

She looked. In a corner of the bar, a figure was hunched over a table.

"Nah .. ." she said, after a long look. "I don't hook up with mysterious strangers in a bar, unless they're paying up front."

She hesitated.

"That didn't come out how I meant," she said apologetically.

He stared blankly at her.

"Oh all right." She swallowed the rest of her mug with one deep draught, and when she could breathe again, she ignored his horrified expression, and staggered over, plopping herself into the chair.

"I hear you're looking for a thief–" but her announcement trailed off as she got a good look at the stranger.

The being in front of her was gray. All gray. Its skin was rubbery. Its head was immense with two huge black almond shaped eyes. The rest of its facial features were tiny, the mouth a mere lipless slit, two tiny notches for nostrils. The rest of it was also incongruously off proportion with its head, the chest narrow, the limbs mere sticks, ending in hands with incredibly long spidery fingers. The sight of those fingers gave Salvra shivers. She wondered if other parts of him were as long and spidery.

"What the hell are you?" she asked breathlessly.

"I'm an Elf?"

"Nope."

"Drow?"

"Nope."

"Dwarf?"

"Nope."

"French?"

"Nope."

"Chartered accountant?"

"No such thing," she thought for a second. "Doesn't matter. Do you have money?"

"Yes."

"Excellent!" Salvra leaned back in her chair, waved her hand, and called, "Another round, the good stuff this time! He's paying!"

Turning her attention to the stranger, she demanded, "So what's your name."

"My species does not use personal names," he said. "We consider it primitive and insulting."

She thought about that.

"Hmm," she said, "we'll call you Darkeyes. Where are you from?"

"My ship suffered a reality core misfunction," he explained. "It descended from overspace, breaking up, and discorporated widely in this realm."

"Sailor then. Darkeyes, the Sailor man, that's you," she announced confidently.

"Not that kind of ship."

"I know all about sailor stuff: Swabbing! Poopdecks!" she said brightly.

"Not—"

"Arr arr matey!" she crowed. "Shiver me timbers! A pocket full of rum!"

"Not—"

"Where's your parrot? All sailors have parrots," she announced loudly.

"But—"

"And a pipe!"

"I left them all at home."

She nodded sagely. "I knew it. When you're a Master Thief, you don't miss much."

"Apparently," he said.

She stared.

"Funny how you talk without moving your lips," she observed.

"Telepathy."

"Pshaw!" she replied, "I know a ventriloquist when I see one."

The big almond eyes blinked once, and then he clearly decided not to pursue it.

"So," she said loudly enough to be heard several tables over, "you need a thief? You've come to the right place. Capable and discrete! I warn you though, I don't come cheap."

There was snickering from a nearby table. She glared, but didn't recognize any of them. Oh wait, that bachelor party! Joke was on them, she'd gotten all their wallets. There hadn't actually been any money in them, just a few coupons. But she considered it a success.

"Actually . . ." Darkeyes began. He made a move, as if to get away. Quickly, she laid a hand on his arm to fix him in place.

"Although my rates are quite reasonable," she followed up hurriedly, "and you won't find a better ninth level thief in the warrens."

"Ninth level?" Darkeyes seemed confused.

"I have a certificate," she said, and passed him over a card.

"It says fifth level."

She passed her other card.

"Fourth level."

"Fourth level plus fifth level equals ninth level," she announced.

"I'm not sure that's how it works," Darkeyes said. "Who certifies you?"

"Oh," she said, "that's simple. No one does. You steal your certificate from another thief. If you can get away with it, you're at that level."

The gray-skinned being stared at her. Its expression was impossible to read, and no ventriloquism uttered forth.

"All right," it said, after a distressingly long pause.

Longlegs brought the drinks. Salvra glanced approvingly at the two mugs. High quality Dwarf Mead. If only she still had taste buds. The bartender gave her another dismissive glance.

"Whatever price you agree to pay her, you pay it to me. I'll pass it on to her," he rumbled, "if anything's left, after I take what she owes."

The huge black eyes blinked, but again, no ventriloquism issued forth.

Salvra grabbed her flagon of mead, just in case the bartender was minded to take it away, and spat in it. Satisfied she'd established her claim, she took a deep drink.

"Don't mind him," she told Darkeyes, "we've got a thing going. There's a lot of unresolved sexual tension."

"No there isn't," Longlegs said. "It took me a week to get rid of the fungus infection."

"Worth every second," she replied.

"I stopped drinking after that," the bartender said, tersely. "I take opium to sleep at night."

He took his leave.

"So what's the steal?" she asked.

The gray-skinned creature's lips quavered, but there was no sound.

"I don't think I need a thief actually," he said.

"What?" she laughed. "Nonsense. Everyone needs a thief for something. Thieving is the biggest growth sector in the economy. If people couldn't steal . . . I don't know what they'd do? Work, I suppose. Buy things. You definitely need a thief! So no more shillyshallying, what's the job?"

"There is a person named Scabrous."

"The Malevolent?"

"Is there more than one?"

She swallowed her drink in one gulp, and tried not to look sick.

"Actually, yes," she said. "It was a popular name with mothers back when the pox came through. There's

Scabrous the Apothecary, Scabrous the Demented, Scabrous the Shoemaker, Scabrous Who Lives with his Aunt, Scabrous the Occasional Prostitute – she doesn't get much business."

She looked up hopefully, and said, "So . . . the deal would be to steal some nice shoes?"

"This Scabrous lives in a tower of black and purple stone, with a dark cloud perpetually above, and surrounded by hellish rape beasts."

"Oh him," she said, "well . . . Could I interest you in shoes instead?" she asked brightly. To emphasize her point, she reached into his robes and felt around. Always a sure-fire winner. There was nothing there. No anatomy. No reaction. Disturbed, she withdrew her hand.

"He has possession of an object I require," he said, ignoring the gesture.

"That would be the Paw of the Golden Monkey?"

"No."

"The Glistening Emerald Eye of Doom?"

"No."

"Nose-Pick of destiny?"

"No."

"Help me out here, Scabrous the Malevolent is a total pack rat when it comes to mystical junk. What exactly do you need stolen?"

Maintaining eye contact with the gray being, she switched her empty mug for his full one, sleight of hand being a particular skill of hers. Satisfied that he hadn't noticed, she spat in his drink and then put it to her lips.

"A tesseract information core," he said finally.

"Ah . . ." Salvra nodded wisely, taking another drink. He still wasn't noticing – she'd gotten away with it. She congratulated herself on being such a brilliant thief. "From the Gods?"

"No."

"Cursed?"

"No."

"Old family heirloom?"

"No."

"Any long and storied history at all?"

"No," he said. "Just a piece of technology."

She made a face.

"Monetary value?" she asked. "What's it worth in gold?"

"Irrelevant."

"So junk! What's the point of even stealing it? Who's even going to care?"

"It is a fragment of my ship," the gray being said.

Salvra rolled her eyes.

The being paused as if thinking it over.

"It holds great sentimental value for me," it said finally.

"Somehow," she said, "you don't strike me as a sentimental sort."

"Nevertheless."

"I charge double for sentimental steals," she said finally, "in advance."

"I will pay the bartender," he said.

Salvra kicked herself, he'd agreed far too readily. Should have tripled the price. She'd have to make it up somehow. She surreptitiously eyed the weightless bag of balloons that he seemed so fond of. Surely there was something valuable in there. Some perk or benefit that she could keep for herself, and that Logo Longlegs wouldn't cut himself in on.

"Go ahead," she waved, "he's right over there."

As an afterthought she called, "And have him bring more drinks. These were so full of foam they were practically empty. The cheat. These should be free!"

There was no expression, but she sensed something vaguely akin to distaste. The small gray creature slid off its chair and ambled over to the bar. Logo Longlegs bent down to talk to him. From his gestures, she could tell he was urgently trying to talk the creature out of something.

Excellent!

While they were distracted, Salvra toed the great leather sack of balloons closer to her. Surreptitiously, she undid the clasps that sealed the cover. Just a quick look inside, she thought, scope out any possible valuables, and then decide later what to take and how to fence it.

Without anyone noticing, very casually, she peeled back the cover, inclined her head, and took a peek. Odd. It was glowing...

And then she didn't have any thoughts at all.

***

". . . So as I was saying," Salvra continued, "you have what is essentially a post-scarcity society. With weak or nonexistent governmental structures, theft is the only reasonable way to effect the necessary equitable redistribution property. Ergo stealing is the basis of civilization."

"Why do you need redistribution in a post-scarcity economy?" Darkeyes complained. "Your whole economic structure makes no sense."

"Because otherwise you develop concentrations of wealth and power, and then you're back to a scarcitybased society. Every society requires a redistributive mechanism, and they stand or fall on the efficiency of those mechanisms. Nothing is more efficient than stealing."

She scratched her bum absently.

"You know," she said thoughtfully, "it's the weirdest thing. First my chrono said it was early-noon, and then suddenly it was mid-noon, my clothes were on backwards, and my bum hurts. Isn't that strange?"

The gray being absorbed this, eyes blinking thoughtfully.

"But aren't there alternatives to thievery?" he said quickly, with sudden enthusiasm.

Salvra shook herself. "Usually that happens when I'm drunk . . ."

"We were discussing economics?"

Drunk Slutty Elf, Page 9

"Oh right! Sure," she said cheerfully, "there are alternatives. Allowing unrestricted accumulation, well, that's never worked out. Mark my words, when a civilization allows a significant proportion of its wealth to concentrate in the hands of a fraction of a single percent of the population, that civilization is doomed. Hah! Primitives more like it.

"The first step to true civilization is robbery. Barge in, chop some heads off, take off with whatever you can carry."

"Seems barbaric."

"Barbarism is the foundation of Civilization," she offered primly.

"That sounds violent."

"And unhygienic," she agreed. "Thieving is much better. No one gets hurt, the rich are liberated from the burden of possession, the poor are ennobled. It all works out."

"It seems rather chaotic," Darkeyes groused.

"What's the alternative?" she asked. "Setting up a state to collect and redistribute wealth? Arrange for public projects? Social programs? Next thing you know, we have record keeping, which leads to bureaucracy, and then . . . socialism!"

She shuddered.

"I'll stick with honest thieving, thank you. You know the old saying... You can always trust a thief. Remember our motto: That hand in your pocket is a friendly hand."

"I thought that was the Prostitutes' Guild's motto."

"Sort of, they claim we're infringing. But we're litigating over it right now."

"You have lawyers?"

"We're a theft-based society! Of course we have lawyers! Oh look, we're here."

The gray being and the thief looked up at the great tower, a full eighty feet in height. Salvra pointed.

"See that window there, with the purple ledge," she told him. "That's the thieves' entrance. All we do is throw a rope with a grappling hook, and quietly rappel up the side."

She looked doubtfully at the gray. He had no discernible muscle on him.

"How are you at climbing? I can haul you up, but it will cost extra."

"Why not just go through the regular door?"

He pointed.

"It's probably locked."

He walked over and pushed. It opened.

"It's booby-trapped!"

The gray looked it up and down carefully. He tossed a pebble through the door.

"It's not."

Just then, a young man came by with a small flat box, from which the odor of cheese and fried meat wafted.

"Oh, hullo Salvra," he said. "Who's your friend?"

"Hi Wendell," she replied. "This is Darkeyes. He's a ventriloquist."

Wendell nodded cheerfully.

"I was just making a delivery," he said. "You setting up to rob the place?"

"You know how it is," she said, "it's the old in and out."

"I thought that was the Prostitutes' Guild?"

"No, we settled that one out of court, joint usage."

He nodded.

"Ah, I'll remember that." Wendell glanced up at the thieves' entrance. "Well, looks like you've got a climb ahead of you. Good luck."

Then he went in.

The gray being stared at her.

"Can we get on with it? My bum hurts when I'm standing still for some reason."

The climb, as it turned out, was not that arduous. The hook caught after only a half dozen tries, and Salvra carefully and quietly scaled the wall, with what she considered to be the epitome of feline grace, knocking over only a few stones, and disturbing a pack of crows, when she accidentally stepped in a nest and crushed some eggs.

Wendell left, waving to her as he proceeded down the path.

The ledge was covered with birdshit, unfortunately, causing her to lose balance, particularly with the egg yolk smeared under one boot. But luckily, she fell inwards, breaking her fall on some old furniture. After a successful penetration, she set up a rope and pulley system, so that she could haul up her thieve's gear and, finally, Darkeyes and his sack of balloons.

"We could have just used the door," the creature protested.

Salvra rolled her eyes, as she scraped birdshit off various parts of her clothing. It was amazing how it spread around.

"This is a lot more inconspicuous." She had to raise her voice because the crows still hadn't settled down yet.

The gray creature seemed unimpressed. Amateur, she told herself. No appreciation of the art and subtlety of a good heist. Why, this one was practically an award winner so far.

"So what now?"

"Now," she smiled dazzlingly, "we sneak into the Wizard's Treasure room, taking care not to disturb him or any of his traps, grab your time–" she hesitated "–and whatever tempting valuables there may be."

No response. Good. She figured she might throw some freelancing in on the side. Some clients were so narrow-minded. 'Take the gold rat, and only the gold rat,' and then later, as they were being chased down a sloping maze by giant rolling boulders, it would be nonstop complaining over some inoffensive trinket she'd pocketed along the way.

"How do we find it?"

Grinning, she produced a parchment from her jacket, wiping a bit of birdshit off. It got everywhere. Her boots were ruined; she'd have to steal another pair. She spread it out on the floor in front of them, pushing aside the broken pieces of furniture.

"All right, here," she said. "We go down three levels."

"So if we'd gone through the door, we'd only have needed to go up one level?"

Salvra rolled her eyes. "Down three levels, past the pit of acid on the left, then past the master bedroom."

"Why does Scabrous the Malevolent keep a pit of acid next to his bedroom?"

She didn't even bother to reply to that.

"Then down this corridor, down these stairs, into this chamber, then up the ladder, into the service tunnel, and then down the laundry chute. Avoiding this trap, of course... Wait, that's just a bug I squashed. Okay, this, this, and these are the traps. Got it?"

Although the creature had no expression at all, she could tell he looked dubious. Salvra grinned and patted him on his boneless shoulder.

"Trust me," she told him, "I know what I'm doing."

***

Scabrous the Malevolent was eating a slice of pizza in the kitchen when Salvra and Darkeyes walked in on him. The foul wizard was seated with one bandaged foot up on a chair. At the sight of them, he leaped to his feet, and began making a series of mystic gestures. Salvra's eyes bulged. Quick as lightning she reached for her pouch, but the dark sorcerer's magic was too fast. Both she and her companion were seized and lifted in tendrils of blue light.

"What are you doing in my kitchen? Why are you covered in birdshit?" Scabrous demanded. He glanced at Darkeyes, did a double take, and looked again. "And what the hell is that?"

"My client," she said. "He's a ventriloquist."

Drunk Slutty Elf, Page 13

"I've heard of those," he said, "in storied tales of yore. Where's his dummy?"

"He said it's with his parrot."

"Aha, a sailor? I'm surprised at you, Salvra."

"Why? I'm happy to accept seamen, for the right price," she retorted.

Scabrous rolled his eyes. "You know I'll have to report you to the Prostitutes' Guild for infringement."

"Oh come on!" she protested, "I've already three citations! One more and I'll be dragged up for a review hearing. Cut me a break."

"Never mind that," he said, "your petty disputes don't concern me. Why are you in my kitchen?"

"It's supposed to be your treasure room," she said. "Your architects have clearly made mistakes."

"What? Nonsense!"

"I have a map," she said primly.

Scabrous harrumphed, "We'll see. Hand it over."

She unfolded the parchment and passed it over to him. He examined it carefully, studying her notations.

"Ah," he said. "Here's your problem. You've been reading it upside down."

The gray glanced at Salvra, great almond eyes squinting. She affected her best 'I'm innocent, it could happen to anyone' look. It wasn't actually very effective.

"Wait," his brow furrowed angrily, continuing to examine the map. "I didn't put a trap here!"

Salvra looked over.

"Oh no," she said, "that's a bug I squashed."

The sorcerer gazed at the stained bit of parchment. "Are you sure?"

"Totally."

"Hmm," the wizard finally said, "all right."

"What happened to your foot?" Salvra asked.

"Mmm?" The wizard looked down. "Oh that? Stepped into one of my own traps."

"It's actually a leading cause of death for wizards," Salvra told the gray being. "Falling into their own traps."

"Perhaps," the gray said thoughtfully, "it might be best not to fill your home with random lethal death traps?"

Scabrous and Salvra stared at each other.

"You see what I have to put up with?" she said. "He's been like this since I met him."

She paused thoughtfully, seeing an opportunity to do some bonding. The ventriloquist was a dead fish anyway. Probably something to do with being a sailor, no sense of humour.

"So," Salvra said, "saw your nephew the other day."

"Oh," Scabrous said, "how's he doing?"

"Same as always," Salvra said, "can't decide what he wants to do with his life. One day it's paladin, the next day it's archer, the day after, he's decided to be a scribe. You know kids."

"He never comes to visit."

"Probably all the ravenous rape beasts," she said.

Scabrous shrugged, "Well, he'll never be a paladin if he's bothered by a few little ravenous rape beasts."

"He'll figure it out – we all do."

"I suppose," Scabrous sighed thoughtfully. Then he seemed to clear his head, focusing on the prisoners. "Well, it's all very nice chatting, but really, I should interrogate you. Why the birdshit?"

"Thieves' entrance."

"What? No! Thieves' entrance is the window on the second level, next to the guest bedroom." The malevolent wizard squinted. "Did you come in through the aviary? I have some prize crows nesting just below that. You didn't disturb them did you?"

"Uhm . . ." she said, "no. They were all out, before we got there. Flown off for something. Quite strange."

Her glance at Darkeyes pleaded 'Back me up!'

"Hmm," he said. "Treasure room. Usually you try to hit the wine cellar."

"Never!" she said.

"Every time," he said. "What do you want in the treasure room?"

He rubbed his chin, then snapped his fingers, with a look of elation.

"The Foreskin of Magnus Groan, Dark God of the Apocalypse."

"What?"

"Magnus Groan, Adversary of the Quoll Pantheon. Was going to destroy the universe, but then the other gods all piled on and dismembered him. His parts have been scattered to the four corners of the cosmos, and his acolytes ceaselessly search to recover and reassemble them.

"The legends say, if he is ever reassembled, then he will destroy the cosmos . . . or give everyone a kitten. The scrolls are obscure on this point, but apparently he was quite fond of kittens."

"No," Darkeyes said.

"No?" The dark wizard seemed disappointed.

"I require the return of a component of my ship," the gray said. He described it in detail.

"Oh," Scabrous said, "that's not in my treasure room. It's in my lab."

The gray turned its unblinking gaze upon Salvra. She shrugged elaborately.

"I like the blinking lights," he said. "They're pretty."

Darkeyes seemed to sigh.

"Each blink of light represents megaterabytes of information," he told them.

Scabrous thought about that. For a moment it looked like he was going to try and count it out on his fingers, but then he shrugged.

"Too bad," he said. "It's mine now."

He smiled.

"We are not pleased with these developments," the gray told Salvra. "We should have simply purchased it."

"If I wanted to sell," Scabrous pointed out. "I've become quite fond of it."

"Where's the fun in buying things?" Salvra sneered.

"Nevertheless," the gray being said, "we are captured, and facing an uncertain fate. This is not optimum. We are in the hands of a wizard."

"Well," she said, "he might kill us."

"I was thinking of it," Scabrous admitted.

"But usually in these situations," she said, "we buy our way free. If we have the gold."

She narrowed her eyes, and tried to whisper towards Scabrous, "He's loaded! Let's cut a deal, you and I, we'll split the take, sixty-forty."

"I'm standing right here," the gray being said.

"Right," Salvra said, sorry, "that's the easy way. Sometimes we'll just get a geas laid out, and have to do some sort of service. Usually it's pretty skill-specific. For me typically it's a mission of thievery."

"That's not what I heard," Scabrous said. "I heard you usually end up shoveling out stables."

He turned slightly as if to whisper, "She's actually quite good with the horses."

Then he did another double take. The gray creature was now standing normally with his sack of balloons. The twisting coils of blue magic, now reduced to threads, were dissipating even as they watched.

"Once!" she snapped, not noticing, "and it was part of my plan!"

She glanced over at Darkeyes, her eyes widened. "You couldn't get me out too?"

"Anyway," she said confidently, returning her gaze to Scabrous, "I'm sure we'll work out something."

She smiled and winked.

"I remember the last time we 'worked it out' after I caught you passed out in the wine cellar," Scabrous snarled. "You got cited by the Prostitutes' Guild, and I got a fungus that took a week to get rid of."

"But it was worth it!" she said brightly.

"I stopped drinking after that! I had to take opium to sleep. Never mind! I will not be distracted."

Scabrous shifted his gaze to peer suspiciously at the little gray being.

"There's no magic in you. You're not a mage, a sorcerer, a wizard, a cleric, an acolyte . . . How did you do that?"

The small gray creature shrugged.

"Any sufficiently complicated form of magic, no matter how ridiculous, is essentially technology," Darkeyes said.

Scabrous looked puzzled.

"What does that mean?"

Salvra had a sense that the little gray being was rolling its eyes, although of course, that was impossible, it was practically all eyes, and there were no whites anyway, so it was just rolling from black to black.

"Primitive cultures embrace magic as an uncontrolled and uncontrollable force. Magic is a thing of mysticism, unknowable, intuitive," it said, "with ambiguous applications and subtle unverifiable results. Advanced magic, no matter how preposterous and ludicrous the underlying principles, achieves measurable and tangible physical results, and thus requires management systems to operate . . . essentially software, and protocols for activation, namely forms of encryption – passwords and instructions, levels of authorization."

Scabrous looked blank.

"To use a phrase from a primitive pre-civilization," it said, "you don't have to be an electrical engineer to flick a light switch. Or computer genius to operate a remote control."

Scabrous looked to Salvra.

"Light switch? Computer? Remote control?"

"It's a sex thing," Salvra said with blithe assurance.

"Did you understand any of that?"

"Totally," she said confidently, "it's a nautical thing. I know all about seamen."

The little gray being stared at them.

"If I had emotions," it said, "I would hate this planet."

It paused, waiting for a reaction.

"You have no idea what a planet is, do you?"

"It's a recipe," Scabrous said confidently.

"No, no," Salvra told him. "Don't try and fake it. A planet is a green leafy vegetable with a pulpy fruit, used by sailors to ward off scurvy. They wear it in their shoes."

She smiled.

There was a long dead pause from the gray being.

"It's very impressive," she said, "how you can intensely not say anything, without moving your lips. That's high order ventriloquism."

For a moment, she felt a flash of irritation from the being's impassive face.

"I am not a sailor. My name is not Darkeyes, I have no name. This is not my world, this is not my civilization, you are not my species, you primitive screwheads. I am not human, or elf, dwarf, drow, stockbroker, halfling, muppet, or any other failure of local evolutionary processes. Any resemblance to human is a rather appalling coincidence. I am not from this section of space and time. Our race comes from Zeta Reticulon, we have crossed light years to assess and catalogue the mysteries of the universe, life in all its myriad forms, which unfortunately includes sample collection and species tagging, no matter how disgusting or hygiene deficient, you self-absorbed mounds of carbon sludge.

"I am not part of your primitive rudiment of a civilization, I have no interest in it. I do not care about your thieving, your enforced servitude, free market economy, socialism, feudalism, nor any other way you have organized your sexual practice. I have no interest in your drinking habits, your endless inane chatter, and the way you all pretend to be experts at everything despite your utter incompetence at anything. As far as I'm concerned, your planet made a horrible wrong turn at paramecium, and it's been downhill ever since, you hemorrhoid-based life forms.

"I crashed, my ship has been dismembered, and I need to retrieve the components in order to eventually return. I will do it, with or without the cooperation of life forms so rudimentary that they believe professional wrestling is real!"

They stared at him, astonished.

"You know," the wizard whispered, shaken, "I didn't see his lips move, not even a little."

"Yes," Salvra agreed, "it's pretty uncanny."

"Did you understand any of that?"

"Sailor talk," Salvra said confidently. "Something about parrots, ships, sea chanties, sails and whatnot. Also, he has to go to the bathroom."

"Enough of this!" Scabrous the Malevolent announced with sudden drama. He made a series of mystic gestures, comprising curling one hand into a claw, drawing the other arm back as if stringing a bow, and then tapping the side of his nose.

With a puff of brimstone, a demon materialized in front of them.

"I await your command," it said.

"A trans-universal automaton," the gray noted. "Simulant variety."

The gray being withdrew a small brightly colored object from its sack of balloons and pointed it.

A bright spot appeared on the demon's forehead. It was there for only a fraction of a second before the demon's brain was cooked. The creature didn't have time to cross its eyes before the laser burned through the bone, instantly turning cerebral matter into a puff of greasy putrid smoke, and punching out through the other side.

The demon toppled.

Scabrous stared at the quickly liquefying body in horror.

"What have you done?" he cried out. "Do you think open-ended service contracts for demonic intervention are cheap? I'm going to lose my deposit! And my insurance deductible!"

Scabrous turned angrily to the ventriloquist, a storm of magic gathering under his fingertips.

"Your entertaining party tricks will not save you now!" he thundered.

But the gray was ignoring him, and fiddling with another object from its bag.

Abruptly, Scabrous was distracted by sunshine coming through the window. He bent one eyebrow quizzically.

"Hello," he asked. "It was night, wasn't it? Does everyone remember it being night? I'm sure it was night?"

Salvra looked out the window.

"Yeah," she said, puzzled. "You're right. That's so strange."

"My ass hurts," Scabrous said.

"There's been a lot of that going around lately," Salvra said.

"Sample collection," Darkeyes said distractedly. Salvra and Scabrous glanced at each other; they had no idea what he was talking about. Somehow, they found they didn't want to guess.

The gray being was sitting on one of the kitchen chairs, his sack of balloons at his side. Salvra was beginning to suspect that whatever objects it contained, those things were not balloons. But if so, how could it be so weightless and bouyant? After a moment's thought, she decided it had something to do with nautical affairs, sails and ropes and funny knots and the like, and dismissed it from her thoughts.

On the table beside him was a strange object whose shape she could not decide upon. On one side, it emanated a series of lights.

There was a warm spot on her forehead. She touched it but there was nothing there. Glancing at Scabrous the

Malevolent, she noted that he had a glowing circle painted on his forehead. He reached up almost to touch it, as if it was warm. Then he glanced at her, and his eyes opened wide. He gulped.

The gray looked up, catching their expressions, and smiled for the first time.

"I believe that we are just about done here," he said. His large black eyes gazed at Scabrous. He held up a sheaf of papers.

"This appears to be the record of an auction manifest?"

"Yes, sir," Scabrous said.

"There are several items of interest here," the gray said, almost seeming to squint, "bid upon by a . . . 'Malbrous the Glandicular?'"

Salvra and Scabrous blanched, their faces going taut with terror. Salvra peed herself a little. So did Scabrous.

"The name rings a bell," Scabrous said, swallowing and looking around nervously.

"Please don't say it out loud again," Salvra said.

"The Masticator of Mazineland, Butcher of Broken Valley, Terror of the Nine Kingdoms. I hear he once ate a god."

"Castrated a god, actually," Scabrous corrected, "and then forced him to sing show tunes. Then ate him . . . slowly. When Malbrous died, they evacuated hell before he arrived, and locked the gates, until he got bored and returned to life."

"Meh," Salvra said. "Hell is a pretty fussy place; it's hard to get in, harder to stay."

"That's our next stop."

"Oh," said Scabrous. "Good luck."

"Oh yes," Salvra said quickly, "you'll do fine. Good luck, have a great time."

The gray looked directly at them.

"I said 'our' next stop."

The wizard and the thief glanced at each other in horror. The gray alien ignored their consternation, continuing to study the manifest.

"We're going to need a much bigger crew," Salvra said, "a fellowship."

The End

***

Waiting For Gorgo

The blacksmith's hammer gleamed in the fierce midday sun. Its final swing buried the seventh nail deep in the living rock, chaining the last of the condemned men to their fate.

Around him the hard-eyed men of the King's personal guard stood and watched. They neither approved nor disapproved; they were soldiers and they did their job. To each of the chained men they left a day's provisions and such weapons as they chose. Then when the smith had finished packing his tools they mounted their horses and rode off into the east.

"He'll be here soon," said the last of the horsemen. "Good luck."

They looked at each other, these seven condemned men.

"Well, here's another fine mess," said the fat one.

The largest of them swore as he grabbed a war axe and began hacking away at the chain that bound him to the canyon's wall. This was Ardaxe who had been a professional hero, and had been condemned to death for mislaying the honor of a no longer virginal princess.

The canyon rang with the frenzied clang of metal on metal. The others watched him apathetically.

"Ruining a fine edge there," commented one of the Rogue brothers.

"Yep," replied the other brother.

"Perhaps we can get free before he comes?" said the shortest and shiftiest of the lot. Blane had been the second-best pickpocket in the realm; his misfortune was that he tried harder. He spoke to Buky Truthteller, acknowledged to have been the cleverest man in the Kingdom, sentenced to death for giving the King a migraine.

From the west came the trumpeting of a war horn.

"I doubt it," answered Buky.

***

It had come to pass that the Emperor Mondal of the renowned Brone Empire had conceived a passion to build a tower to heaven. Heaven of course lay a good way off, and the edifice was less than half completed before he had exhausted his treasury.

Now a thing like this would have stopped a normal man. But Mondal was a man unlike other men, a hero as out of ages past, and not to be deterred by so trifling an obstacle. He resolved to war upon the other kingdoms of the world, stripping them of their wealth and enslaving their people. The tower commenced to grow again.

Now as things happened Mondal trampled almost every nation in the known world but one. So enthusiastically did Mondal pursue his project that he did what plague and famine could not in reversing the progress of civilization in the world. The one exception was the tiny Kingdom of Dumaund which lay at the eastern edges of the civilized world. Neither prosperous nor mighty it was obscure even to its neighbors; its trade was negligible, having but one gateway to civilization, a single tortuous canyon that gave passage through the Sheetrock Mountains.

So there came a time when Mondal, having still not completed his tower, and having looted almost every single kingdom in the world turned his eyes to the east...

Drunk Slutty Elf, Page 25

Now, as it happens, Dumaund in the east was well aware of Mondal's quest to reach heaven, which philosophers and theologians applauded and shopkeepers and masons considered a senseless waste of good building stone. Being largely out of the way made Mondal's undertaking a largely abstract matter for most people. They were aware as well of the activities he carried on to support his project and it is safe to say that the disapproval was universal. But there was no sentiment to act on that disapproval.

That Mondal might someday come for them, they did not for a moment imagine. The people of Dumaund were tranquil in the notion that disasters were what happened to other people.

Thus it came as a great and very public shock to the nation when a spy (Dumaund had always believed in keeping a prudent eye on its neighbors) came tearing through the stifling heat and swirling dust. He galloped through the capital's gates without so much as a by-your-leave and literally up to the steps of the palace before the horse died of exhaustion.

Bloody and broken, the spy staggered past startled palace guards and burst upon the King in the middle of his court. In an unforgivable breach of etiquette he blurted out his story and promptly died of his wounds.

Mondal was coming, and he was only a day away.

The King of course, panicked, and the nation followed suit. Mondal was coming.

The King's generals were by and large a more laconic group. True, Mondal had never lost, but it seemed reasonable to assume he had to do it sometime, and this was as good a time as any. They were confident of their ability, in an abstract way, to defend the Kingdom. The trouble was that a day or less was simply not enough time to properly prepare a defense. Perhaps the King, as one ruler to another, could ask Mondal to wait a day?

The King briefly contemplated making this request of a man who had raged up and down the civilized world like a mad dog, in a quest to build a tower to a place he had already sent thousands of his enemies.

He panicked again.

Well, said the Generals, perhaps he could be delayed. It was pointed out that there was only one entrance to the Kingdom, and while it could not be blocked, there were points here and there where a handful of men might hold a vastly superior force for a day or so. There would be no question of supplying or rescuing such a force and their ultimate death would be as horrifying as it was certain, but it might save the Kingdom.

Out went the call.

Nobody answered.

It is not to be said that the people of Dumaund are any less brave or heroic than the people of other nations. In fact, they come off quite well on that score. But the task called for far more than mere heroism. Specifically, it called for stupidity of the highest order.

Faced with less than twenty-four hours to live, the people of the Kingdom decided that there were far more important things to do than prematurely give it up facing a horde of bloodthirsty maniacs in the middle of nowhere. It has been written that during that night in the Kingdom more people found God or lost their virginity than any other day in the Kingdom's history, before or since.

The King, having no volunteers, selected ten condemned criminals. To ensure that they would not run away, which he certainly would have done in their position, he commanded that they be chained to the Canyon.

The people were disappointed by this news as there is nothing like a good public execution to take your mind off your problems. But war called for sacrifices, and they bore it well.

Drunk Slutty Elf, Page 27

There was little likelihood of the convicts surrendering and granting easy passage. It was well known that if there was anything Mondal hated more than enemies, it was cowards. Much of the devastation that Mondal had wreaked could be attributed to the fact that at some point or other while he was pummeling them, his foes would try to surrender, and really make him mad.

Which brings us back to our reluctant heroes.

***

The scouting party burst into view. As their horses reared in surprise, they briefly assessed the situation and then retreated back to the main army.

Ardaxe, sweating and strained, had given up trying to chop through the chain, but otherwise their attitudes were unchanged.

"Maybe we should surrender in exchange for a quick painless death," Blane wondered out loud.

"Perhaps I can get us out of this," said Buky.

The others looked at him with a flicker of hope.

"But to do so, you must all drop your weapons and do not speak except as I give you leave."

***

Thus it was that when Mondal, riding a pure white charger at the head of his host, came upon the convicts they were sitting in the sand, weapons of all sorts scattered about them, their heads hanging in despair.

"Who are you?" boomed Mondal who had been expecting more spirited resistance.

"We are dead men," answered Buky, looking up.

"How perceptive," snarled Mondal as he drew his sword and advanced on them.

"Who are you?" Buky asked, without apparent enthusiasm.

This stopped Mondal for a moment; he could not imagine anyone not having heard of him. Truth be told, Mondal was a bit full of himself. He certainly could not fathom what these men might be doing chained in to the gray rock of the Canyon if not for some purpose meant to frustrate him.

"I am Mondal the Destroyer, Ravager of Nations, Despoiler of Kings, Mondal the Great, Mondal the Fearless, Mondal who shall one day walk into heaven and sit with the gods, Mondal who has come to destroy your land and bend your wealth and people to my quest . . ." This was said with some enthusiasm, and truth be told, went on for quite a long time. Although he would never admit it, Mondal loved the sound of it all, and introduced himself at every opportunity. This was why he loved parties, although he was saddened that he wasn't invited as often as he would have liked.

"That's interesting," said Buky, without apparent enthusiasm.

Mondal had received many different responses over the years. But indifference was a new and intolerable one. He cantered his charger forward and raised his sword for a blow to send the insulting fool's head rolling from his shoulders.

That was when he made his fatal mistake.

"What are you doing here?" he asked Buky, just as he was about to cleave his head.

"We're waiting for Gorgo," Buky replied, and shuddered.

It was that fateful shudder that stopped the death blow. That put Mondal on the road to ruin. He could still have recovered, could still have taken a mighty swing and then rode with his army over the bodies. He could have taken the Kingdom unprepared and crushed and looted it. He could have done all these things.

But instead he asked the question.

"Who's Gorgo?" he asked.

And was lost.

"Gorgo," Buky answered, "is the giant monster that terrorizes our land. He is fond of human flesh, so we are chained out here as sacrifices to the beast."

Drunk Slutty Elf, Page 29

Now Mondal was no more stupid than the next man. He knew very well that there were monsters, and that many of them prized human flesh. Why, he had slain a few dragons himself in his day. But this seemed a bit much.

"All seven of you?" he asked incredulously.

"A light snack," explained Buky, who seemed the only one willing to talk. The others were in a thorough funk over their fate.

Mondal hemmed and hawed suspiciously.

He wanted to pluck the kingdom like a ripe fruit. This delay was intolerable. He looked around.

No sign of a monster.

But quite a lot of gear.

"What are all these weapons then?" he demanded. "You look pretty well armed for sacrifices."

"It's a tradition; our families bring them to us so we can kill ourselves before the beast devours us."

"All these weapons?" he asked suspiciously. "It looks like you have enough to fight an army here."

"Well, of course we are not the first to be sacrificed to the monster."

Buky stood up, sighing as if rousing himself from despair, in order to be a good host to a rather demanding guest.

"Each fallen weapon represents a noble sacrifice. Each tells a story."

Buky grabbed Mondal and pointed, "See that great broadsword there . . . it belonged to Omab the Mighty. Of his own free will he came here to slay Gorgo. But the sight of the monster so terrified him that he cut off his head."

"He cut off his own head?" repeated Mondal suspiciously. He stared hard at the man. Buky seemed absolutely sincere, but it was too much to grant.

"It is said that he waited until he could smell the fetid breath of the creature, watch the drool dripping from that cavernous mouth, before he finally did it."

"It looks nicked, and its edge seems blunted." Mondal said with what remained of his critical faculties.

"That's because Omab was wearing an Iron Collar. They say it took him two or three strokes to cut off his head," replied Buky glibly.

Mondal searched his face, looking for any hint of falsehood. Buky figured it was time to move along. He picked up a small knife.

"This," he announced, "is the knife of Bittindon the famous carpenter. In the face of the beast he whittled himself to death."

"Well then, where are the bodies?" Mondal asked.

Buky shrugged laconically. "Gorgo leaves nothing but the weapons behind. We think he spits them out."

Mondal could scarcely credit this; all the monsters he had ever heard of had been messy eaters. Truth to tell, his own table manners were far from the best, but he hadn't thought of any connection.

"That's all he leaves behind! I don't believe it!"

"Gorgo is quite voracious. Did you see smooth areas on the canyon walls as you came in?"

Mondal replied that he had. He had never heard of water erosion.

"That" Buky assured him "is where Gorgo espied something, perhaps a small lizard, perhaps a scorpion, perhaps merely a hanging lichen, and licked it off with his rasping tongue. Gorgo's hunger knows no bounds."

It was at this point that Mondal noticed that the canyon walls in this area were almost universally smooth. In spite of himself he was getting nervous. It was time to attack.

"Rot this," he boomed. "I'm here and I have my army with me. I'll slay this beast and be on my way."

To his surprise Buky embraced him. Technically, he embraced his leg, since Mondal was on horseback, and laid a series of passionate kisses from his thigh to just above his ankle. It made Mondal feel rather peculiar in his trousers, and truthfully, he was a tiny bit disappointed when Buky stopped kissing parts of his body. Shaking his fist in the air, Buky sang out.

"Three cheers for great . . . err what was your name again . . . (the Emperor gave it.) Mondal! Three cheers for Mondal the Mighty! He has come to free us from the beast."

The other prisoners showed animation for the first time as they got to their feet and cheered loudly.

Buky embraced Mondal's leg again, while Mondal's horse looked askance, and then the young man fell to his knees. He kissed Mondal's feet and looked up, tears brimming in his eyes.

"Oh, I should have known you were a hero like those out of legend. Why, you are the spitting image of the great hero King Lokadion (though not so tall or broad), who went out to slay the monster with thirty thousand horsemen and fifty thousand pikemen."

Mondal did a quick calculation. That was a force fully two thirds larger than his own.

"How did he fare?" Mondal asked.

"Magnificently – why for a full month Gorgo was spitting out weapons and hardly ate anyone. I'm certain that you will do even better. After all, Gorgo has gotten older," Buky paused thoughtfully, "and bigger, much bigger as well. But more importantly older. So it stands to reason he has slowed down. Perhaps become weaker with age. Theoretically."

"Mmm," mmmed Mondal. "Just how big is this Gorgo?"

"Ahh," said Buky "that is a good question, for none that get a good look at Gorgo live to tell of it. It is my considered opinion that he is probably smaller than a medium sized mountain."

"You just said he eats small lizards?" Mondal accused.

"As a man eats sesame seeds," Buky replied.

But Mondal's skepticism had returned.

"People have visited Dumaund for hundreds of years. How is it that nobody else has reported this monster?"

"We keep it a secret of course. Otherwise no one would come here. For many years visitors have helped us feed this monster," Buky shrugged eloquently and continued. "But what of it? You are on your way to slay the beast, I'm sure you must be quite eager. Don't mind us, just go on through. We'll wait here."

This was almost too much for Mondal.

"Are you saying you sacrifice visiting foreigners to the beast?" Mondal was not particularly outraged; it was the sort of thing he would have done himself.

"Some. Others Gorgo finds for himself."

"Wouldn't your neighbors notice that people weren't coming back?"

"Well of course we don't sacrifice them all. Why for each foreigner sacrificed a second and even a third are well treated and allowed to go their way, to lure more foreigners back. It's worked quite well so far."

Buky sighed happily.

"But now all that is over. You are here to slay the Monster." He looked up at Mondal. "A word of advice, Gorgo's hearing and scent are extremely keen, if you wish to sneak up on him you must do so quietly."

"My spies didn't report this monster." he said petulantly. There was still doubt in his mind, but if in fact there was such a monster he was going to have his intelligence chief executed.

"Have all of them returned to you?" Buky asked.

Mondal suddenly realized, with a sinking certainty that three had not.

Now in truth, the first of these spies had slipped on a patch of scented oil while exiting the public bath with very important information. He was never exposed as a spy. Instead, he was buried with full honors and had many powerful and important personages as mourners.

The second agent had taken the gold, which he was to use for bribery, and entered Madame Livonia's House of a Thousand Illicit Pleasures (cynics said it was only seven hundred or so, but that is neither here nor there) and had not at this date exited. In fact, at the moment Mondal was speaking in the dust of the Canyon, the spy was taking advantage of some extraordinary "end of the world" sales.

The third had, through no fault of his own, become completely lost, and now wandered far beyond the boundaries of the known world. He was about to embark on a terrific series of adventures, which unfortunately are not the subject of this story.

Mondal knew none of these things, of course. What he did know was that before him lay a ravenous and seemingly invulnerable monster, and behind him lay his beloved tower, still not completed, and crying out for his attention.

Without a word, Mondal mounted his charger and trotted back the way he came. His mighty army followed him.

"Wait! Wait! Where are you going?" shouted Buky. "The monster is the other way!"

Mondal ignored him, except to pick up his pace a bit.

"Come back. Please come back!" screamed Buky. Around him his chained companions were rising in a chorus, yelling for the army to return and slay the monster.

"Or at least feed it!"

"I lied," yelled Buky. "There is no monster. Really. We were chained here to stop your progress. Please, won't you come back?"

If Mondal heard this it only added paranoid fire to his delusions. He spurred his horse onward. As the shouting of the men behind grew louder the whole army broke into a dead run, lest the noise attract Gorgo prematurely.

Slowly their calls faded as they watched the dust settle behind the fleeing army. Buky licked his lips.

"I told them the truth at the end," he said.

***

It has been written that Mondal returned to Brone to continue work on his tower. His subjects finally tired of him, and assisted him in arriving at heaven in a more conventional manner than he had planned on. However, as he had always believed that the ends justified the means, it could not be said that he had been wronged.

The people of Brone, without Mondal to drive them on, lapsed into a friendly and contented tranquility. Civilization eventually returned to the known world. The unfinished Tower became a major tourist attraction. Many said that from its top they could just make out Mondal in heaven being pursued by legions of his victims.

The Kingdom of Dumaund waited three full days for the attack that never came. Finally they investigated and found no trace of an invading army. They concluded that it had all been an elaborate hoax. The rest of their history is one of peace and prosperity, though sometimes they did stop to wonder why no one ever came to visit anymore.

Of the seven who were chained and waiting, only a few broken metal links were found. Nothing more is written.

The End

***

The Romance of the Undead

Rutger's coffin lay in its new resting place for four days before the Vampire hunters discovered him. They were all waiting around the coffin as the sun vanished beneath the horizon.

Rutger pulled himself from his casket, mouth fuzzy with that moldy smell that came from lying dead on top of your grave soil. He heard the whir of a cheap camcorder. Baring his teeth, he looked from one to the other. They were all there, Bran, Leroy, Contessa, Bela, Ihor and the others, all dressed in black with their sepulchral pancake makeup. Bran, he noted with particular disgust had sprinkled glitter.

"Can't you leave me with at least a little bit of dignity? Why are you here?" he snarled. "Don't you people have lives?"

"So, what will you be doing tonight?" Ihor asked. They were immune to insult, Ihor particularly. He was a fat and ungainly lout with coke bottle glasses, and an appalling command of trivia.

"I hunt," Rutger said simply. He wished they would go away.

"Can that thing record me?" he indicated the camcorder suspiciously.

"Actually," Bran said, "all we get is a blur, but it's a neat effect."

"Can we come with you?" Leroy asked, licking his lips. "We'd like to watch."

Leroy had a straggly mustache, but otherwise was nondescript. He needed to bathe more often. Rutger thought of Leroy as the pest most likely to become a serial killer.

"No," he told them.

I should kill them all, he thought, not for the first time. I should have killed them the first time I noticed them skulking around.

But it had been too late even then, he thought sourly. It had all been recorded and referenced. There were detailed descriptions of him and his activities in sealed envelopes and hidden places, all ready to reach interested parties should any of them disappear.

They'd made that clear in those first encounters.

Not that they were threatening him, they'd hastened to add. They were big fans of his, or of what he was. They'd seen all the movies, read all the books, they even tried to dress the part.

"Actually," Bela said, "we'd like you to come to my place. We're going to hold a special ceremony."

Bela was small and weasely. Rutger was sure that Bela was not his real name, but rather he chose to model himself after his favorite character. To Rutger, he looked more like a Renfield.

"About your clothes . . ." Ihor was saying as they tagged along after him.

Not that again.

"What?" It was no use trying to ditch them; they'd shown a disquieting ability to find him wherever he hid. He could, he supposed, outdistance them. But you can't feed at a dead run. There was nothing to do but hope they would go away.

"Why don't you dress better, like in the movies?" Ihor asked.

"Yeah," Leroy put in, "cool threads, a bitching leather jacket and some hot cowboy boots."

"No," Ihor said, "I mean something classy, like a tailored suit, or a tux."

Perhaps with an opera cape? Rutger thought. No thanks. He didn't want people noticing him because he was well dressed. He preferred something plain and unassuming. Blue jeans and a bomber jacket worked nicely.

"Jet black," the Contessa said huskily, "like night."

Like your lipstick, Rutger bit back. The Contessa was the tallest of the group, edging out Bran by a good couple of inches. As far as he could tell, her entire wardrobe was black, all her tops and dresses were low cut, and she didn't seem to own a bra. She cultivated a superior reserve that was abandoned any time one of them came up with an idea.

"Can you transform into a wolf?" Bran asked.

"Yes."

"What about a Rottweiler?"

"A what?"

"It's a kind of dog?"

"I don't do dogs," Rutger said brusquely.

It had been a mistake to let them coax him into the arduous transformation into a bat.

"What about a goat?"

"I don't know," he said irritably.

"A giraffe?" Ihor asked.

Rutger stopped and starred at him.

"You know," Ihor whimpered, "an animal bigger than you."

Rutger looked at him coldly, and then started walking again.

"Can you transform into any animal," Bran was asking, while Rutger did his best to pretend that he wasn't in the group, "or are you restricted to predators?"

Rutger stopped again, and faced them all.

"Look," he said, "stop following me. I have to hunt."

"If we leave you alone, will you come to our ceremony?" Bela quavered.

This is what I am reduced to, Rutger thought, bargaining with imbeciles.

"All right," he said grudgingly.

Bela grinned. "Eleven thirty, my place, apartment thirteen thirteen, six sixty four, the Rice building."

The 'Rice' building? Rutger rolled his eyes. Bram Stoker Estates must be full. Where did they find these things? Why?

"I'll be there."

"Do not feed too deeply," the Contessa whispered, "There will be . . . refreshment."

He turned his back on them and stalked off, listening for footsteps after him. There were none.

How did they keep finding him? he wondered. Perhaps they'd hidden one of those radio transmitter tags on his person or coffin, like they did on Wild Kingdom. He found the idea profoundly disquieting.

Hunting was lousy. Hunting had been lousy since they had started following him around. Once again, he contemplated pulling up stakes, moving to another city.

Around ten thirty he found a victim, a man walking back from a convenience store. It was usually best to disguise these things as muggings. Rutger raced up behind the man, clouting him under his left ear as he turned. The blow opened a small wound. Rutger pulled the limp form behind a dumpster and spent five minutes licking blood from the wound before a passing car drove him away.

As he flitted down shadowed back alleys, Rutger checked the man's wallet. Only fourteen dollars. He almost threw it away.

He sighed. It was almost time to go. He wondered about the 'refreshment.'

He found the Rice building without difficulty. For a split second he considered scaling the outside of the building and entering that way. But no one put apartment numbers on their balconies or bedroom windows, and that had resulted in awkward moments in the past. He took the elevator and walked down the hall counting apartment numbers.

The door opened before he could knock.

Of course.

"Enter freely and of your own will," Bela told him.

Had he obtained that from some book? Rutger wondered.

"Stuff it," Rutger said as he shouldered past.

"I'm so glad you came," Bela gushed.

Rutger walked into the modest one bedroom apartment. They were all there, the whole cursed gang of them. The walls were lined with bookcases, above which were movie posters. Coppola's Dracula, Langella's Dracula, Bela Lugosi as Dracula, Abbot and Costello meet Dracula ad infinitum ad nauseam. Next to the television, there was a thick stack of antique DVD's, Rutger hardly needed to guess. Beside the stack was the Twilight Special Memorial Commemorative Blue Ray package, still in the original wrapper.

They went into the bedroom, it wasn't much better.

"I've got such things to show you," Bela was saying, "you wouldn't believe some of the things I've collected."

"A rare first edition of Bram Stoker's laundry list," Rutger sneered, "or perhaps an autographed Anne Rice paperback?"

Bela's eyes got huge. "Wow, you're good."

The bathroom door opened. Rutger turned as a figure stepped into the bedroom.

"A little whore d'evour," the Contessa said.

He hated puns.

The rubenesque blonde with her tittered in with excitement.

"We kind of had the impression hunting hadn't been going well lately," Bran explained.

I wonder why, Rutger thought, but bit the words back.

Drunk Slutty Elf, Page 40

The blonde grinned and waved.

Huge hair was the first thing he noticed. Massive peroxide locks, rigid from hair spray. The second thing was immense and improbably buoyant breasts spilling out of a tight sequined dress bursting at the seams. She had blunt features obscured by makeup. He decided she'd never be beautiful, but in the right light, might have been pretty.

"Rutger van Helsing," Ihor introduced him.

"Halsey," Rutger corrected.

"Van Halsey," Ihor amended.

Rutger gave up. Might as well go with it.

"Let me introduce you to Crystal Bathory, who gives her blood for your revel," Ihor concluded.

"Charmed," she said, holding her hand out, knuckles slightly arched. Did she expect him to kiss it? He had no idea where that hand had been or what she'd been doing with it. He shook it gently.

Just because he drank blood, he wasn't supposed to be fastidious?

"Actually," she simpered, "that's my Vampire name. My real name is Ruth Anne Simpson."

Vampire name? Rutger wondered. What was he supposed to say to something like that?

"I will drink your blood," he mumbled, trying to be polite.

She almost swooned.

"I will be yours," she moaned.

Rutger stepped toward her, uncomfortable in the circle of gawkers. He felt way too exposed and awkward. Feeding should be a private thing, he thought, most of the time even his victims were unconscious.

What if they scored him? Feeding and technique, he had a horrible mental image of them holding up cards with numbers, like in figure skating contests. He hoped at least he'd get a good score.

"Wait," she said, "I have to take off my clothes first."

"What?" he asked, looking around.

"I need to be devoured nude," she said.

Rutger was confused.

"That's not really necessary," he tried to explain. But she was already peeling out of her overtight dress, sequins were literally flying off. Did she want him to bite some particular area? The possibilities made him blanche. He'd draw the line; he had to draw the line somewhere.

Leroy stepped forward, as Ihor helped Crystal or whatever her name was, struggle out of her dress.

"She wants to be sky clad for it. This will be the first time Crystal's been bitten by a vampire and she wants the ritual to be perfect."

Ritual?

"Very well," he replied with misgivings.

Naked, Crystal proved to be a slightly fleshy girl with a large muscular rump. No underwear. He noted that her thatch of pubic hair was an entirely different shade.

Is this supposed to arouse me? He wondered.

Stretch marks on the hips, skin blemishes, fugitive body hairs standing black and defiant, dimpled knees, the smell of deodorants and shampoos, and under that armpit scents and a fast nervous sweat. He found nothing appealing about the human body and its cavalcade of imperfections.

Ah well, he'd had worse, he decided. The trick was not to dwell on these things when feeding.

"I have a poem I'd like to read first," she said. She cleared her throat, closed her eyes and began to recite.

Oh my God, he thought, kill me now.

Still, the poem with its infantile symbolism and fractured meter was mercifully short, so he stood awkwardly trying not to focus on any of the words and fixed his eye on the light stand on the bedside table.

She crawled to the center of the bed and assumed a half supine pose.

"I'm ready to surrender myself to the kiss of darkness," she quavered.

It was lucky, he decided, that Vampires didn't blush. Still, he found himself lowering his head and scratching at his hairline.

They were all gathered around the bed waiting expectantly.

"Very well," he said. He climbed onto the bed, clambering until he was next to her. Standing on his knees he towered over her as she batted cow eyes at him.

What did they expect? He wondered. Experimentally, he bared his fangs and grasped her shoulders.

She gasped, "His hands, like ice from the grave, seize me in bonds of iron."

Please stop, he thought.

What if she had another poem for when he was biting her?

It was lucky Vampires couldn't vomit.

He bent down over her, she threw back her head, exposing her neck, artery pulsing.

No way, he thought. In movies they always went for the neck. In real life, that was disastrous. For one thing, it would be hard to leave a more obvious mark. For another there was always the danger of crushing the esophagus, inflicting inadvertent whiplash, or worst of all, hitting the artery. You could lose a good shirt hitting the artery. Necks were bad, they were messy, obvious and, all too often, ultimately fatal for all involved.

He usually preferred to make a scratch on some less obvious area and suck away slowly. Scalp wounds were good, they bled like the dickens. Of course, that wouldn't be sexy enough for them. Mind you, torsos weren't too bad, nor were arms and legs.

Someone coughed.

Where to bite? They'd probably want him to sink right in, like in the movies. It wasn't an especially efficient way to draw blood. He much preferred a superficial incision with one fang.

Drunk Slutty Elf, Page 43

They'd probably want him to use both fangs. Why not just tattoo "Vampire" above the mark, he thought sarcastically. But he held his tongue; no point in giving them ideas.

He eyed her form doubtfully.

He hated it when his fang scraped bone, it was like biting tinfoil, he could feel the vibration all the way to the back of his skull. No one ever realized how delicate and sensitive a Vampire's fangs were. The breasts looked safest. Gingerly, he bit down.

She arched her back and let out a deep sigh.

Give me a break, he thought, rolling his eyes.

"Teeth penetrate my flesh; there is a sharp stabbing sensation, which is fading to a warm ache. Cold shivers run up and down my spine. My nipples harden and I feel an electric tingling in the pit of my stomach."

Please shut up, he thought. She was doing it.

He'd been afraid of this and here it was.

Was that poetry? It didn't rhyme. Free verse? He wished she would stop. His jaw worked slowly as he began to suck.

"I am mere sustenance for the beast at my breast. How can I describe the sensation as my being, my essence, passes remorselessly into him. He battens on my soul."

Abruptly his mouth filled with a strange viscous liquid. Gagging in panic he detached from her, staggering off the bed. Bent over he hacked and coughed, expelling what seemed like a thick translucent medium.

"What?" he snarled, gasping. "What was that?"

From the bed, she screamed in what was now genuine terror.

"Oh my god, he bit my implant. I'm leaking. I'm leaking."

He looked back. She was screaming and writhing around in bed as Bran and Ihor attempted to comfort her. As she clutched her breast he could see more clear thick fluid oozing out like transparent toothpaste.

"These things cause cancer!" she screamed.

"It's okay," Bela yelled back at her, "I've got a repair kit in my bicycle; we can just patch it for you."

"Are you stupid? Get me to a hospital."

"Stop squeezing it like that," Brain cautioned, "you're forcing it out."

As he watched amazed, he realized that, yes, her breasts were now noticeably lopsided. The humans thrashed about on the bed as it became increasingly slippery with blood and silicone. The rising level of panic engulfed them all.

He realized, suddenly, none of them were paying attention to him.

As quietly as he could, he turned around and walked out of the room. Bela rushed past him into the living room to grapple with the lock on his bicycle's emergency kit, blocking the doorway. Casually Rutger stepped through the sliding glass doors to the balcony.

The cold night air greeted him like a friend. He could scurry down the side of the building and be gone an hour before they noticed.

"What fools these mortals be," a husky voice murmured.

He jumped.

The Contessa stood there, leaning against one wall of the balcony, smoking a cigarette from a long holder. She wore black satin evening gloves that came half way up her arms, and her usual low cut black gown.

They looked at each other.

"I came out to get away from the confusion," he told her, hoping she would believe him.

"I'm sure you aren't impressed with that childish display any more than I am," she said, "the puerile acting out of adolescent fantasies."

He suspected that she knew a lot more about puerile adolescent fantasies than she would have admitted. He remained silent.

"They're so hopeless," she said, "I don't know why I even hang out with them. 'The Contessa, Queen of the Nerds.'"

She laughed.

"Still," she intoned, "they brought us together."

"Well . . ." he said carefully.

Here it comes, he thought sourly.

"Take me," she said, baring her breasts. Rutger noticed she'd apparently stained her nipples black. He shuddered. "Make me one with you! Initiate me into the mysteries of darkness! Make me a Vampire so that we may hunt the eternal night forever. Seduce me."

I could just push her over the balcony, he thought desperately. It could pass as a regular accident. But he realized that it wouldn't work. The others inside would know, and sooner or later, he would be destroyed.

"I can't make you a Vampire. It doesn't work that way," he said desperately. "You've got it all wrong; It's not a romantic existence."

"Listen," he tried to explain to her, "I don't seduce my victims. They're food. I don't have relationships with them any more than you have relationships with Big Macs.

"Who wants to have a deep spiritual dialogue with a Thanksgiving turkey? You eat it, that's all. You don't take it home and make friends with it. I don't relate to my victims, I don't talk to them. I don't even like talking to people."

"But you can't deny the intimacy of the event," she persisted.

"What intimacy?" he asked desperately. "Who do you think my victims are?" he asked. "Actresses and models? Beautiful people?"

"Why? What for? Blood is blood. I don't take risks. I don't need to have an emotional experience, I just have to eat. I look for the easiest, fastest, safest prey.

"I prey on old people. Drunks. The sick. I spend a lot of time in skid rows and hospitals preying on people who are too out of it to notice, and in such bad shape that other people won't spot the mark. I mug people.

"I have to go out of my way to disguise my bite, as a blemish, as the remains of a sore, as a scratch or a scrape.

"Do you have any idea how many knees I've sucked! The elbows! The noses! There's nothing romantic about that.

"There is no society of vampires. We're like tigers, we require our own territory. We don't like each other. We are solitary parasites. We hunt. That's all."

"The loneliness of the tiger, burning bright," she whispered. "We are of the same spirit, you and I, let me ease your immortality."

Had she listened to a word he said? He shouldn't have mentioned tigers.

He was appalled.

Inside, the level of chaos continued to rise as the rapidly deflating Crystal used a fire extinguisher to defend herself from her rescuers. He heard a whoosh of compressed air, and for a moment a white mist puffed through the balcony doors. Inside someone was yelling about a damage deposit.

The Contessa's breasts were still bared.

Oh well, he thought, if you can't beat them . . .

He bent over her as she shivered at his touch. At least there was no poem.

The racket inside was reaching new proportions. He rolled his eyes.

"Creatures of the night," he whispered, "what music they make."

The End

***

Alice in the Mirror

I had not seen my dear friend, Sir James Fitz-Sterling, since the horrific affair of the Lancashire Mummy, over a year ago in the closing months of 1994; so I was quite startled and pleased to receive his invitation.

As I drove to his country estate, I reflected on what a threat to the world had been posed by that unholy union of Celtic Druidism and ancient Egyptian sorcery. Sir James had, for crucial moments, been a solitary bulwark, singlehandedly preserving our world from a host of newborn and nameless gods until we could contain them.

Since then great changes had come into his life; he had retired, married, and, quite startlingly, gone blind. Oddly, none of his associates could really agree on the order of things. Sir James, though consulting on occasions, and offering timely and welcome advice, seemed to have become a bit of a recluse.

I must confess, I myself had engaged in speculation as to his circumstances from time to time.

It was mid-afternoon that I arrived, and parking in the usual spot, I jaunted up the marble steps of Stormway, Sir James's estate.

I rapped three times sharply, with the intricately sculpted brass knocker, and waited. The door knocker tried to make conversation, but I ignored it. The door opened.

Sir James was standing there grinning jovially. Time had been kind to this great man, a father figure to all of us in the trade. Only his jet black glasses suggested that he was not at the peak of physical condition in every possible respect.

His wife I did not see at first. Then I caught sight of her in the huge hallway mirror. She was standing just inside the doorway, almost behind the door. No wonder I hadn't spotted her, especially with such an imposing physical presence as Fitz-Sterling bearing down on me.

"Welcome, Charles, my boy, it is good to have you around." he said, unerringly seizing my hand and pumping it vigorously.

"It's good to be here, Sir James," I said quite sincerely, shrugging out of my greatcoat. In the mirror I caught the reflection of his wife assisting me, taking up the coat as it slid off my shoulders.

"I'll just put that away for you," she was saying, as I turned to look at her.

She wasn't there.

The coat fell to the ground in a heap.

I looked straight away to the mirror. There the three of us were, reflected. But though her reflection was present, she was not.

A cold sweat broke out over me. My fingers immediately and subtly wove through the Carnavon Sigils, guaranteed to provide a painful, if temporary, defense against anything short of a twelfth level Sumerian Deity/Demon. My knuckles immediately began to ache, for it is well known the sigils were crafted for the use of dexterous tentacles.

Sir James frowned briefly, and then stooped to gather up my coat himself.

"I see you've just met my wife Alice, and encountered her condition. Let us repair to the sitting room and all shall be explained."

"I think that would be appreciated," I answered him slowly. My gaze darting back and forth from her reflection in the mirror to the place where she should be, but inexplicably was not.

"I must admonish you," he said sternly, "in the strongest terms to abide by certain rules of my house, for reasons which shall become clear to you."

Saying that, he turned and swept down the hallway. I had no choice but to follow him. The reflection of Alice followed us in the numerous mirrors distributed freely along the hall, and infesting every room we passed.

Wisely, unlike Orpheus of Greek myth, I did not turn around. I did not fear danger, of course, certainly not in the home of my friend. But a breach of etiquette, there was a risk even I feared.

We arrived in the opulent sitting room, tastefully furnished in Victorian style with just the slightest traces of oriental influence. The biggest shock was that the whole of the east wall, facing away from the fireplace, had been covered with a huge mirror. I moved to examine the glasswork. It was exquisite; I could not find a single seam. The mirror made the sitting room, already large, positively cavernous.

"Sit," he waved to one of three overstuffed lounging chairs which faced the mirror with nothing but a small coffee table and a tea server between them.

"Face the mirror at all times. On no account look directly at anyone or anything in the room," he instructed me as he settled into the chair nearest mine.

His wife Alice was standing at the tea server, pouring a cup. She passed it to Sir James, who accepted it with thanks. She smiled at me in the mirror.

"Mister Smith?" she asked.

"Charles, please," I told her. "And black with one lump of sugar."

She passed me a cup, and just as I reached for it, I glanced away from the mirror towards the cup in time to see it suddenly fall to the floor, inches from my fingers.

"Oh bother," she said with some consternation, looking at the spilled tea and shattered cup. "James, I am sorry, this is just not working out well."

"Nonsense," he said. He performed a mystic gesture. Instantly I held the steaming cup of tea.

"A simple time displacement spell, elementary and useful for parlor tasks like this," Sir James explained graciously.

"Sit my dear, and soon it shall all be sorted out with Charles."

Dutifully, she took her seat on his opposite side.

He sipped his tea and turned to regard me.

"By now, I am sure that you have divined my wife's condition. Quite opposite to Vampires, who cast no reflection, she can only be seen in mirrors. She can move about and affect things in what we so humorously call the 'real' world, only so long as no observer looks directly at an object, rather than a reflection. Thus my instructions."

"An Alice through a looking glass," I expostulated. "Surely not the girl from the Lewis Carroll story?"

"Quite right, my boy, this is a decidedly different Alice. Though you are right to wonder about the correspondence of the names. We both know there is no such thing as coincidence."

"But this is so remarkable," I went on, "I hardly know where to start."

"Then, best we start elsewhere," he said with perfect grace, "rushing blindly into a subject is often the fastest path to ruin. How have you been?"

Alice echoed his comment, her voice coming sweetly. "Yes, James has told me so much about you. We would dearly love to hear more from you. The last report placed you in the centre of the Isswitch Church matter."

I watched my face fall. It was the dashed oddest sensation to be watching ourselves in the mirror as we chatted. I felt almost disembodied.

"I'm afraid that ended quite badly. We lost several people to the thing in the pit and could not banish it at all."

Sir James reached over to put a fatherly hand on my shoulder.

"Don't blame yourself, son. In cases such as these, it is all anyone can do to contain the horror. Certainly if not for you and Renfrew the loss of life would have been intolerable."

"How is Renfrew?" Alice asked sweetly. "James has spoken so highly of you two. I feel almost as if I know each of you."

"I thank you, Ma'am," I told her, "but I fear after Isswitch, Renfrew and I may no longer be considered associates."

An ineffable sadness washed over me. I tried to shake it off.

"But what of you, Sir James? So much has happened to you these past few months. How are you dealing with this lack of sight?"

Sir James, with characteristic wisdom and compassion, allowed the conversation to turn to his blindness.

"It is a surprisingly small handicap. Most people fail to appreciate how acute the remaining five physical senses . . . and the seven metaphysical ones can be, if applied. Most times, I hardly notice it."

"But still, there are qualities peculiar to sight," I said.

"How do you read?"

"I read for him," Alice said, reaching forth to put her hand on his knee. He turned towards her.

"With the voice of an angel," he said. In the mirror I watched them gaze at each other with the most honest love I had ever seen.

I thought of Renfrew, a lump rose in my throat. I washed it away with a swallow of tea.

Sir James must have sensed my mood.

"Of course such a condition would be a rather critical handicap in our profession, so my retirement became rather a matter of necessity."

He turned back to me, sipping his tea.

"Not that I minded. Once I had found my Alice, I discovered I could not bear to leave her side."

Drunk Slutty Elf, Page 52

"He is not completely inactive," Alice said.

"I do some small consulting," Sir James chuckled, "after all, the decades following a millennium are dangerous time. Things have been born, that should sleep, and things wake that should require a hobby."

"His advice was quite instrumental in the Japanese case," she said proudly.

"I heard of it," I recalled. "At the time Renfrew and I were involved in an exorcism on a member of the Royal Family. Otherwise we would have lent our aid."

"That was a close one. The tendency for events to repeat is a powerful one," Sir James murmured. "May the good people of Hiroshima never realize how close they came to another holocaust."

"Robeson and Savage sent us the kindest letter," she told me.

I found myself with a powerful urge to look directly at them.

"Confound it, Sir James, I can stand no more. Your wife's condition is singular. How did it come about?"

Fitz-Sterling settled back in his chair and stared thoughtfully at the mirror.

"Well, it seems to me that all cultures have understood, in some fashion or other, the power of images. Even the barbaric Americans, with their Hollywood and Madison Avenue, grasp this," he spoke thoughtfully.

"Why in supposedly primitive cultures it is believed a camera can steal your soul into a photograph, or a mirror can trap your spirit. I've often wondered at the truth in this."

"I quite suspect that in our own culture we are exposed to cameras and mirrors on such a continuous basis that we have grown immune to certain of their effects, almost like developing calluses from physical exertion. I think they could have quite dramatic effects on those peoples who had never developed a resistance."

"I suspect that somewhere in the English character there was a certain affinity, perhaps merely a lack of immunity, to image magic. That we would throw up people from time to time, who were like hemophiliacs in a way, in that they lacked a certain element that isolated them from their images."

"There are stories, after all. Consider the famous Lewis Carroll 'Alice' and her adventures in the looking glass. Or look at Peter Pan and his difficulties keeping his shadow attached, there's a suspicious case if ever there was one. Or consider the tragic case of Dorian Grey. All situations of images taking on a life of their own."

"A life of their own," I broke in, "then where is the real Alice?"

"Oh, this is the real Alice," Sir James chuckled, "she's definitely real enough, I can attest to that."

Alice giggled demurely.

"I have confirmed that she was born, quite happily, on this side of the mirror, and spent her first few years in schools as a physical girl. Somehow, as she got older, she slipped across the mirror's face, and found herself unable to get back."

"It sounds quite silly to say so," Alice said, pouring herself another cup of tea, "but it happened so gradually that I never really noticed until it was far too late. James speculates that I was actually slipping in and out of mirrors from a very early age, so that it was done without the particular self-consciousness that comes with growing up. In some ways, there really is so little difference between here and there."

She paused to think.

"I suppose the problem should have become apparent in my teenage years, but aren't all teenagers eccentric or rebellious in some manner? I was a sheltered girl, and my dear mother simply chalked my increasingly odd requirements up to adolescent vaporings and fashions."

She stood to attend at the tea server, reaching beneath it.

"But now I think it is time for some refreshments." She handed a bowl of biscuits to Sir James, who set them on the table. Then she produced a flat, exquisitely wrought, wooden box, handing it again to Sir James.

"Works?" he inquired, passing it to me.

I laid the box on my lap. Eighteenth century French mahogany, I judged a case for dueling pistols. I opened it. Inside, laid out on red velvet was a polished antique syringe, fitted out with a gleaming modern needle, I noted the fresh surgical tubing, the clamps, and of course the three rubber sealed vials.

"The mixture of the solution is heroin eighty per cent and mescaline twenty per cent, as per your preference. Should you prefer to do your own dilutions I have included the pure solutions," Sir James told me.

I could barely trust my voice.

"Really, Sir James, you are the perfect host. Alas, I would prefer to wait until later in the evening."

"Of course," Fitz-Sterling replied as I closed the case and placed it on the coffee table.

"I must say, this calls Renfrew to my mind. He could not abide this little pleasure, you know."

"I can hardly say I am surprised," rumbled Sir James, "much as I like Renfrew, I'd always felt that his choice of dress and hormones, coupled with his refusal to pursue surgery, spoke of a person unwilling to commit fully to life. I'm sure it must have been a barrier in your relationship."

"Actually," I said reflectively, "I found the androgyny of his physical aspect quite exciting. It was actually my limitations that came between us. I could not abide certain of his tastes."

Sir James and Alice nodded sympathetically.

I pulled my handkerchief from my vest pocket and wrung it in my hands, staring at it.

"When we admitted to our feelings for each other, we both agreed that to be together, we would each refrain from what the other could not bear to tolerate."

I looked fondly at the case on the coffee table.

"I put my friends away. Renfrew could not tolerate the thought of needles. He gave up certain . . . pleasures as well.

"We were quite happy together. If our home was unusually free of vermin, well, Renfrew was a meticulous housekeeper. If I smelled the occasional roach on his breath, I simply chose not to think about it.

"It was Isswitch that ruined it for us. I feel certain of that now. It was such a drain on the both of us. Poor Renfrew was a wreck.

"I had taken to long solitary walks to get my bearings. On one of these walks, Renfrew, left alone, could stand it no more.

"He must have gone out to a pet store and purchased a box of kittens."

I daubed at a tear that had sprung unaccountably at the corner of my left eye.

"When I returned early, he was half way through them. I still remember him looking up in surprise at me. His face smeared with red like a child caught at the jam. I simply could not bear it, not after Isswitch."

Sir James reached out a hand, resting it on my shoulder as if to steady me. Alice left her seat, crossing behind me to lay her hand on my other shoulder.

"There now, it will work out," she assured me.

"The greatest trial of love," Sir James whispered sincerely, "is learning to abide with that which is intolerable in your companion. It is something we must all face. We cannot be what we want each other to be, we must be who we are, and we must love that. We must transform at least that part of our selves that cannot accept the whole."

"Yes," I whispered, almost not trusting myself to speak, "of course you are right. It's just so hard."

"But you have it in you," he urged, "you and Renfrew both. If you wish to, you can transcend this, as Alice and I have done."

I gathered myself up. I did not want to seem unmanly in their home.

"You seem so happy together. Tell me, how did you meet?"

In the mirror I watched them exchange fond glances.

"Actually," said Sir James, "it was her mother who brought me into it."

"Mother was getting on in years, you see," Alice told me, "and she had finally decided that something should be done about my condition. For years we had simply made allowances and accommodations, purchased mirrors and positioned them cleverly."

"Indeed," Fitz-Sterling said, "the principal handicap was her inability to affect the material world when someone was gazing upon it. Her mother had grown quite skillful at where and how to look at things, to allow her daughter freedom. Why, I remember when I first arrived, Alice's bedroom was off limits, but mirrors were arranged so cunningly in the hallway that you could see the whole of the bedroom without ever actually looking directly into it."

"Just so," she agreed, "but finally, she determined something more substantive would have to be done. How would I make my way when she was no longer around? There are not a lot of career prospects available for a girl in a mirror."

"As you can imagine," Sir James continued, "I found the whole thing quite without precedent, and completely beyond my experience. It was a major effort even to understand her condition."

He looked directly at me for a moment.

"I found the works of Bohr and Heisenberg on quantum mechanics of invaluable assistance. The paradox of Schrodinger's Cat helped greatly in grasping this phenomenon."

"But he could do nothing for me," she said, crossing over to stand behind him, and running her fingers through his hair.

"Her condition was too far advanced. Too much time had passed. Perhaps in the early stages . . ." he shook his head.

"Mother was reluctant. She was afraid that they might try to exorcise me. She wanted me brought closer, not sent away. That was why she waited."

"Still, I gave it the old college try, and spent quite a bit of time thereabouts. Alice and I became quite familiar. You must admit, Charles," he seemed to glance directly at me, "that it is a most fascinating case.

"I kept returning to it again and again," he said.

"Until one day, I realized that I was drawn back as much by Alice as by her condition. More so. For I had long determined that there was nothing I could do, and yet, I kept returning."

"I still remember that joyous day he proposed," I heard her voice behind us, glowing with happiness, "only a year ago. He completely swept me off my feet."

Sir John chuckled with pleasure and she answered with her own happy giggle. I watched the two of them in the mirror.

"I am happy for the both of you. If what they say is true: that for every loss there is a compensation, then your blindness has been more than recompensed, Sir John," I told them.

"Love isn't all roses my boy," Sir John said. "Like you and Renfrew, we had our tribulations.

"The source of our own trials lay in Alice's unique condition," he explained, "though you must not think her disabled. Through the affinity of images, Alice can touch and affect anything in the material world that whose image she can reach inside the mirror. Provided, of course, that there is no observer of the material world, thus alone, or with us gazing straight into the mirror she is quite competent."

"Anyone, with just a glance, however, can render me impotent and helpless." Alice stated. "It is the most wretched thing. Worse by far, I think, than being a quadriplegic in a hospital bed or wheelchair. At least then you cannot feel and touch only to have it stolen away in an instant."

"Yes, it was hard on us at first. Especially on poor Alice. I cannot tell you of the cups and glasses which were shattered, the moments ruined, when I would look away from the mirrors. Her mother had received a lifetime of practice, and had never been so intimate as we were."

"I had a mirror installed over our bed, so that we could share our nights. I cannot bear to speak of the times passion would draw back my eyelids, and suddenly her touch would vanish."

"I found," Alice said softly, in the mirror she was leaning down over the chair, behind him, their arms entwined, "that I was of a passionate nature. The frustration became unbearable."

"I took to wearing veils over my eyes to block my sight, but these proved to be inadequate," Sir John said.

"I realized," she said, "I could not live with a sighted man."

"Dear Lord God in Heaven," I gasped, as Sir John slipped off his dark glasses and I looked into his empty sockets, "you don't mean that she . . ."

"Of course not," Sir John told me, "I did it myself."

The End

***

Armageddon When?

The Pope was going over the Vatican's quarterly financial statements when the phone rang.

He looked at it curiously, turning his head slowly. He had to move his head slowly because of the inertia of the three and a half foot tall papal hat. It was called a Mitre, he was told, or something like that. The Pope wasn't actually all that sure what his hat was called. The Pope only knew it made getting through doors a nightmare.

It kept ringing.

Finally he sighed and pressed a button.

"Yes," he said.

"You have a call," his secretary told him.

"I said I wasn't to be disturbed," the Pope replied with that mixture of gentle serenity and solid firmness that had won him the papacy.

"I do have to get through these records," he chided the secretary.

"But it's the Archangel Gabriel on the phone."

"Oh."

The Pope sighed and stared at the speaker.

"He said it was urgent, he had news concerning the coming apocalypse."

The Pope considered it for a moment, but there seemed no easy way around it.

"Very well," he said finally, "I'll take the call."

There were a couple of clicks on the line, and then the voice of the Archangel was heard.

"Our father's greetings," said the Archangel Gabriel. The voice of the angel was beautiful, the very tones richer and somehow purer than the sounds from coarse human throats.

"Archangel," the Pope said by way of greeting. A while back when Angels had begun to manifest, there had been substantial debate as to the proper terms of address. Eventually, the simple economies of this utilitarian age had resulted in their being addressed by basic titles.

"We need to talk about the Antichrist," Gabriel announced, "and about his pernicious plans."

The Pope rolled his eyes.

"The Antichrist?"

"He must be stopped!"

"I already told you," the Pope replied exasperatedly, "I'm not returning his phone calls. I've issued an encyclical on the subject. I don't know what more we can do."

There was a pause on the other end of the line.

"But still," Gabriel said hesitantly, "the struggle against evil is never ending . . ."

The Angel went on like that for a while. The Pope listened politely, mumbling noncommittal answers from time to time. In spite of himself, his eyes glanced over the financial reports.

"Uh huh," he said aloud, for the benefit of the Angel. He picked up the financial statement, and started flipping through it quietly.

"I see," he said, in response to the Angel's petulant whining.

Good lord, look at the catering bill! That can't possibly be right. He picked up a red pen.

On the phone's speaker, the Archangel Gabriel's complaints continued.

* * *

The Antichrist spent the entire morning in his Agent's waiting room.

He knew this was not a good sign.

Still, as the lord of Evil, he was not unacquainted with patience. He'd been waiting a thousand years and more for his time to come. He could afford to wait a few hours.

Occasionally he checked with Genevieve, his Agent's pretty secretary. She would smile at him and politely check his schedule.

No, I'm sorry, he's in a meeting. Oh, right now he's on the phone, I can't interrupt. That person, well, he'd been scheduled well in advance. Her? That's an emergency. Right now? I'm terribly sorry, but he takes his massage now, I'd really like to but . . ."

"That's all right," the Antichrist smiled, "I suspect being the agent for the Antichrist is very stressful."

She gave him one of those glossy lipstick stretched toothy expressions that are used for jokes that aren't really funny.

The Antichrist sat down.

He noted that Genevieve had never offered him a cup of coffee.

Not even a glass of water.

When he had reached for a mint from the bowl on her desk, she'd casually moved it out range.

That was definitely a very bad sign.

Around noon his agent breezed out. The Antichrist leaped to his feet grabbing the Agent's sleeve. A look of distaste flickered over the Agent's face and was quickly replaced by a plastic grin.

"Hey it's the Great Satan!" the agent said. "How's the Holocaust coming?"

The Antichrist thought his Agent's grin looked a lot like Genevieve's polite smile.

Drunk Slutty Elf, Page 62

"It's the Apocalypse," the Antichrist said. "The Holocaust was a few years ago, and it was someone else's."

The Agent slapped his head.

"Ouch, and me being Jewish too! I guess I should get down to the synagogue and say a few Hail Marys."

"Don't worry about it," the Antichrist said.

"So, what 'deviltry' have you been getting up to? Raising a little 'hell,' eh?" the Agent asked, pumping his hand in a too firm shake.

"Well . . ."

"You can tell your Agent. Anything big coming up?"

"Oh yeah," the Antichrist said. "I've got some big plans. People are really going to sit up and take notice."

"Uh huh," the Agent replied. "Like what?"

"Uhmm," the Antichrist mumbled. "Things."

"Uh huh," the Agent said, his smile visibly losing wattage.

"Big things," the Antichrist said desperately.

"Right." The Agent retrieved his hand. "Look at the time! I'm already late. Well, it was great meeting you. Don't be a stranger, drop by any time."

The Agent threw a mock punch at the Antichrist's jaw.

"I'm here for you baby," he told him as he turned away.

"Wait," the Antichrist said.

The Agent paused for a second.

"Can you get me on the Late Show?" the Antichrist blurted. "I need a little exposure."

The Agent's plastic grin slid off and on.

"I'm sorry," he said, "that's a little out of your league right now."

"But you got the Whore of Babylon on Kimmel! Twice!"

The Agent frowned.

"Listen, you put out three hit singles and a banned music video, and we'll talk about putting you on Kimmel."

There was a moment of awkward silence.

"Can you get me anything?" the Antichrist asked plaintively. "Oprah?"

The Agent hesitated, wavering.

"Maybe I could get you onto the Jerry Springer show . . ."

The Antichrist bit his lip.

"How do you feel about drag?"

"What?"

"Jerry's big on drag queens. Show up in a dress, you'd be a cinch."

The Antichrist was speechless.

"Think it over," the Agent said. "Drop me a line, let me know."

Then he was gone.

"I take it you'll be going now," Genevieve said to the Antichrist, giving him her best plastic smile.

She said it in a friendly way. The sort of friendly that would call security if he didn't leave immediately.

"Sure," he mumbled, and left.

***

"Excuse me," the Angel asked, his white wings resplendent, "could I talk to you about the Apocalypse."

This was rural Kansas. The Angel had come out here in the hopes that the solid moral values of the Bible belt might provide more manna. If the teachings did not find firm roots here, then where?

"We'd like to," the farmer said, "but it's harvest time and we're really busy."

"Oh Joshua," the farmer's wife said, "have some pity on the poor thing."

She turned to the Angel.

"You go right ahead, dear. What's on your mind?"

The Angel almost wept with relief.

"It's about the Antichrist," he told them. "He walks among us even now. The skies will rain blood . . ."

The farmer grunted.

"Damn," he said, "we'll have to irrigate some, blood rain's hell on the crops."

The Angel winced. The Farmer's Wife elbowed her husband.

"No profanity in front of Angels," she hissed. "What will people say?"

The farmer grunted.

". . . and the dead will rise for the coming Judgment Day."

"Well," said the farmer, not quite rudely, "whether the dead rise or not, the pigs still got to be fed. Now, if you'll excuse us, we got chores to attend.

"Come on Martha," he said.

Martha smiled apologetically, and the Angel took the opportunity to put a tract in her hand. He'd picked that up from the Jehovah's Witnesses. They were unbearably tedious, but they'd been doing this longer than he had.

The Angel waved goodbye to Martha and her husband. He stood on the street corner trying to make eye contact.

These were trying times, the Angel thought, not for the first time. The forces of evil sure did have it easy.

A man in a business suit didn't look away quickly enough.

The Angel clutched his tracts and stepped forward.

"Excuse me . . ."

* * *

The Antichrist sat outside the petting zoo.

He'd gone to visit the seven-headed, ten-horned beast of the Apocalypse. It always cheered him up. But the line-up was so long he'd given up.

Instead, he sat on a park bench with an exotic dancer and her five year old son.

She should have been one of his people, he thought. One of the legions of the damned. He just had a hard time, though, seeing her as anything but an ordinary person trying to cope as best she could with her circumstances.

Drunk Slutty Elf, Page 65

"I feel really cheated," he told her. "I mean, when the Christ came, everyone was into it, everyone believed. He made miracles, he could raise the dead. It was easy then. People flocked around him."

"I wanna see the beast," the little boy whined, "the one with seventeen heads."

"Seven heads," the Antichrist corrected automatically.

The dancer smiled apologetically.

"He's been looking forward to seeing it all week, ever since that segment on Sesame Street with Ernie and Bert."

"Seventeen," the child sang and started to count loudly.

The Antichrist nodded.

"Well anyway," he continued, "we start manifesting now . . . devils and angels, signs and miracles, the whole ball of wax . . . and for a while, we're a big deal."

"So," the dancer asked, "do you really know the Whore of Babylon?"

The Antichrist shrugged.

"Sure."

He tried to continue.

"But then, something happens and suddenly everyone's talking about this sex scandal, or that economic summit, or some 'shocking' fratricidal murder, and I'm not on page one of the news anymore."

"I have all her songs. I think she's so talented."

"She is. So I think, all right, I'll be back. But things keep happening, and nobody's paying attention. It's like that Mars mission. They landed a robot on Mars. I was astounded, but a week later nobody could be bothered with it. I mean . . . It's the flipping Apocalypse, and nobody seems to care."

"Well," the dancer said, "I think people do care, it's just that everyone's so busy."

"Too busy for the end of the world?" the Antichrist asked.

"You know what they say: Life goes on."

Drunk Slutty Elf, Page 66

"I'm talking Armageddon here bitch!" the Antichrist snapped. "Life does not go on, not if it knows what's good for it."

Her face froze.

He knew he'd said exactly the wrong thing. He was going to be sleeping alone tonight. Again.

"Come on, Timmy," she said coldly. "We have to get back in line. It's been nice meeting you."

"Seventeen heads," Timmy sang. "One, two . . ."

"Yeah," the Antichrist yelled, "well they've got it doped to the gills on Prozac."

Which wasn't exactly factual. The Beast, the Antichrist reflected sadly, just wasn't what it used to be.

A petting zoo, for Christ's sake.

The forces of good, he reflected, must sure have it easy.

* * *

The Antichrist drove a Porsche. He was very proud of that. When he was reduced to driving a Toyota or a Hyundai, he'd promised himself that he'd throw in the towel.

Not that you couldn't be profoundly evil in a Hyundai. He wouldn't reject a potential follower just on the make of their vehicle. But for the Antichrist personally, it was a matter of style.

All right, so it was third hand and the warranties had expired, so the paint was scratched and the right fender was dented, so the tires were bald and the transmission jumped and the engine was making increasingly disturbing knocking sounds. It was a Porsche.

He parked in front of the soup kitchen. Stepping out of the car, listening to the engine wheeze erratically before finally shutting off, he checked himself briefly in the driver's door mirror to make sure he was the picture of sartorial evil. Slick, well-groomed, and deadly.

He grinned, his teeth flashing wickedly.

Believe it, he told himself. Believe.

Who is the Antichrist?

Drunk Slutty Elf, Page 67

You are!

Time for the big showdown, he thought to himself.

It wasn't what he'd originally planned on, he thought sourly, but things had drifted too long. It was time to take matters in hand.

He strode through the doors of the soup kitchen like a gunfighter entering a saloon.

"I'm looking for Jesus," he announced.

The room went silent. Everyone recognized him from his brief time on newspaper front pages, and television news programs. They knew something heavy was going down.

"Here," someone said, raising their hand.

Unlike the Antichrist, Jesus had never actually made the front pages. It had been the Angels and the Archangels who'd hogged the coverage. The Antichrist had no idea what Jesus looked like.

Jesus, it turned out, was a small man, about five foot five, with straggly hair, thick eyebrows, a full beard and bad teeth. The Antichrist was disappointed.

"How's your dad?" Jesus asked.

"What?" the Antichrist said surprised. "Oh him. Same as always. Bitching and complaining. Never happy about anything. And yours?"

"Vague," Jesus said, "creating everything really took a lot out of him – the Universe is a lot to watch over, but it's gotten worse the last few thousand years. Nowadays, he really only pulls himself together long enough to announce 'Nietzsche is dead!' and then he starts giggling."

"Sorry to hear that," the Antichrist said with more sincerity than he wanted to feel.

Jesus shrugged.

"He seems happy enough."

The Antichrist worked up his nerve.

"It's time we had it out," he announced.

"Is it time for the Armageddon?" Jesus asked.

"Screw the Armageddon," the Antichrist said, "it's just you and me. We're going to settle it all once and for all, here and now."

The silence in the room impossibly deepened. People looked around nervously.

"Oh," said Jesus. He rocked thoughtfully on his heels. "I hope you weren't planning on incinerating the whole place in a holocaust of hellfire."

"I could do that," the Antichrist said defensively. Actually, he couldn't. He just didn't want to admit it.

"I'd consider it a favor though, if we just found an empty table and settle it quietly."

"I could do that too," the Antichrist said.

Hell, it wasn't every day you could get the Son of God to owe you a favor.

Jesus led them to a table at the back. The Antichrist sat down.

"Get you something?" Jesus asked. "Glass of water?"

"No thanks."

Jesus sat down.

"What's on your mind?" he asked.

"I didn't expect to find you in a place like this," the Antichrist said, looking around.

Jesus smiled.

"What did you expect?"

"I don't know," the Antichrist shrugged. "I expected a mansion, like Elvis's. Or a giant cathedral. Thousands of followers hanging on your every word. I expected you to be ten feet tall."

"Disappointed?" Jesus asked, half smiling.

The Antichrist thought about it.

"No."

"Churches aren't me," Jesus said. "In my life, I never built a church. I wandered where my feet took me, teaching where I could, ministering where it was needed."

A derelict shambled close, the Antichrist wrinkled his nose.

"I've never actually been inside one of my churches," Jesus said.

"Excuse me." An old derelict came up to them. The side of his face was covered with bandages where an abscess had burst. The bandages were soaked and stained with yellowing pus.

"Go away," the Antichrist snapped. The derelict retreated.

"This isn't going to be one of those 'I'm in the sunrise, I'm walking in the sand beside you' sort of parables?" the Antichrist asked. "Because if it is, I'm going to throw up."

"No," Jesus chuckled. "I just prefer places like this."

There was a pause.

"So what's wrong with a Church?" the Antichrist asked. "If I had them, you couldn't pry me out with a crowbar."

"I guess," Jesus said slowly, "if it's doing its job of helping people be closer to God, then I don't need to be in there, and if it doesn't do its job then it's not a place for me.

"Every now and then, one of these Evangelists seeks me out and offers me his congregation, like it was his to give. I always tell them the same thing: Renounce everything, feed the hungry, care for the sick. They nod and look serious and go away, they never come back."

Jesus hesitated.

"Although I thought about visiting the Sistine Chapel. I hear it's nice."

"It is," the Antichrist agreed. "Yeah. I saw it when I did Italy. I was visiting the Pope. Now," he finished bitterly, "he doesn't return my phone calls."

"He's a busy man," Jesus said sympathetically.

"Yeah," the Antichrist said, "that's part of it. Nobody returns my calls. I'm the Apocalypse made flesh, and nobody seems to care. Armageddon is turning into a big fizzle."

Jesus nodded sympathetically.

"It must be tough," he said. "I've been there. Metaphorically."

"So cut it out. I'm doing my part," the Antichrist complained. "Let's get this show on the road. Let the Beast out of the petting zoo, loose the four horsemen, let's do it, before people lose interest completely."

"Excuse me?" The derelict again.

"Go away," the Antichrist snapped, and then to Jesus. "It's time."

He tried to keep that small note of desperation out of his voice.

Jesus shook his head.

"I can't."

"Are you chicken or something?" the Antichrist snarled. "Your father wrote the damned book, for Christ's sakes."

"Don't take my name in vain," Jesus snapped. He softened and tried to explain. "Look, it's not your fault. You've heard that we are sustained by the beliefs of Mortals."

"Are you telling me that I'm a figment of the imagination? That the Apocalypse isn't going to happen because nobody believes in it?"

"No," Jesus said, "it's a little more complicated than that. It's not just a matter of belief; it's of focus, of attention. People don't believe or disbelieve the Apocalypse.

"They just don't have time for it. They can't be bothered. All the spiritual energy that would have powered Armageddon, it's just not there. It's taken up for other purposes. All the Angels and Devils hover around reduced to buzzing like insects."

"That's it then?" the Antichrist sneered, "the end of the world has been canceled due to lack of interest?"

"Perhaps it's for the best," Jesus said sympathetically.

"I don't notice you doing too poorly out of it," the Antichrist snapped.

Drunk Slutty Elf, Page 71

"I'm not driving the Porsche," Jesus replied.

"Bite me, Jesus," the Antichrist snapped.

Jesus smiled. "You think I'm immune from the changes."

"You're the Son."

Jesus laughed. "These days, I do a few minor cures, but the dead stay dead. I may make a few extra bowls of soup, or improve the drinking a bit, but no more loaves and fishes, no more water into wine."

"Damn," said the Antichrist, he'd hoped that the divine being would be more . . . divine. "So what's the point of going on? Why do we bother if nobody cares?"

"You'll have to figure that out for yourself. Mine was always a simple message. Travel where I may, teach what I can, minister to the sick, feed the hungry. I never needed miracles for that."

"Excuse me?" The derelict returned.

"Oh for Pete's Sake," the Antichrist snapped, losing his temper completely. He turned and healed the bum. "Now get out of here."

"Nice work," Jesus said.

The Antichrist shrugged.

"Maybe it's time to get out of the damnation business and look for a new line of work."

"Well," said Jesus, "I'm thinking of taking a vacation, if you'd like to pinch hit for a while."

The Antichrist thought about it.

"Would I have to wear a dress?"

"Only if you want to."

The End

***

Simulaw

Two green cavemen were bonking each other's heads with clubs on the Holo. Susan Flanagan opened one sleepy eye and groaned.

Manually she adjusted the tint until both cavemen were cartoon pink and their clubs a proper brown. She wondered how her lawsuit against the manufacturer was going. Then she groaned again and pulled a pillow over her head. It was too early!

On the Holo the cartoon cavemen continued their mayhem, as they chased each another, gouged eyes, and threw spears. Being cartoon Neanderthals, they bore a vague resemblance to earlier animated cavemen. This too was the subject of a lawsuit. As they maimed each other the announcer's smooth masculine voice overrode the grunts and groans.

"Yes, it's a jungle out there, but you've come a long way from the apes, baby. Your life is too important for monkey business, don't be a victim of simian justice. Get SIMULAW the first and finest legal program, now with an advisor function.

Perfect defense, perfect offence, SIMULAW!"

On the Holo the cave men continued to inflict senseless violence on each other. Normally, she would have just laid there with the pillow over her head blocking out the offending world.

She did that a lot these days.

But the adblurb had reminded her of the day's assignment. She pulled herself out of bed and walked the half dozen steps across her one room apartment to her work/entertainment console. She pulled a cigarette out and almost lit it, but at the last second thought better of it. Instead, she screened her SIMULAW index. It took the console five minutes to scroll through the update of the thirty-two legal suits she was defending or prosecuting. She noted a new lawsuit against her with interest, but couldn't recall the incident that the factum set out. She keyed a motion for disclosure.

Maybe it was a case of mistaken identity? Briefly, she set her program to compiling briefs for a counter claim focusing on Abuse of Process, Malicious Proceedings, and Defamation.

She chewed her nails thoughtfully; an old smoker's reflex, and then went into the General Proceedings database. The only tobacco related case that was going on was a class action against the State by a group of Nicotine Addicts alleging that the government had violated the Human Rights Codes by levying excessive tobacco taxes, thus singling smokers out for punishment.

It was safe then. Good. She lit the cigarette and closed her eyes, taking a long sensual drag. She luxuriated in the sheer joy of a good cigarette and finally began to feel human. She thought about going for a walk later that day. Meteorology scans predicted a nice day. She ordered a legal projection and advisory.

Her program accepted the command, then returned to its display of the Nicotine Addicts class action suit. The console displayed predicted chances of the actions resolution in success or settlement and the likely cash award. Tapping her keys she joined the class action.

It was time to go to work. She set her SIMULAW on automatic, with scan and recall functions in case something popped up that she should know about. Then she cleared her console and instituted word processing and accessories on the first screen, and called up her notes and research on the three subsidiaries.

She scrolled through her notes looking for a good lead. This one seemed likely.

"The Colt .45 was history's first equalizer."

Was this accurate? She wondered. She put a check mark beside it. Cautionary review.

"In the Wild West the man with a gun need submit to no other. The cowboy's egalitarian society was based on the premise that man could not be oppressed when the means of violence were universal."

She flexed her fingers and spun the idea . . .

"But this equality, based on arms and courage, was a fiction. All men were not equal. Speed, recklessness, military and paramilitary organizations, even property, undermined the foundations of the Wild West myth."

"The gunslingers became heroes, because in a society based on the notions of freedom and equality through strength, they were more equal than their fellows and achieved transcendent freedom."

This was going nowhere, she thought. She saved the opening, dumped it into the notes file, and tried again.

"The twentieth century Lawyer was the ultimate civilized mercenary. A 'hired gun,' knowing no honor or loyalty past his own duty to clients, the lawyer walked into the courtroom the way ancient warriors had walked into the Colosseum."

Flanagan sat back and thought about that one. She liked it. It started off with a punch, and followed up with a reference to the distant past. It was close enough to remind people of the famous SIMULAW cavemen, but still distinct enough to avoid litigation.

"All men were equal before the law. Contingency fees made legal services available even to the poor, and people throughout the developed world became increasingly aware of and insistent upon their legal rights. Led by the United States, western nations experienced a litigation explosion. Actions in contract and tort led to revolutions in civil liberties, workplace safety, and environmental protection."

She wasn't as happy with that one.

"But a more fundamental revolution was under way. Computers were creating the information society. By the late eighties programs had been designed for such different uses as medical diagnostics and stock trading. In fact, the stock market crashes of '87 and '08 were attributed, in part, to computerized trading."

Susan stopped and wiped the last sentence. The market programmers were very touchy. Even whispering the words "Madoff" or "Trump" in certain buildings would get you half a dozen civil actions. It was the modern equivalent of yelling "fire" in a crowded theater.

Instead, she focused on the technical developments that had computerized law. It had been simpler than many people thought. Legal wording and phraseology had been developed over the centuries to eliminate many of the imprecisions of colloquial speech. The price had been to make legal jargon boring and incomprehensible to the lay person. But this same process had made it very easy to fit into software formats. Many legal processes, once commenced, were predictable chains of notices, pleadings, and limitation periods.

The bell rang for an incoming call. It was John, her lover. She smiled at his face on screen, but it didn't smile back.

"Susan, we have to talk," his image said urgently.

"Can we do it later, John? I told you I'd be working today," she said with a hint of reproach in her tone.

"You're suing me!" he accused.

"It's not personal," she told him. "Now really, I'm in the middle of work, we can talk about it later."

"Not personal!" he roared, "Not personal! What do you call personal if not–"

She cut him off. She called up her dateminder and fixed a note to call him when he calmed down.

On one of the screens, an out of sequence note told her that 87% of the North American population owned or leased SIMULAW or one of its competitors, which was roughly equivalent to three hundred and ninety million twentieth century lawyers. The numbers continued to climb. She tagged it for an insert box.

The big problem had been in writing programs intelligent enough to apply real life incidents to legal process. But the true revolution had come when these programs became available to the average consumer.

The litigation explosion had gone nuclear.

Suddenly, almost everyone used or had access to a personal legal programmer. More importantly than that though, they used it.

Her SIMULAW program beeped, attracting her attention. She fixed and forwarded. The latest lawsuit had been withdrawn; she prompted her own countersuits and reviewed the settlement return projections. Then she fed the results to her financial planner.

Nowadays 76% of personal income was derived from lawsuits. Perhaps she should use that. North America's productivity had plummeted, but continual lawsuits had resulted in the more nearly uniform distribution of wealth than all of the social programs in history. Poverty was almost a thing of the past.

"Computers changed society in fundamental ways," she wrote. "Incredible precision became the rule in mediums as diverse as art, music, and business. The concept of approximation vanished."

That was safely generic, she decided – she could slide it in anywhere. How to relate it to the subject . . .

Drunk Slutty Elf, Page 77

There was an incoming call. She flagged it. It was John, again. Irritated, she blocked it and initiated a second action against him for Telecommunications Harassment.

"SIMULAW systems made it possible to apply this precision to human relationships," she typed. "Overnight, the social lubrication that had sustained humanity vanished. People simply no longer gave each other space. It was as if everyone had begun walking around with loaded guns pointed at each other, and trigger fingers started getting itchy."

She paused thoughtfully. It would be best to attribute this analysis. Preferably to someone who was already being sued. On the other hand, the part about loaded guns looked good. Maybe she should work the Wild West metaphor into it somewhere.

Susan toyed with the idea as she began her second cigarette.

It would put a more positive slant on the article, and emphasize SIMULAW as an ultimate expression of personal freedom and equality.

Her program beeped again. She checked it. John had launched his own lawsuits against her.

Good. Maybe it would make him feel better.

"Constant litigation has changed the way people react to each other. Many kinds of crime have all but disappeared. To avoid lawsuits, elaborate forms of courtesy have emerged, but some feel that there is less human contact, less friendship, and people have become more isolated. Social paranoia has taken root."

Was that really true? She wondered.

"SIMULAW systems have made society more ruthless. Law ceases to operate as a moral force. People and organizations often choose to do what they want, factoring the costs of lawsuits as part of the price of doing business."

Balance was all right, she decided, but she hardly wanted to sound negative. That could expose her to liability.

Susan stopped and scrolled back. Something was missing.

She did some quick spot checks through her research base and noticed a promotional brochure from SIMULAW.

". . . formal legal systems had become hopelessly overloaded. The courts simply could not cope with the volume of computer assisted lawsuits. Built in settlement features allowed the programs to negotiate out of court settlements, but real life and real time courts still had an impossible burden."

"SIMULAW solved the problem by creating SIMUCOURTS. Programs modeled on real judicial processes which computer assisted litigants could refer their disputes. Instant law could lead to nearly instant judgment. Of course, any real court could overturn a SIMUCOURT judgment, but studies had shown that a vanishingly small fraction did, so accurate was the software. The last barrier to the litigation explosion . . ."

She paused. Should she mention the expense of the real court process, the unreliability of human triers of fact and law? No, the National Association of Judicial Officials, embattled and obsolete as they were, were notoriously touchy. Best to avoid setting them off.

Her console beeped, signaling it was time for a coffee break. Flanagan did a quick survey of related product liability, and health claims. She had so many cups of coffee that she had reduced its potentially complex search and review spectrum to a few keystrokes. Assured that it was safe, she punched up a steaming cup of Sumatran Coffee.

She thought about John. Susan hoped that he wasn't too angry. She really liked him, and it was hard these days to find people who were really compatible. Something about her lawsuit had bothered him. She sipped her coffee. Perhaps she should drop it?

Susan dismissed the thought. If she withdrew the action things would never get resolved. John would just have to act like an adult.

The computer tone called her attention back to the console.

An opinion was ready indicating that an afternoon walk would offer minimal litigation exposure. Good. She backed out of SIMULAW and ordered a diagnostic check on her SecMan harness.

Then she punched up news of the world.

The big story was a class action suit, PEOPLE OF THE WORLD v. GOVERNMENT OF BRAZIL, ET AL. The decision finally had come down from the live Justices of the Brazilian Supreme Court. The Brazilian government was now committed to repairing the damage to its rain forests, the screen rolled through costs and tertiary awards.

America had achieved world supremacy in an unexpected way with the advent of PEOPLE OF IRAQ v. GEORGE W. BUSH ET AL, back in 2029. Even though it was a "real law" case, it had extended American jurisdiction throughout the world, allowing literally anyone to sue anyone else in an American court. Third world leaders had used it to redress the perceived injustice of the world economic order, and had themselves been devoured by civil rights and pro-democracy lawsuits. Today, the third world, with a lower level of litigation was pulling itself up to western standards, but the richer they became, the more lawsuits developed.

The destruction of the rain forests had been halted long ago, but the Brazilian government had dragged its heels for years. This decision was seen as a vindication for SIMULAW systems, as it was 97% on point with SIMUCOURT decisions.

A beep advised her that the diagnostic of her SecMan had been completed. It was in perfect working order. She turned to regard the heavy harness with its cameras, microphones, and biomonitors.

The need for an accurate record in litigation was vital. Camcorder and audio recording systems had originally been restricted to things like business meetings. But as the litigation explosion went nuclear these recording devices had been installed in and around all personal homes, stores, offices, and public buildings.

The final step had been the SecurityMan harness which allowed people to carry recording devices everywhere they went, ensuring total coverage. Nowadays, almost nobody went out without their SecMan.

Susan was reminded of a book she had read once. "1984" by an Orwell or Blair or something. It had featured cameras everywhere recording everything for a brutal totalitarian state.

She had never seen the parallels others talked about. After all, the incessant cameras were there at the insistence of the individuals who constantly prosecuted or defended themselves from endless lawsuits.

Cradle to grave surveillance and recording by everyone of everything was the price of the virtually unrestricted liberty the people of today enjoyed. The data could only be extracted by Court or SIMUCOURT order, and then only with due restrictions. She, for one, was glad to have the cameras.

Besides, she thought, unlike the book, she could turn off her Holo at any time. All she had to do was be prepared to defend against an action for Unreasonable Restraint of Artistic Expression.

"1984" was no longer available. The SecurityMan Corporation had succeeded in its suit of Retroactive Libel.

Over on the Holo the two cavemen were bashing each other's heads again. She tried to ignore it.

Still, there was an interesting idea. Her fingers spun again.

"The hidden foundation of SIMULAW and its competitors is our faith in the all-inclusive pristine incorruptibility of the Evidence and Security databases. No court can make a reliable decision without reliable evidence, and even the suspicion of tainted evidence can undermine the system."

"Thus, not only must our Security/Evidence systems gather every piece of potential evidence, and store and retrieve it correctly, but the database must be pure, and be seen to be pure."

She stopped typing and stared at the screen.

Nice, Susan thought, a touch controversial but not especially litigable. She spent the rest of the morning working on the article. Then she put it through stylecheck, and finally had her SIMULAW program vet it for minimum litigation exposure.

Then she eFAXed it through and stretched out on her recliner. There was nothing like the satisfaction of a good day's work. On impulse, she called John. His face appeared on the screen, reserved and wary.

"I'm going for a walk in the park, would you like to join me?" she asked.

He seemed to think it over.

"Sure," he replied.

"But let's not discuss any lawsuits we have against each other," she suggested.

"All right," he agreed, "But you have to promise me that you won't sue me during our walk."

Susan hesitated, he was asking a lot. But then, didn't special people deserve special considerations?

"Fine," she told him, "I'll meet you at your place."

Smiling, they signed off. She loved the little dimples in his cheeks when he smiled. She sighed.

John was so reactionary sometimes. He seemed to yearn for the good old days and sometimes complained that the immense wealth of a technological civilization should have a better use than supporting endless petty squabbles.

She loved him, but she couldn't see his point. To her, the old days were a litany of endless oppression. States oppressed their citizens, businesses oppressed their workers, husbands oppressed their wives, and parents oppressed their children.

Even the waiters were rude.

The modern age, she thought, was one of a clean environment, free of poverty and crime. The worthwhile parts of life hadn't changed; people still went for walks in the park. John argued that things could be achieved more cheaply, but he missed the point.

The founding fathers had understood that liberty had to be defended or it would be lost. Their principles had merely been extended to their logical conclusion. Freedom was based in the right to attack without significant personal risk or cost, anyone, anywhere, at anytime, for anything and everything.

She couldn't understand why John was so upset, simply because she was suing him for substandard performance in bed.

She pulled on her SecMan harness, and checked the latest updates for the Etiquette & Courtesy index. Stepping out of her apartment, she exchanged extremely polite greetings with her neighbor, Gladys. She set off down the street, into a beautiful sunny cloudless day, listening to the music of birds chirping.

To Susan Flanagan it was the best of all worlds, and she wouldn't have it any other way.

Deep in the bowels of the SIMULAW Corporation's resident legal program, her article was being reviewed. Better safe than sorry, the program decided, as it sued her.

The End

***

Drunk Slutty Elf, Page 83

Courtesy Call

"Hello."

"Stan Jones of 366 Pocklington?"

"Yes?"

"Mr. Jones, I'm Staci from Customer service at S-Mart, Shop smart shop S-Mart. This is just a complimentary courtesy call to our valued customers. How are you sir?"

"Uh . . . Fine, I guess."

"That's excellent; we're pleased to hear that."

"Well great, listen I have to–"

"According to our records you purchased a quality Mark VL Trinitronic Macrodolby Wall Entertainment system a little over three years ago."

"Uh . . . yes . . ."

"And has it performed to your satisfaction?"

"Uh . . . yes . . ."

"And how is it right now?"

"Well . . ."

"Yes?"

"Well it exploded actually, caused quite a fire."

"Good! And this would have been on the Nineteenth."

"Twentieth actually."

"Oh that's fine, well within tolerances for a unit of that sort. We were just a little worried about the product remaining functional beyond the warranty period."

"My son was badly burned."

"Well, I'm sure your medical coverage was adequate. Had you received our flyer about our courteous and safe disposal service the week prior?"

"Uhm . . . yes."

"We're very disappointed with you Mr. Jones."

"I didn't think it would—"

"Thinking is not required. It said so right in the product warranty manual. How are we to maintain a productive and mutually beneficial relationship with you, our valued customer, if you aren't going to cooperate with us?"

"I was busy . . . It was—"

"Now Mr. Jones, we're not criticizing you. You're a free individual entitled to make your choices as you see fit. We're just a little concerned."

"I'm sorry."

"Mr. Jones, you don't have to apologize to us. You did what you thought was appropriate and your son suffered for it. We don't want your apologies, we want your business. Did you know that according to our records, you hadn't made a visit to one of our stores in over three months?"

"I've been working a lot lately. Two jobs. It's been rough. And between the hospital and the fire . . ."

"I know, sometimes it can be hard to make time. Should I schedule you for some make up appointments? We'll make a sales representative specially available for your shopping needs."

"Really, don't trouble—"

"No trouble Mr. Jones. It's just the S-Mart way, shop smart shop S-Mart. It's why we're number one in Customer service. I'll just pencil you in."

"All right."

"Thursday all right with you?"

"Maybe Friday or Saturday—"

"Thursday it is then, 6:00 pm, so it won't interfere with your jobs. Your sales representative will be Brad."

“. . .”

“Mr. Jones?”

“. . . yeah. Brad. Okay.”

“Excellent! Mr. Jones, may I call you Stan?”

“Uh . . . sure.”

“And may I ask you a question?”

“. . .”

“Stan, what are you watching now?”

“What?”

“Your television exploded right? On schedule, right?”

“Yes.”

“So what are you watching now?”

“. . .”

“Stan, answer the question.”

“Nothing. I’m not watching anything.”

“Don’t lie to me Stan.”

“I’m not lying. I’m not–”

“Our credit check shows that you purchased a Kaijurama Megascreen Unit two weeks ago.”

“Jesus Christ!”

“That’s right Stan, we know. How was it Stan? Did you like it? Japanese, Stan! You couldn’t even buy American?”

“Oh God, listen–”

“No, you listen, Stan! Here at S-Mart, shop smart shop S-Mart, we work hard at providing you with quality service and products. Quality, Stan! It’s not just another word!”

“I know but–”

“We don’t appreciate this Stan. Sneaking around behind our backs like that. We just don’t like it.”

“Listen, I had to. They infected my wife with a nerve toxin. We had no choice.”

“We don’t want to hear your fucking excuses, you worthless piece of shit! You think we give a damn about nerve toxins? You think we’re playing here? You think you can play games with us? You aren’t taking us seriously? Don’t fuck with us! Are you fucking with us, Stan? Because it looks to me like you’re fucking with us!”

Drunk Slutty Elf, Page 86

"No no no–"
"Your house is pretty flammable Stan."
"Jesus no! My firefighting premiums have lapsed–"
"Your negligence isn't our problem, Stan."
"Jesus, please–"
"Fuck you Stan. Do you think we won't take your wife? You want to receive her thumbs in the mail? Oh and by the way, we've got an excellent medical coverage plan that includes reattachments for only a nominal fee, we really recommend you subscribe. You think we won't do it again?"
"Please–"
"We know where you work. We know where your wife works. We know what hospital your son is in. How about a courtesy alcohol bath for him, Stan? How about we just go out and finish the job? Is that what you want?"
"No no not Jimmy–"
"You listen to me you fucking cockroach. We nuked Baltimore, you remember that? We fucking nuked them! So don't you think for one second that we give a shit about some pissant junior account executive!"
"Oh God, don't, please don't (copious weeping). God, I'm sorry, I'm so so sorry. Please, we'll do anything, anything–"
"Stan?"
"Oh God, oh God, oh please, please, not again."
"Stan. Calm down. Listen to me!"
"Oh, oh oh."
"Stan?"
". . ."
"Stan?"
"Yes."
"I've been looking over your credit records, Stan, and you qualify for our special preferred customers' line of credit, which would allow you to buy our new Century 3000 MegaTelevision Entertainment Unit with all the

features. It's the buy of the millennium, available at low low interest with easy monthly payments."

"..."

"We're going to make this once in a lifetime offer because we value you, Stan, and we want to be your store. Remember, shop smart shop S-Mart."

"I can't–"

"Don't go there, Stan!"

"Will you at least protect me from Kaijurama?"

"Stan! We don't do that sort of thing; we're a consumer products and services corporation. Besides, our projections show that you'll be able to make our monthly low reasonable payments without interfering with your financial obligations to Kaijurama, or to any of your other secured service providers, including Jimmy's hospital."

"Uh . . ."

"So what about it Stan?"

"All . . . all right."

"Excellent, Stan. It's now legally binding. Brad will make the arrangements for delivery and custom service at reasonable charges. It can probably go in the bedroom. Or you could keep it in the living room for comparison with the Kaijurama. Have them face off against each other."

"Okay."

"Well, it's been a pleasure speaking to you."

"Yeah."

"Stan, aren't you forgetting something?"

"..."

"Stan?"

"Yeah."

"Well, Stan? We're waiting."

"Shop smart . . . shop . . . (sob) S-Mart."

"Excellent. Glad to have you back in the S-Mart family Stan."

"Yeah . . . thanks."

"Just doing our job, after all, you're our valued customer!"

* * *

Staci leaned back in her chair, head resting against the wall of her booth. Another successful call, another satisfied customer.

She stared in satisfaction as the call logged and her performance index moved back from red to green. She heaved a sigh of relief. It had been close there for a while.

The fucking Japanese! How were they supposed to compete with nerve toxins? It just wasn't fair.

There was the sound of faint screaming, the soundproofing making it seem far off. The sudden odor of roasting flesh made her acutely conscious of her own leads jacked into her body and connecting to the Workplace Incentive Unit.

Who had it been? She wondered. Elaine? Susan? Mary?

The screen blinked. The next call was due. Staci sighed and got back to work.

* * *

Stan hung up the phone and rubbed his temples.

The door opened.

He looked up quickly, in sudden fear.

It was just his wife, returning from her second job. He watched her move gingerly, her frame wasted by chronic malnutrition. She shut the door with awkward movements, although her thumbs had been reattached, she'd never recovered full sensation or use of them.

They stared at each other, despairing, gaunt, hollowed faces mirrored in each other's eyes.

"We bought a new TV," he told her, tonelessly.

"Oh good," she said, tonelessly.

The End

***

Drunk Slutty Elf, Page 89

Silver Giant Sexy

The giant monster, Gorgoron, roared, the sheer kinetic energy of the sound waves shattering windows in nearby skyscrapers. Junichiro Takahashi, Captain of the Science Rescue Force, swore as he wrestled with the skyhopper, darting in and out between buildings, catching glimpses of the immense saurian.

"We have visual," the lovely Lieutenant Tomiki Sakano yelled, activating the recording devices.

The creature loosed an incandescent jet of flaming plasma, slicing through an office tower. As the building began to collapse, Takahashi pulled the skyhopper up, searching for a stable rooftop. Then he felt it, the tremor in his soul, the flutter of an alien presence.

An iridescent beam of shimmering light shot down from the sky into an open plaza barely a quarter mile from the rampaging Gorgoron. Where it touched down, a ball of light settled, lightning arced all around the ball. As the light faded, an unearthly giant stood in its place, tall among the office buildings. It stepped forward, its slender limbs full of unearthly grace.

The Silver Giant had arrived.

"We're saved," Tomiki cried out. "The Silver Giant will stop the monster.

Gorgoron roared at its enemy as the Silver Giant eased into a combat stance. The titans prepared to do battle.

Takahashi surveyed the buildings, looking for a stable location to set down.

***

The Silver Giant was flung back, its purple ray blasting harmlessly into the sky. The momentum from the giant Saurian, Gorgoron's, blow sending it spinning around, crashing through buildings, until it found itself on hands and knees.

"Get up," Junichiro Takahashi whispered. "Get up! Get up!"

He and Tomiki Sakano were the designated monitors for the Science Rescue Force, keeping tabs on the Monsters, even as the operational members of the force engaged in evacuation and rescue. Takahashi was the spotter, piloting the Hopper and guiding the craft to secure locations, while Sakano operated the recording equipment. They had worked well together through many Kaiju incursions.

But despite their friendship, Takahashi kept two secrets from her. The first was his unspoken, romantic, but somehow chaste, love for his colleague. And the second was his psychic link to the Silver Giant, the alien presence always in the back of his mind. He would have been hard pressed to say which one was more vital to him.

Gorgoron was closing in fast behind the Silver Giant, its lumbering bipedal stride almost comical, were it not for the massive trail of destruction behind it. The blue and green dragon's dorsal spikes were already glowing, lightning arched around its eyes.

But the Silver Giant was barely moving. Was it stunned? Painfully, its palms flat on the ground; it tried to get its feet under it, elevating its hips. And remained there, as if waiting.

Smoke was tricking from Gorgoron's jaws. The behemoth seemed to pick up speed, like a colossal walking

Drunk Slutty Elf, Page 91

freight train, bearing down on the Silver Giant from behind.

"Get up!" Takahashi screamed. "He's right on top of you!"

Then, suddenly, shockingly, they collided, with a sound like thunder cracking out. Gorgoron clamped its paws on the side of the Silver Giant's hips, and in turn, the Giant arched its back. The first crack of thunder was followed by another, and then another as it settled into a series of rhythmic booms.

In the seconds that followed, a horrified Takahashi knew he had only one choice. He placed his hands over Tomiki's eyes.

"You shouldn't see this," he said, horrified.

But instead, she pushed his hands away.

"Dolt! I'm not a little girl," she said. "I grew up on a farm. Now let me do my job, you whiny custard-brain!"

In front of them, the rhythmic booming continued, the ultrasound shockwaves making their diaphragms vibrate. But Takahashi was having a hard time focusing. His mind was being overwhelmed with feedback from his Silver Giant, images and sensations were crashing through him.

"Oh my," he whispered, and then passed out.

***

The Science Rescue Force had assembled in the auditorium. Takahashi looked around. Practically the entirety of the base was here, field operatives, offices, even mechanics and support personnel. He nodded to Tomiki. She glanced at him, and looked away, uncomfortable. Hurriedly, she plucked a wet nap from her valise, and wiped her hands.

Things had been awkward between them ever since the incident. After he had passed out, she had tried to render first aid. And he had stained his pants.

Over a dozen times, actually.

He'd had no idea that a human body could contain that much fluid.

Drunk Slutty Elf, Page 92

Apparently, it had surprised Tomiki as well. She'd been obsessively washing her hands ever since.

The Director came forth.

"I am Shigeru Onodero," he began. "And when I was a very young boy, playing with my friends on the shores of Tokyo Bay, I witnessed the rising of the first Kaiju, Ogazar. To this day, I still don't know what made me stop and look out over the bay. Perhaps it was a flight of birds taking off from the water. Perhaps a strange swelling on the surface of the waters, as of something rising from the deep. But I was watching, and I believe that I was the first to see that monstrous head, those horns, those glowing eyes, come out of the sea as it headed to Tokyo in 1954."

"I was perhaps five years old then. I knew that I was looking at something terrible, and I knew that there would be great suffering. I could do nothing but watch. I promised then that I would spend my life trying to save humanity from this monster, and the ones that followed. I have done my best to keep that promise."

He seemed deflated.

"Now, it seems that the recent field work of Tomiki Sakano has given us all much to think about."

Then the lead scientist, Fumiko Oto stepped forward, her lab coat blazing white. She tapped the microphone.

"Ahem," she said. "Is this on?" She gazed out over the assembled throng.

"I am sure you have all heard that reports and rumors of the Gorgoron encounter, some of you are undoubtedly eyewitnesses. We have Ms Sakano's recording, but before we review it, I want to revisit some of our data.

"We are all aware that the Age of Kaiju began in 1954 with King Ogazar, the radioactive dinosaur tyrant. It devastated Tokyo, and then, under attack from defense forces, returned to die in the sea.

"As it turns out, every assumption was wrong. It was not a dinosaur, it was not the creation of atomic testing or radiation, and it did not die.

"Instead it reappeared, as did more and more of its kind. Dozens of them. Creatures of enormous, impossible size and destructive abilities, many of which featured reptilian or arthropod traits, or even combinations of these qualities.

"At first, these creatures were attributed to many sources – chemical spills, atomic testing, radiation leaks, pollution, mad scientists and secret government projects. But eventually, analysis of isotope residues demonstrated that they were not of this Earth. All of these monsters were from outer space.

"In 1967, the first of the Silver Giants appeared on Earth, fighting the Kaiju. Since then, there have been several Silver Giants. While they do not always appear during Kaiju outbreaks, whenever they have, they've battled Kaiju, saving tens of thousands of live, and preventing immense property damage. It is not an exaggeration to say that the Silver Giants have saved human civilization. We believed that they had come to save us from alien menaces . . .

"We were wrong," she announced. "Play the recording."

The lights dimmed, the giant screen behind Doctor Oto lit up. Calmly, she walked to the edge of the stage.

The Silver Giant appeared fifty meters tall, thousands of tons in weight, an almost slender humanoid figure with a flat face and glowing insect-like eyes appeared, its silver body almost metallic, iridescent with purple, red and green highlights. The giant flashed through a series of poses as the stock footage played, displaying its anatomy.

Somehow the footage conveyed a sense of a creature as much insect-like as humanoid, something whose resemblance to men and women was as coincidental as it was startling.

Next flashed Gorgoron, one of the most terrifying of the giant monsters, over seventy meters tall, festooned with spikes, horns, protrusions, all sprouting from a reptilian, dinosaur-like frame. Triple jointed jaws opened as it roared, and luminescent stripes glowed. It released a stream of fire from its mouth.

Takahashi knew what was coming next, and he sank down into his seat. Sakano automatically pulled another wet wipe from her valise to wash her hands.

The two titanic beings appeared together in Sakano's recording, the Silver Giant, clearly on all fours, hips elevated, waiting as the monster bore down on it. It was the wait, those long seconds of hesitation as the giant reptile approached, that made it awful. Takahashi had always remained pure, he avoided pornography. But even in his own personal innocence, there was no denying what that position signified.

A moment later, Gorgoron had borne down. The rhythmic booming had begun, as well as other sounds that might have been moaning or roaring. Takahashi couldn't bear to watch. He looked away. Also, he'd stained his pants again.

The screen went dark, and Doctor Oto once again strode to the podium.

"They're having sex," she said bluntly. "That's what it's been this whole time: Sex."

Behind her the screen lit up, showing frames from previous recent battles between the Kaiju monsters, and their enemies, the Silver Giants. Each captured pose was somehow more licentious and provocative than the last. Takahashi knew these were life and death battles, but these frozen images suggested other interpretations.

"In hindsight," she said, "we should have figured it all out long ago. The Kaiju and the Silver Giants . . .they're the same species. That has become clear as we've re-examined the isotope traces. The isotope ratios were identical, creatures of the same world. Same species. Same origins

"Just different genders. Like the birds of our world, the male gender has become large and colorful to attract the notice of potential mates, they've become tall, grown elaborate horns, feathers, spikes, scales, brilliant plumage to display and attract attention, while the opposite female gender is plain and smooth.

"The posturing gender does not just develop plumage, it demonstrates itself. Among birds, it builds nests and constructs elaborate songs. Among Kaiju it engages in wanton destruction to show its power and might, to prove its sexual worth.

"For the last four decades, we have not been witnessing battles between good and evil races of giant aliens. We have been watching courtships. Elaborate mating dances, as the females select among their suitors. Tens of thousands of people have died, so they can 'get jiggy.'"

From the audience, a ripple of protest emerged.

"Why come here?" someone protested.

"We don't know," Doctor Oto said. "Perhaps our cities and landscape are simply delightful to destroy the buildings crash and fall apart satisfyingly. I can't imagine kicking around rocks on barren worlds is much fun. Perhaps it's as simple as that."

Oto hesitated. "Or perhaps it's the fact that humans resemble tiny versions of their female's base forms. Maybe that inspires them. Perhaps they're just kinky. It would be like humans having sex in the middle of a complex of termite mounds filled with Barbie dolls. Who knows? The point is that our planet is now hostage to giant alien sex rituals."

Takahashi suddenly felt unclean. He reached back along the psychic link he'd had with the Silver Giant. Was it really that? Not good versus evil, not heroism, not paragons of light saving a fragile humanity from the outer darkness. Could it really be so tawdry and vulgar? For a second, the link opened and he had a sense of what the Silver Giant was doing right at this moment.

He broke the link. But even that glimpse had been too much. His body was shaking, his skin felt clammy and sweaty, and he was distressed to notice he'd stained his pants again. Carefully, he picked up his file folder and laid it across his hips, hoping no one would notice.

"It's clear," Doctor Oto said, "that this interpretation suggests that we are on the verge of a new pattern of behavior, one which will have major impacts on the pornography industry, public morality, and perhaps pose vast challenges to explaining to children."

Takahashi didn't want to hear another word. He wanted to shrivel up and die, although one part of him was decidedly refusing to shrivel. He had always believed he was special, that he had been touched by something divine, enlisted in a noble, righteous purpose.

Now, it turned out that he was just a puppet of space perverts.

He noticed Tomiki talking to a few other women, she pointed at him, and they all looked in his direction. Takahashi blushed deeply and pretended to look away.

He tried to concentrate on blocking out the Silver Giant's psychic connection. The feelings were bad enough, but once in a while an image of monstrous anatomy slipped through, and he really didn't want that in his head.

"So . . ." someone was saying, "our whole world is just a cheap love hotel for alien monsters? What do we do? How do we deal with this?"

Director Shigeru Onodero stood resolute. "As disturbing as this knowledge is, it changes nothing. We must continue as we have been, evacuating, rescuing, rebuilding, saving who we can, and fighting. The only shame is surrender."

He paused.

"This awful knowledge offers us hope. We know their motives and motivations now, and we can only hope that once they all have it out of their system, they will depart the world and leave us in peace."

The assembled members of Science Rescue Force rose for a standing ovation, as Onodero bowed his head in acknowledgment.

Drunk Slutty Elf, Page 97

All except Takahashi whose pants were in far too awkward a state to permit him to stand.

Instead, he sat damp and miserable. Surely there was more to it than kinky alien sex, he thought desperately, although from the images and sensations coming in, it was definitely kinky.

But sex involved reproduction.

He could only hope that the wherever they laid their eggs, settled their larva, or birthed their young, whatever those things were, they'd do it far, far away.

***

As Onodero had hoped, both the Silver Giants and the Kaiju monsters faded away, their courtships climaxing again and again in unnatural acts. Sated, both genders drifted away from Earth, leaving nothing but ruins and destruction behind. Mankind breathed a deep sigh of relief and life seemed to return to normal.

***

Deep beneath the earth, in hidden chambers scattered across the planet, pulsing golden eggs glowed with lambent light.

Suddenly, in one chamber, the surface of one of the eggs rippled. A clawlike hand struck through, surging out. More eggs rippled. Slowly, beings began to struggle out, human sized and human shaped, but with their bodies smooth, resembling the shapes of the Silver Giants, their heads somewhat oversized, some of them bearing insect like antenna and plates.

One by one, they struggled and stumbled, gazing at each other in wonder. But they were already prepared to exist in this world, thanks to the Silver Giant's psychic links to humans like Takahashi. Takahashi's human form had provided the template for the newborns to shape themselves, so that they could blend with humanity.

Unconsciously, they picked up the telepathic emanations from the human world above, temporarily shaping themselves as young men and women, forgetting

Drunk Slutty Elf, Page 98

their alien natures for a time. One by one, they began to stumble out into the world above, where they would find each other, and discover their strange forms and powers.

Out in space, proud fathers began to hear the squalls of their newborns on faraway Earth, that world of tiny beings whose edifices and activities invited such delightful destruction. Newborns who would mimic, the local species, but who would slowly come into their powers, reverting to natural forms, some of them lone 'riders,' others clustering together as groups of powered 'rangers' and superb 'sentai.'

The newborns would have to be taught, to be cultivated, to be challenged so that they could develop their abilities and fully mature.

The proud fathers began the long journey back to Earth. Things were about to get interesting on that planet, and like proud fathers everywhere, they didn't want to miss a minute of it.

The End

***

A Hard Day's Blight

The devil had gotten into the habit of dawdling by the water cooler.

"So how about them Mets?" he said.

To be fair, it wasn't really THE DEVIL, but rather 'a devil.' To be completely specific, it was a rather minor devil in the bureaucracy of Hell. He liked to think that his friends, if he had any, would have called him Hideous.

By the same token, it wasn't really a water cooler that he dawdled by. For one thing, it was designed to maintain its contents at a scalding and unbearable temperature even in the inferno. For another, the corrosive and acidic liquid within could scarcely be called water, even by the souls of damned goldfish forced to swim within.

Hideous had never thought about what a goldfish could possibly have done to be sentenced to eternal punishment. Hideous avoided thinking about anything at all, especially his work. Thinking was frowned upon in Hell.

Thinking had resulted in most of Hell's arrivals, including Hideous's own kind. If Hideous had paused to consider it, he would have considered it a clear case of burning the barn after the horse had escaped. But Hell didn't bear second thoughts.

"Pretty awful," said Roadkill, "losing every game."

Roadkill shifted his general shape, but usually resembled a collection of animals that had been run over by heavy vehicles and reassembled in a rather freehand style.

"Yeah, but remember, most of the team is on drugs, and the star is having carnal knowledge of a twelve year old boy. I expect that we'll see most of them down here, when that tour bus crashes." This was from Vomit, who resembled a spiny lobster turned inside out.

In spite of his best efforts, Hideous had noticed more and more of his fellow devils tended to congregate around the water cooler. Sometimes there were so many that the boiling liquid would be entirely consumed and the damned goldfish would be forced to flop about on the hot plate. He hoped they appreciated the change.

He slapped a mosquito. As near as Hideous could determine, every mosquito that had ever lived had gone straight to Hell.

Alone of all Hell's denizens, they seemed to like it here.

"What's all this then," boomed a terrifying voice. An unspeakable apparition appeared. "I turn my back on you lazy goldbrickers, and you all goof off? Back to work!"

It was their supervisor. A ferocious demon who had once terrorized the Aztecs as 'The Baked Potato of DOOM.' As demons went, this was a fussy and officious personage. It imagined that its superiors respected its work, when they did nothing of the kind. It treasured the 'The' of its nomenclature, fondly imagining that it had a uniqueness it would have lacked had it only been known as 'a baked potato of doom.' The true ranking and status of this demon extended little further than lording it over such minor devils as Hideous and his kind.

"It's still our coffee break," ventured Vomit timorously. Which had an element of truth in it. Time was as endless in Hell as it was in Heaven, and so an earthly minute could be an eternity.

"Your coffee break was over two eons ago. Now back to work." The Baked Potato cracked its whip. "A soul enslaved is a soul burned. One Two Three Four – Torture Torture Torture."

"One Two Three Four," the devils mumbled as they shambled away from the water cooler.

"Torture Torture Torture," chanted Hideous under his breath, as he slouched back to his chamber of torment. Thompkinson would be waiting there. He almost looked forward to finishing the day and getting back to his wife, and then shuddered at the thought of his wife.

"Remember, eternal punishment is the price of damnation," called The Baked Potato.

Hideous had noticed that it seemed to resort more and more to desperate cheers and slogans.

"Hello Thompkinson," said Hideous as he came through the portal.

"Hello Hideous," said Thompkinson, who was chained to a rack. "What shall it be today?"

A surge of hatred bolted through Hideous, followed by an undercurrent of fear.

"You miserable worm Larvae," screamed Hideous with his most terrifying aspect, "First, the flesh will be seared from your body by the flaming whip of Aspodel, and then red hot pokers will be inserted into your nether regions."

"Fine," yawned Thompkinson.

For an instant Hideous's blood turned to ice.

Thompkinson went on, "Listen, I think I'll take a nap for a while, wake me when you get to the bit about the hot poker."

"You will not sleep," roared Hideous bravely. "You will scream in eternal torment."

"I can scream in my sleep," said Thompkinson mildly, stifling another yawn. "It's one of the first things we learn to do around here. Besides, I'm very good at it. You'd swear I was awake and screaming."

"That's beside the point. When I'm tormenting you, you will be awake. I'm only saying it once. When I'm tormenting you, you WILL be awake!"

"That's twice," Thompkinson pointed out.

"Do you have any idea what I'll do to you if you go to sleep on me?" Hideous gnashed his teeth and breathed hellfire, his hooves struck sparks, and his head spun right around. He thought that last one was a pretty good effect.

"If you do it again!" he warned. "I'll . . ."

"You'll pluck out my eyeballs," said Thompkinson wearily.

"I'll pluck out your eyeballs," screamed Hideous.

"Then you'll rip out my tongue," monotoned Thompkinson.

"Then I'll rip out your tongue," screamed Hideous.

"You'll pluck out my fingers and toes one by one," said Thompkinson.

"I'll pluck out your fingers and toes one by one," screamed Hideous.

"Then you'll tear me to pieces and sew them back together backwards and throw me into a vat of molten lava," said Thompkinson.

"And then I'll tear you to pieces and sew . . ." Hideous stopped abruptly.

He stared suspiciously at his victim.

"How did you know that?" asked Hideous.

Thompkinson sighed "You've threatened to do that two hundred forty eight thousand five hundred and sixteen times."

Hideous digested this information with a familiar sinking feeling.

"How many times have I actually done it?" he asked.

"One hundred seventy two thousand three hundred and eight." replied Thompkinson.

Hideous thought for a moment.

"How about if I put you through the Cuisinart of perdition, slice, dice, and have horrid insects replace certain internal organs?" he suggested hopefully.

"Six hundred and twenty one thousand, nine hundred and seventy two, counting all the variations," Thompkinson conveyed an impression of incredible weariness.

"That's a good one, eh?" the devil grinned evilly, plumes of sulphur spurting from its nostrils.

"Actually," replied Thompkinson, "It's pretty tired. But you usually fall back on that one when you run out of ideas."

Hideous let out a terrific bellow and plucked out both Thompkinson's eyes, then for good measure he ripped off his arms and ground them underfoot.

"Oh, very good," retorted Thompkinson, "I suppose I should be impressed."

"That's supposed to hurt," growled Hideous.

"Well it does," said Thompkinson reasonably, "but trust me, after the first five million times the shock sort of wears off."

Hideous moped.

"Besides," went on Thompkinson, "I've had my eyes plucked out by experts."

"What's expert about plucking eyeballs?" snarled Hideous jealously.

"Hah," Thompkinson laughed, the viscous jelly on his cheeks had dried, and soon the eyes would reform. "A lot you know. Why, when Satan plucked mine out I screamed for a month. And then . . ."

"That's it," screamed Hideous, "I don't want to hear it. I don't care. You are damned and I'm going to torture you for all eternity."

"Sure," said Thompkinson affably. "But Satan . . ."

"No Satan," screamed Hideous, well into a tantrum, "I'm sick and tired of Satan. Satan this and Satan that. To Hell with Satan, that overrated windbag."

Drunk Slutty Elf, Page 104

Which in Hell is exactly the wrong thing to say; because at that moment a bolt of black demonic lightning appeared out of nowhere, fried him into cinders and split him evenly in two. The powers of Hell were not to be mocked.

"At least," thought Hideous, "I'm not a pillar of salt this time."

It was high time for another coffee break.

The gang at the water cooler had grown larger. Hideous noted that the condemned goldfish had been without fluid so long they had finally grown little legs and now hopped about the plate. He sidled up to Vomit.

"Vomit, dear fiend," simpered Hideous in what he thought was an ingratiating manner. "My damned simply offers no challenge anymore. Perhaps you would consider trading?"

Vomit stepped back; he always disliked the smell of Hideous breath, as well as everything else about Hideous.

"Who have you got?" asked Vomit hopefully.

"Thompkinson."

A shudder ran through the group.

"I'll trade," an upstart devil called Sump answered.

"Terrific," said Hideous, unable to believe his luck, "who have you got?"

"Waldorf."

Hideous cringed.

Still by the time The Baked Potato had arrived to exhort them all back to work, Hideous had settled on a new approach.

"Thompkinson," he called as he came through the portal, "have you ever considered the philosophical basis of evil as the source of suffering?"

Thompkinson peered at him thoughtfully; the eyes had grown back completely.

"Are we talking manifest evil or structural evil, and are you approaching this from a Hegelian dialectic?" Thompkinson asked.

Hideous screamed.

Finally, Hideous went back to the flaming whip. Though what little enthusiasm he had dissipated entirely as the sound of snoring reverberated through the chamber.

"It wasn't always like this," Hideous reflected, on the way home.

Originally, after the fall Hell had been a decent place. It was still a flaming pit of everlasting suffering, but it had been THEIR flaming pit. The devils could suffer and rage in peace. They'd almost managed to become comfortable.

But then HE had started sending down these rejects from Heaven and suddenly everyone had to rush around and get organized to torture and punish the incoming.

He supposed that the bureaucracy of Hell was necessary. Without it, some of the damned might escape their just punishment. He remembered how, during a sudden influx of immigration, a band of Germans had gone unnoticed. Until they managed to set up a country club, and had gotten on everyone's nerves with their incessant singing of "Deutschland Under Alles."

Now Hell was crowded and polluted and getting more so with each day. His partners in the car pool were especially obnoxious.

Hideous idly crushed a cockroach under his hooves. Cockroaches were a good example. Since coming to Hell, they had somehow managed to reproduce and were now omnipresent. Whole classes of imps had been assigned to cockroaches, and now found themselves outnumbered and on the defensive.

His wife Blanche met him at the door by ripping off his face. Hideous was pleased. She was in a good mood for once. Blanche was a loathsome mixture of Lizard and Tarantula and she had a face filled with rows of rotating needle-like teeth.

"So," screamed Blanche, "Mr. La De Da finally deigns to come home. Perhaps I should bring out the fatted calf. Some of us actually work, you know. I could at least expect some consideration. But nooo . . ."

Hideous listened with only half an ear, the other half had just been bitten off by Blanche. But his mind kept returning to the problem of Thompkinson.

Perhaps the molasses and red ant treatment?

No, it felt disturbingly familiar. He wasn't sure how often he had employed it, but he suspected that Thompkinson would be able to tell him.

Maybe a Chinese water torture using molten lead? That sounded good.

No, he had used it last week. Thompkinson had merely counted the drops of lead and used it to calculate square roots. That had been a bad experience.

Blanche was still going on, pausing only to hit him with large spiked objects. Blanche. Now there was an idea.

"Blanthe, deareth." he lisped, she having just broken his lower mandible, "have you ever heard of Thompkinthon?"

She paused, "Thompkinson?"

Abruptly he remembered he had tried this before. After a short time Blanche and Thompkinson had begun to get along famously. Then they had teamed up on him. He changed the subject. Time for a reassignment, he decided.

The next morning he marched straight into what passed for The Baked Potato's offices. The Baked Potato glowered at him.

Hideous quailed, but stood firm.

"I want a transfer!"

"You and everybody else," The Baked Potato snarled, and handed him a handful of forms. "I wish you yellowbellies would look around and realize this is Hell. Fill this out."

Hideous looked incredulously at the small number of forms in his paw. Could it be this easy?

"Those are the forms requesting the forms for permission to apply for the forms requesting the forms to requisition the application to transfer forms," The Baked Potato told him. "Everything has to be filled out in quadruplicate and individually dated and co-signed in proper sequence.”

Whatever Hideous had in place of a heart sank like a stone.

“But I’ll tell you right now, the only openings are on the pit bull squad.”

Hideous quailed again. While it surprised no one that pit bull dogs should be condemned to Hell, the dogs had been severely peeved by their new abode. So much so that they immediately set upon and tore to pieces every demon sent to torment them. Their temper was legendary throughout the underworld. At one time the powers had decided to offer them positions as minor demons, but they had devoured the emissaries.

Finally, a band of clever devils had decided to approach the maddened dogs by shape shifting into less provocative guises, like little girls and fluffy kittens. Hideous shuddered at the thought of how that turned out.

Thoroughly defeated, Hideous returned to Thompkinson.

They were well into the torment of the thousand cuts when Hideous finally screamed out.

“Cut that out.”

“Cut what out?” Thompkinson asked pleasantly.

“That whistling! You were daydreaming again,” Hideous accused.

“I was not daydreaming.” Thompkinson responded placidly.

“Was too!”

“Was not.”

“Was too! How many cuts have I inflicted?” Hideous questioned.

“Five hundred and thirty two,” Thompkinson answered.

“Ah hah!” crowed Hideous, “you were daydreaming. It was five hundred and seventy seven.”

"No, it was five hundred and thirty two. You missed several important cuts," replied Thompkinson.

This was just too much for Hideous.

"Are you accusing me of sloppy workmanship?" Hideous screamed.

"Look for cut eighty five," replied Thompkinson smugly.

Hideous looked. Cut eighty five was a deep incision just over the left kidney. It wasn't there. In a fit of pique he tore out both Thompkinson's kidneys with his bare claws.

"Well, I guess that ruins it completely now doesn't it?" Thompkinson commented.

"Maybe I'd do it right if I had a victim who properly appreciated these things," roared Hideous.

"I think," said Thompkinson, "that you are going at this wrong. You should change your approach."

"Oh?" said the devil.

"Your problem," said Thompkinson, "is that I am on guard against anything you might do. What you need to do is lull me until I let my guard down and then pounce."

"And, uh, how would I do that?" asked Hideous, interested in spite of himself. Thompkinson might be on track here.

"Just be nice to me." Thompkinson explained, "Then, once my guard is down, BOOM!"

It made perfect sense, Hideous thought. With rising excitement he began to plot how best to lull Thompkinson. And then just as quickly, his balloon was punctured as he recalled that he had tried this one many times before.

He had brought Thompkinson sumptuous banquets, fine wines, plied him with works of art and literature, brought him television, stereo, a pinball machine, had even brought imps in the forms of a succession of beautiful women.

Thompkinson had blithely eaten the banquets, drank the wines, admired the art, read the literature, listened to the stereo, played the pinball machine, and made love to the impish women with happy insouciance. All without ever for an instant displaying anything that could be remotely mistaken for a lull. Thompkinson had not suffered at all.

Which was more than he could say for himself, when the powers had noticed what he was doing.

It was time for a coffee break.

Over at the water cooler it was crowded as never before. Some enterprising devils had set up a track in the water cooler's plate, and were now taking bets on the different goldfish. It took a Herculean effort on the part of The Baked Potato to drive them back to work.

But this time, Hideous had an idea. One that was sure to work.

"Thompkinson," said Hideous as he came through the portal, "we have to talk."

"Sure," replied Thompkinson cheerfully, "I've got some time."

He laughed at his own joke. Hideous hated that.

"I think we should clarify our relationship," Hideous told him. "You are a damned soul, judged and found wanting, and cast down to Hell to suffer eternal torment and damnation. Are we clear on this part?"

"Got it," answered Thompkinson brightly.

"I, on the other hand, am a fallen angel who rebelled against HIM and was flung down to the fiery pit. How are we doing so far?"

Hideous was being very calm.

"Fine," said Thompkinson affably.

No sarcastic remarks about what an incredibly bright idea the rebellion had been. No philosophical ruminations on the futility of waging war upon an omnipotent being. No pointing out that Omniscience guaranteed the result since before the beginning of time.

Not even a simple 'So what exactly were you thinking?'

Hideous hated it when Thompkinson pointed out his mistakes, and by any measure, the rebellion had been a spectacular blunder.

Thompkinson was being pleasant for a change.

Hideous was almost grateful.

"Now, it is my mission to see that you suffer everlasting torment and ceaseless agony for all of eternity. Got that?"

"Yep," nodded Thompkinson.

"So what in Hell is the problem?" Hideous screamed.

"Well," said Thompkinson reflectively, "I guess there's just a limited number of things you can do to torture someone. Eventually, given eternity, you will do everything so often that the effect just wears off."

"Just so!" chortled the devil, and hurled his spell.

Thompkinson convulsed on the rack and went limp. The spell began to relentlessly wipe away his memories.

For the first time in eons the devil allowed himself a laugh, a long rolling booming thing.

To remove all memory of previous suffering was a radical and dangerous step. Technically, it was forbidden in hell, but Hideous was all out of options. It was tricky; one had to leave a tail end of a past to the victim, otherwise he might be cleansed of his sins and catapulted straight out of Hell.

Randomly launching formerly damned souls into Heaven did not go over well in either realm.

But it was worth the risk. When Thompkinson opened his eyes, it would be as if it was his first day in Hell.

Hideous contemplated an eternity of roasting, of gouging, of plucking and burning and a million other torments, each one fresh and new as a summer flower in spring. It was wonderful.

Thompkinson raised his head and looked at the devil with childlike innocence.

"You know," he said, "I have no idea who you are or where I am. But I have the strangest feeling that this has happened three hundred thousand two hundred and ninety three times . . ."

And it was at that moment that eternity yawned before the devil like some vast and empty cavern and he began to scream. He finally understood the cruel and merciless justice of a Creator who would instill in his creations a capacity for boredom and then grant them eternal life.

And particularly, who that Creator had actually set out to punish.

He could almost admire HIS imagination and sneakiness.

This really is Hell, thought the devil.

The End

***

The Furry Tentacles of Menace

Collision Peters stood turning the antique Pictish fertility rod over in his hands. He turned to the other men in the room.

"Perhaps," he told them, "perhaps our greatest strength is the limitation of the human mind. For surely, if one could, for one terrible instant, perceive the cosmos as it must be, one would go raving mad!"

His gaze fell on the two men sitting in the elegant drawing room with him. A thin and snappish young blade was engaged in pouring tea, and glanced up at him. The distinguished older gentleman, peculiarly wearing sunglasses despite the dim lighting, sat back easily in his comfortable chair. Presently he spoke.

"I have seen it happen," said Sir James, the elder of the two listeners. "That is a certainty. Even in my trade, we develop certain eccentricities."

"Like not taking off your sun glasses indoors," Collision spoke suddenly.

"We have not gathered to discuss my apparel," Sir James said frostily.

"Sir James," Charles said hastily, "is without the gift of sight."

"Oh," Collision paled, "was it a tragic accident?"

"It was a result of his marriage," Charles explained.

Collision's brow wrinkled in confusion.

"And for that reason, not tragic at all," Sir James chuckled. "They say that love is blind. That's not quite true, but certainly blindness helps. This handicap has allowed me

Drunk Slutty Elf, Page 113

to largely retire from my practice of 'psychic investigation,' and devote my best years to my wife."

"Oh," said Collision. "Perhaps I've come to the wrong place. I'd asked Charles for the very best help available."

"Indeed," said Charles, the younger gentleman. "You have presumed upon our old school friendship to bring you here to Sir James. I believe that you said it was a matter vital to the freedom and security of the realm as we know it. Perhaps we should get on with it."

"I am principally retired, but I consult from time to time," Sir James reassured Collision.

"Oh very well," said Collision, sitting down, "I am here on a matter of gravest urgency."

He stood up again, exclaiming, "People wonder why I can no longer stand the sight of sunflower seeds. Why I wear a hat of tinfoil. Why I keep meticulous records of the grocery lists of members of parliament. Why I have thirty-five cats."

"And walk them everywhere in groups of five," Sir James commented, listening to the sounds of a faint but distinctly feline racket in the cloakroom.

"People wonder why I no longer have sexual intercourse with my wife!" This was an anguished cry.

"You're married?" Sir James asked, mildly surprised. He sipped his tea.

"Oongawa Peters," Collision explained. "Surely you've seen her at social occasions."

"Oongawa . . . Oongawa," Sir James murmured, then he brightened. "Native girl, huge bone through her nose, filed teeth. From the forbidden reaches of the Amazon, if I recall my accents."

"That is my beloved," Collision said stiffly, "I've been trying to get her to wear a smaller bone."

"Capital girl," Charles said, "I remember I was sitting next to her at Lady Chichester's tea, some months ago. She had some amazing recipes for Mapaya."

"What is a Mapaya?" Collision asked, puzzled.

"Oh," Sir James looked up, "sluglike creature, about six inches long with spines. It lives in tropical pools and burrows up the nether entrance of warm-blooded creatures, where it deposits its eggs."

"How horrible," Collision shuddered.

"Actually, the experience can be quite exhilarating," Sir James replied. "The trick is not to let these things go too far. With the Mapaya, one should pursue a dalliance rather than a consummation."

He seemed to glance towards Charles, who blushed.

Sir James sighed wistfully, contemplating the vagaries of human invertebrate relationships, and then turned back to Collision.

"So tell me, Mr. Peters," Sir James began.

"Collision," Collision corrected.

"So tell me, Collision," Sir James continued, "I am astonished. How is it that people learn that you are not intimate with your wife?"

Collision looked startled, and thought hard on the matter.

"I guess," he said finally, after due consideration, "I tell them."

"Ahh," said Sir James.

"But that's not the problem," Collision fretted.

He handed Sir James a scrawled drawing of particularly repellent aspect. It depicted unnatural entities with yellow skin, eyes on one side of their heads, protruding upper teeth, and heads of jagged spikes or bizarre pillars.

"You wouldn't by any chance be an artist of some sort?" Sir James asked, smoothing the crumpled paper, and passing the sheets to Charles.

"Actually no, I'm an accountant,"

"Thank God!" Charles said, as he examined the drawings.

"But my real avocation is as an adventurer and explorer. I yearn to cross uncharted vastness and wrestle lions with my bare hands."

"These trades, I hear, are quite similar to accounting," Sir James ventured.

"But as to the drawing," Collision persisted, "can you take my meaning?"

"I confess that I cannot. What is it?" asked Charles.

"It is the Old Ones," Collision whispered, "those formless and stygian monstrosities that wait outside the borders of time and space as we know it."

"Ahh, I see," said Charles, holding it up to the light. He began to rise from his chair. "Drawings of formless beings. Thank you for bringing this to my attention. You've done the proper thing. Just leave it to us to set things right."

"But there's more," Collision said, seeming to advance on them from his seated position.

"I supposed there would be," Sir James said regretfully.

He seemed to glare at Charles, who blushed audibly.

"I must say first, that save for the horrific thing I stumbled onto, there is nothing at all out of the ordinary about me.

"My parents had me after but a single occasion of intercourse and thereafter lived quite proper lives. I was a precocious youth of course," Collision continued, "raised by the coal shuttle and growing up on tales of adventure and exploration.

"In due course, I went off to a very good school, where I was caned regularly, as every young boy should be. I grew to the fullness of manhood, and commenced upon my career."

"Accountancy?" Sir James asked.

Collision coughed, "Exploring actually. But there were no openings, so I turned to accounting as an interim occupation, as I waited for something to become available."

"Ahh, and how long have you been an accountant?" asked Sir James.

"About twenty years." Collision paused. "Dry tedious years of adding up numbers starved my soul of the romance and adventure it needed. Even as I calculated capital gains amortization tax, some part of me was imbibing hallucinogenic slime with the Yanomano in the jungles of Brazil.

"Thus, when I noted some old school colleagues were getting up an expedition to the Andes, I knew it was my chance. I had to go."

"Indeed," sighed Sir James.

"The expedition, in its initial stages, could only be considered a success, as we spotted and identified many new species of insects and fungi. Encouraged, we pressed on into the Andean jungles, going where no white man had gone uneaten.

"On the fourteenth day of our expedition, we unwittingly blundered into a waterfall, and were near drowned. Capsized, we swept down the wild currents, and as I sank for the third time, I realized that I might never see England again."

Collision paused to take a sip of tea.

"I must say, then, that it came as a shock for me and the other members of the expedition to wake to grinning sunburned faces and sharpened teeth staring down at us. I remember my lungs being rudely emptied of water, and one particular pair of soft lips, pressing against mine, to give me the breath of life, and a little bit of tongue."

"Oongawa?" Charles asked.

"Her brother, actually," Collision said. He smiled wistfully. "We had been rescued by the TShoo TShoo people."

Charles leaped to his feet. "The Tcho Tcho people," he cried, "not those notorious cannibals and bloodthirsty worshippers of nameless forms from beyond."

"Their cousins actually," Collision corrected, emphasizing the words, "the TShoo TShoo people are kinder gentler cannibals."

"Indeed," said Sir James.

"Well, they are not really cannibals, except in the technical sense that they eat human flesh," Collision said.

"Regrettably, that is all too often the technical definition of cannibalism," Sir James observed, nodding in Charles direction.

"It's just that they are so refined and sensitive that they are unable to procure their meat by violence – that is, hunting and killing it. Instead, they consume only that flesh which has come to its natural conclusion. Alas, since it is somewhat difficult to follow a water buffalo through the jungle for years waiting for it to die of natural causes, the meat they most commonly consume is found more readily at hand. So in a sense, they aren't really genuine cannibals."

"I see your point," Sir James said, "but I would pray that it relates to something."

"Ah well, I will get on with the story. Most of the expedition quickly recovered and moved on, except for me and the Vicar. I had found true love, my blessed Oongawa. I am happy to say that our feelings were mutual, and were soon consummated. Happily do I recall the day that we were married over the Vicar."

"Married over the Vicar," Charles mused, "what a strange turn of phrase."

"Actually, the Vicar had passed away, but as was the village's custom of waste not want not, he found a final nuptial role as the wedding feast."

"Broiled?" Sir James asked.

"No, roasted. He was a bit gamey actually," Collision confessed.

"Don't I know it. Human flesh can be inedible unless properly spiced," Sir James chuckled.

"I have heard that basil and garlic works well," offered Charles.

"Garlic works well on most things, but for human flesh eucalyptus and chamomile are best. Nothing else is civilized," Sir James responded.

"I shall keep that in mind. Thank you," said Charles.

"Think nothing of it," Sir James rumbled, "but I believe Collision here was relating his story."

"Well yes. I must confess that I spent a certain amount of time in the village, a honeymoon of sorts. During that time, I got to know the village witch doctor, Oongawa's father, quite well.

"Many is the afternoon we sat under the shade tree, contemplating the noonday sun and discussing the arcane secrets of our respective trades. He was, I recall, quite taken by the accrual method of accountancy and double entry ledgers, but he could never see where the lions entered into it.

"For his own part, he revealed what I was to discover was a sophisticated metaphysical outlook. The tribal belief was that the physical universe was but the tiniest fragment of true reality, created by formless beings of unimaginable dimensions as a plaything. These beings had, as he put it, 'gone for a nappy,' but when the stars were right, they would wake to reclaim all that was once theirs."

He looked directly at Sir James.

"Clearly, he was speaking of the Old Ones."

Sir James nodded slightly; his face had taken on a grave cast.

"He even shared with me certain holy images, which I have tried to reproduce for you, and the ritual protections of their tribe, such as 'fla grn, fre gnafn hr/lyara."

With those words, Charles and Sir James leaped from their seats.

"I must ask you never to repeat those words in this house again," Sir James thundered.

"But what do they mean?" Collision asked.

"It is a reference to the dentures of the Old Ones!"

"Objects of such unimaginable geometry that no living man could floss them without going completely mad!" Sir James exclaimed.

Drunk Slutty Elf, Page 119

"If you sought to convince us of some secret knowledge of the Old Ones, you have succeeded," Charles said. "Just don't utter those words again."

"Very well," Collision's voice dropped, "the village witch doctor–"

"I believe that they prefer to be properly known as Shamans," Charles pointed out. "They prefer it to the outmoded and racially charged term."

"But he did have a PhD from Cambridge," Collision revealed. "He quite insisted on the title."

"Perhaps," Sir James offered, "we could set this issue aside. Continue Mr. Collision."

"Yes, of course," Collision agreed, "the tribal witch doctor, Phd, emeritus and head of the divinity studies branch of the University of Caracas, and my father-in-law, revealed that amongst the Old Ones, was one, reputed to be a . . . light and restless sleeper."

"This one, whose name I fear to repeat, was known as 'the being with many furry tentacles.' So otherworldly was it, that barely the tips of its being could intrude into our world at different places."

"I know of the entity to which you refer," said Sir James soberly. "Pray go on."

"You must understand that at the time, all of this was in the nature of friendly banter between father and son-in-law. I thought nothing of it, and soon we returned to England, where I resumed my career.

"Exploring?"

"Accounting, but now in a bold and daring way."

"Accounting can be quite adventurous," Charles admitted. "Or so I am told."

"It was shortly after my return to the firm that I was introduced to a bland fiend named Chetworth. Chetworth was a member of the titled classes, and hence, we administered a large portion of his funds.

"Chetworth and I seemed to hit it off nicely, and my superiors at the firm encouraged me to develop a friendship with what seemed to be a valued client.

"As I recall, he was fascinated by my Andean adventures, and quite entranced by Oongawa. Oddly, he seemed to have no interest in exploring or bare-handed lion wrestling. I was later to recognize a lack of enthusiasm for felines as a dead giveaway.

"These beings," Collision paused, "or perhaps I should say, this being, cannot abide the presence of cats in any fashion. But I get ahead of myself.

"Although I did not realize it at the time, Chetworth, and I shall continue to call him that, showed unusual interest in the native lore I brought back.

"Over and over he would coax me to repeat the syllables of the native tongue, and those incantations I was taught. The sounds would throw him into unaccountable paroxysms of humorous explosions.

"Chetworth himself, I found strangely dull."

Collision laughed deprecatingly.

"I know you'll scarce credit this, but as an accountant, I think I meet more than the usual share of dull people."

"That seems inconceivable," Sir James replied with careful neutrality.

"But there was something odd about Chetworth's dullness. There was something unusual, dare I say it, unnatural about his boringness. I found myself, with that natural repulsion of all things real and organic for all things sidereal and metapsychical.

"Nevertheless, Chetworth continued to attend at my home. Perhaps sensing my reticence in his presence, he began to pay increasing attention to my dear wife.

"Was it my imagination, or did Chetworth grow ever more vapid! Each conversation became more inane than the next. At first, I feared that I had a rival for my wife's manly affections. Although a foreigner born, she wielded the cane like an English schoolmaster. I began to observe Chetworth secretly . . .

"And these observations . . ." Sir James prompted gently.

"That was when I noticed the overbites," Collision said ominously.

Charles looked up, startled.

"Good heavens!" Sir James exclaimed, "You don't mean . . ."

Charles quickly crossed to the bookshelf where he selected a tome.

"That's right," Collision affirmed, "Chetworth had a pronounced overbite. Remarkable really, with two huge protruding front teeth. I swear to you Sir James, no upper lip could be stiff enough to conceal those cyclopean incisors."

"Oh," said Sir James quietly.

Charles quietly replaced the Vampirium Compendia in its regular spot and returned to his seat.

Sir James and Charles exchanged glances as Collision's voice hushed to a whisper.

"But that wasn't all," Collision continued. "As I surreptitiously followed Chetworth, I noticed something quite disturbing."

Collision paused.

"Many of his so-called friends . . . had overbites."

Collision laughed, a sad and maniacal sound.

"How flexible the human mind is in its own defense. How grim the truth is when it is finally faced. I had found the first piece of the horrible puzzle, and like a child, I turned it over and over in my hands, unsure of its meaning.

"Gradually, I realized that these telltale malformations were not particular to Chetworth and his friends. I began to see them on the street, in shops. Walking through crowded London, I came to a deadly certainty that people with overbites were everywhere, even following behind me. I was literally surrounded every time I went outdoors."

Collision leaped to his feet, hand shielding his eyes.

"I cannot bear to tell you of that damnable day when I opened a magazine, the sight that so innocently met my eyes drove all reason from my head and I keeled over senseless."

"What was it?" Sir James asked.

"It, whatever it was," Collision's voice almost broke, "had reached its slimy tentacles in the highest reaches of our national soul. It was a picture of . . . of . . ."

"What?"

Collision leaped again from his seat and strode to the window, posing theatrically with his arm flung across his eyes.

"I cannot bear to say the name. I can only tell you that this vile infestation, this appalling mutation, has reached even unto the members of the house of Windsor, our very Royal Family!"

"No!" gasped Charles.

"No!" gasped Sir James.

"Yes!" repeated Collision.

"But surely this sounds more like a job for an Orthodontist. An army of Orthodontists perhaps. But certainly not a supernatural intervention to trouble an old spook chaser like me," Sir James said.

"I would that it would be so simple, Sir James. But I know that you yourself have faced the footsteps of the beast with a thousand shoes, so you are well aware of the nameless forces at work in the unknown reaches of what we call existence.

"In any case, wasn't that the crowning irony? Look in any yellow pages, and you will find the army of Orthodontists you have referred to. How is it then that this unnatural dental plague should continue? Unnatural, I was to discover, was the nature of the condition. Or should I say . . . supernatural?

"I began to make careful notes on these strangers in our midst, following them where possible. Watching unobserved, I could tell right away that they knew each other, these strange inhuman mongrels. Often I observed them exchanging strange signs and clasps in greeting.

"Often did I spot Chetworth's bobbling uncoordinated walk. As often did I find Chetworth's particular style of locomotion on those of his companions or peers.

"I grew to loathe Chetworth, his cheerful high pitched greeting of 'What Hey Peters.' It was all I could do to offer tea to that inoffensively hateful visage.

"I began to notice common features, a strange clumsiness or ungainliness, as if unused to human form. Their voices too were strange, high pitched and grating, and they made a whinnying inhuman sound that passed for laughter.

"In specimen after specimen, I saw the terrible repetition of Chetworth's characteristics. I say further that many of them held important positions, bankers, lawyers, politicians. Why, they formed a solid unbroken mass in the Conservative party!

"You see where I am leading, Sir James," Collision's eyes burned into the seated man's dark glasses, "you see how this proliferation of details can only lead to one conclusion."

"Inbreeding?" Sir James asked.

Again, Charles blushed.

"If only," Collision sobbed. "If only it was a simple case of inbreeding on a national scale. I confess, I harbored such thoughts myself, and it was only slowly and with much reluctance that I forced myself to the truth."

"The truth?" Charles asked.

"Yes, the unthinkable truth."

"Certain heretofore unremarkable facts began to take on a new significance. Did you know that Guinea Pigs were discovered in the Andes in 1920, Sir James? A mere eight specimens, who have somehow transmuted into the millions of millions of so-called pets who have wormed their way into homes across the western world!"

"No, I did not know that," Sir James said gravely.

"Or that damnable American mouse, I dare not speak the unspeakable name . . ."

"M . . ." Charles began, but stopped at a raised finger from Sir James.

"That's the one. This horrid rodent has garnered a larger international cult than Elvis himself!

"Oh yes," Collision continued, "and there's more. So much more!"

"As I observed these . . . creatures. Yes! Creatures! I must use that word; I dare not call them human! As I observed these creatures, it occurred to me that their behavior was quite rodent-like."

Again Collision laughed sadly.

"What a damning observation, for the more I observed them, the more it rang true. Their fear of cats . . . they claimed to have allergies, bah! Their appetite for certain foods. Sunflower seeds, peanuts, cashews, macadamia nuts, it all followed a horribly consistent pattern.

"Only then did I break through to the next level of horror. These new signs introduced me to the true magnitude of the inhuman conspiracy that threatens to overwhelm us all . . .

"Did you know that England imported two hundred and fifty thousand pounds of sunflower seeds last year!"

Collision's voice dropped to a conspiratorial hush.

"Who . . . or what . . . is eating them?

"As I looked about me with enlightened eyes, do you know what I saw?" Collision asked, without pausing for an answer. "I saw children eating sunflower seeds, being fed them by their mothers. Otherwise ordinary people who didn't have cats. As I carefully watched the people around me, I realized that even my closest friends had been contaminated by at least one of the many pernicious symptoms of the supernatural incursion.

"The vile Chetworth! His influence had pervaded literally up to my doorstep.

Drunk Slutty Elf, Page 125

"One midmorning over tea, just after a visit from the damnable Chetworth, I looked up at Oongawa, eating her breaded tart. Her nose wrinkled as she consumed the delicacy. My blood froze.

"I'd had a guinea pig once, whose nose had wrinkled exactly like that.

"I realized suddenly, the meaning of furry tentacles from outside dimensions. Suddenly, I knew what the faces on the ends of those tentacles of menace, poking into our reality like separate creatures, were!

"I knew then that I'd lost her, and must take steps to preserve myself."

"Hence the cats?" Charles offered.

Collision nodded briefly.

"What about the tinfoil hat?" Charles asked.

"Obviously to stop telepathic intrusions," Sir James explained, "I often wear one myself. Terrific things, and easy to make. But go on, Collision, what happened next?"

"Well, no actually," Collision explained, "I've always worn tinfoil hats. They're quite stylish, proof against rain, and accentuate my features properly. I didn't discover their . . . supernatural benefits until recently."

He cleared his throat.

"In any case, finally having isolated myself in a rented apartment with my collection of tinfoil hats and my cats, I found a measure of safety. But I began to realize it wouldn't be enough.

"These evil entities would sooner or later convince my more naive colleagues that I was overcome with a mental spell or some such nonsense.

"Similar to a good barrister or lion tamer, I knew that I would need evidence to back my case up. Proof so indisputable that none but the blind . . ."

Sir James coughed politely.

Collision hesitated and then continued.

"None but the unspeakably blind could possibly dispute it."

Drunk Slutty Elf, Page 126

Sir James coughed politely again, but Collision continued.

"Slowly, I began to amass my evidence," he paused, "masses of newspaper clippings and grocery lists. Surreptitious photographs of people's teeth. Statistics on cat ownership. Discarded sunflower seed wrappers. All of it carefully indexed and cross-referenced. Would you like to see it? I brought it just in case. It's in a couple of Lorry Cars outside, just have a couple of men bring in the boxes."

"Perhaps later," Sir James said politely.

"Oh right," Collision said tactfully. "You're blind. Perhaps you could have a manservant read it to you? I'm told that some are quite clever."

"If I feel the need," Sir James said, "I'll have Charles read it all for me."

Charles blanched.

"Emboldened by my pitiful defenses and my scraps of evidence," Collision continued, "I returned home to rescue my beloved Oongawa. Perhaps it was not too late to save her from the slimy embrace of furry incisor teeth. As I arrived home, I was confronted by the sight of Chetworth's automobile. Fearing the worst, I raced up the stairs and burst through the door."

"There was Chetworth, offering my wife," Collision's voice quavered with outrage, ". . . macadamia nuts!"

"The cad!" Charles ejaculated.

Sir James waved him silent.

"I confronted Chetworth, we exchanged harsh words. He reached into his vest pocket. My heart leaped!

"What was he reaching for? Perhaps some adjunct of elder sorcery! I grabbed his arms. We struggled, and with a desperate surge of strength I threw him down. As he fell, his forehead collided with the mantelpiece. I heard a sickening crack, and then he lay still!"

"I must confess, at that moment, all my careful suppositions fled. The evidence I had painstakingly accumulated vanished from my mind, and I felt a sick sensation in the pit of my stomach. As I looked at the prone body of my friend, lying face down, I knew that I had become a murderer.

"Oongawa had fled, whether to call the police, or just in unreasoning fear I knew not. Slowly I bent down. With trembling hands I turned the limp form of Chetworth over . . ."

Again, Collision leaped to his feet.

"Sir James, I know that you are a man who has seen much and done much, but I must warn you to brace yourself. I too had thought myself wise and worldly. I too had thought my researches had prepared me for what I was about to face, but I was wrong. Nothing could prepare any man for the sight that met my eyes in that moment of lurching vertiginous horror.

"Chetworth's skull had caved in completely, and I saw, aghast, that it was hollow. Completely hollow. But more than that, towards the front of that bone white ruptured dome, there was what appeared to be a tiny instrument panel with an object that startlingly resembled a steering wheel. But that wasn't all . . ." Collision's voice broke.

"Slumped unconscious over that steering wheel was a hamster, wearing yellow plastic goggles and white riding gloves."

Collision broke down, heaving great sobs.

"Now, now," Sir James said, "you've done the right thing, bringing this matter to us."

"Uh, right," Charles coughed, "I'm glad you exposed it now, these things are best caught early."

Collision looked at them, his eyes searching.

"You mean there's yet hope?"

"There's always hope," Sir James said sternly. He stood up and began to lead Collision to the door. "Now you must return home to your wife."

"But what shall we do?" Collision asked.

"Leave everything to us," Sir James instructed. "Go back to your wife and trust us to deal with matters. I cannot ask you to forget what you have seen, or to ignore the signs now apparent to you. But I tell you that these should trouble you no more, for we will attend to them. You may count on that."

Collision seized his hand with a grip of desperate gratitude, before turning and stepping through the doorway.

As the door closed, Sir James returned to his seat and unfolded a newspaper.

"Well," Charles asked, as he poured another cup of tea.

"He's mad, completely mad to think it's the Old Ones," Sir James said dismissively, as he flipped through the paper to the sports page. "It's a shame to see a good man so completely lost in his own delusions."

"And his story?" Charles prompted.

Sir James shrugged eloquently.

"It's just hamsters trying to take over the world again," Sir James said. "Nothing to worry about."

"Indeed," Charles said, "sometimes I wonder why they bother?"

"Who knows with Hamsters?" Sir James asked rhetorically.

The End

***

Duty

"Are you a hero?" the villagers had asked as he passed through. He had not answered, and left them behind.

The Nemedian beast, a nightmarish combination of lion and alligator, reared on its heavy hind legs, lashing out with razor claws. Its hooked beak opened to screech its rage, exposing vicious rows of needle shaped teeth.

Hrothgar Wolf Slayer, hero of a thousand sagas, danced back warily. Keeping the beast of the cursed lands away with his lance, he waited for it to expose itself. Abruptly, seeing his opportunity, he leaped forward, impaling its tender belly.

It screeched in agony, black unnatural blood spurting, but did not die immediately. Instead, it began to work its way down the lance that impaled it, closer and closer to Hrothgar. Its claws flashed inches from his face, as he wrestled the lance.

Finally he leaped away, pulling his dagger to defend himself. The beast reached for him, but he nimbly evaded it. It fell on its side and began to kick convulsively at the earth.

Hrothgar wiped its black blood from his face and stared up at the mighty walls of the tower. Pitch dark it was, a blackness that seemed to absorb all light, hence is't name. Few outsiders had ever come this close. You could almost see the air shiver with the eldritch energies that corrupted the land and created monsters such as this.

The thing still convulsed and tore at itself, he noted with disgust. It's awful shrieks might draw other monsters, or even the followers of the serpent who maintained the Black Tower.

There were many monsters, and many followers. Only a month ago, Heothane's great siege of the tower had been broken, his followers crushed. Heothane himself had been torn limb from limb.

Hrothgar grabbed up his gear, glancing again at the tower. Armies had tried and failed. But perhaps . . . perhaps one clever warrior, working by stealth and subterfuge, could succeed where armies, by brute force, could not. Perhaps there were hidden entrances, or ways that could be won by stealth rather than force of arms.

He had to try. Hrothgar, moving quietly for so huge a man, lit a small torch and left the dying horror to howl in the night. He ventured into the dark hole in the living stone of the tower from which the creature had issued.

A warm smoky breeze blew out at him from within, as if to confirm his theory that this portal gave access to the nether regions of the tower.

Carefully, Hrothgar explored the winding passageways within, marking his course, retreating, advancing, doubling back. He avoided a dozen traps, brushing past giant spiders and toxic slimes. Finally he came to a room.

"Are you a hero?"

Hrothgar Wolf Slayer paused, his massive thews rippling uncertainly, the Godsword Warseer ready in his hand. With a single glance he took in the heavy stone walls of the labyrinth chamber, the rough-hewn wooden furniture, and the withered elderly man sitting at a table in the middle of the room. There was no sign of a trap.

He had been wandering the labyrinth for hours, using all his skills to find the secret entrance to the fortress of evil, the Black Tower, center of the Cult of the Serpent, home of the very Serpent God itself. He had not seen so much of a trace of a person, until now.

There was just an aged man, head shaven, eyes peering about weakly, dressed in the red and gold ceremonial robes of the Cult of the Serpent. The table at which he was sitting was strewn haphazardly with books and scrolls of every description.

"Excuse me?" Hrothgar asked.

"Are you a hero?" the old man asked. He pulled a heavy, leather bound tome from the pile.

Hrothgar cleared his throat.

"I have come to put an end to your evil cult, and destroy the devil you worship."

The ancient priest wrote in his book.

"Hero," he said. He looked up. "You're a northern barbarian, aren't you?"

"How can you tell?" Hrothgar asked.

"You said 'excuse me,' very courteous. Northern barbarians make a fetish of being polite. Not like the ones from Nork Nork or Jawsa," the priest said. "Bloodthirsty maniacs all, you barbarians, but I prefer the courteous ones."

"I don't imagine it makes much of a difference in the long run," Hrothgar said, examining the man and his surroundings.

The man was ancient and stooped, clearly useless in battle, with few years left to him. Something about that sunken frame suggested that in his prime, he might have been a terrible adversary. But those years were long gone.

The room and furnishings appeared plain; there was no apparent device to give a warning. No signs of any hidden traps or dangers.

They posed no threat and Hrothgar could not see how a warning could be issued.

"Very clever of you to find the back entrance to the Black Tower of the Pit of the Serpent," the priest ventured.

"It seemed reasonable that there would be one," Hrothgar replied. "Now, to business, which way to the accursed Serpent?

"Oh," said the priest, gesturing over his shoulder, "down the next hall, take the first left and you can't miss it."

"Thank you," said Hrothgar advancing with drawn sword. "I'm sorry, but I cannot leave you behind to give a warning."

"You're planning to kill me?" asked the priest.

Hrothgar noted that the priest betrayed neither surprise nor terror. His voice was steady, his features expressionless. He merely made a check mark in his book, and pulled a new volume out of the pile on the table.

"It seems expedient."

"Before you do, could you answer just a few questions, for our records, and you can be on your way," he said briskly, flipping open the thick book to a blank page.

"You keep records?" Hrothgar asked, mildly surprised.

"We have endured a thousand years, I cannot see how we could not," the old man snapped. "We live for administration. Even gods may die, but bureaucracy is eternal."

"Oh," Hrothgar considered this decidedly anti-heroic viewpoint. He decided to cooperate with the old geezer before he lopped his head off. Respect for elders, even if you had to kill them eventually, was a time-honored barbarian tradition. He sheathed his sword.

"Bureaucracy?" Hrothgar asked blankly.

"It's a system whereby our lives are ruled by pieces of paper containing endless rules and bits of information," the old man explained.

"I see," Hrothgar said, brightening. "Magic!"

"No, no!" said the old cultist. "It's . . . Actually . . . It's more like . . ."

Hrothgar waited patiently, as the priest thought about it.

"Yes," the old man said finally, "magic."

"Ahhh."

"Name?"

"Hrothgar Wolf Slayer."

The ancient priest looked up sharply, and then thumbed through a smaller, but still massive book. As he opened it, Hrothgar glimpsed the word 'Index' on the cover.

"We've had nine Hrothgar Wolf Slayers over the last twenty years. A popular name with mothers where you come from?"

"It is the name of a great hero of the plains tribes. He was a huge deal before he disappeared. I take the name to honor him," Hrothgar replied with as much dignity as he could muster.

"I see. Divinity?"

"What?" asked Hrothgar, his heavy brow furrowing in confusion.

"Divinity," the Priest explained. "Do you claim divine beings within your recent ancestry?"

"How recent?" Hrothgar asked.

"Within five generations," the priest explained.

"Well," Hrothgar said doubtfully, "it is rumored that my grandmother consorted with a demigod, but my grandfather denies this."

He paused before going on.

"It's kind of a sensitive thing in the family. I'd rather not discuss it."

The priest shrugged and made a note.

"Blessings?"

Hrothgar cleared his throat and belched ceremonially. "I was blessed by Huffu, God of War, when I became a man. I have since received the benedictions of the Goddess of Storms, the Goddess of the Hunt, the God of Health and Potency. I have been specially blessed by Cheora, God of Gods of my people, and by Nig-Sitha God of Gods of the heathen Tcho.

"Tcho Tcho?"

"No, just Tcho . . . they cured their stutter."

The priest nodded in approval.

"Very good," the ancient cleric said. He looked at his list again.

"Amulets, sorceries, enchantments, potencies or consecrated or sorcerous weapons?"

"I'd rather not say," Hrothgar replied, offended.

"Uh huh."

The priest looked him over critically.

"That looks like a belt of strength," the priest ventured.

"It might be," Hrothgar replied evasively.

"And a Godsword."

"A Godsword?" Hrothgar said, surprised.

"Certainly," the priest told him, "you didn't think yours was the only one, did you?"

"Uhh . . ."

But then the priest saved him from an embarrassing response.

"Deeds?" the priest asked.

"Deeds?" Hrothgar asked.

"Deeds. You know: Conquests, prowess, monsters slain, princesses deflowered, battles won, that sort of thing."

"Oh," said Hrothgar with some relief. It was at least a subject he knew exceedingly thoroughly.

"Well . . ." Hrothgar launched into a detailed recitation of his long and illustrious career. For the only thing a true barbarian loved more than doing bold and heroic deeds was talking about them. It took the better part of an hour . . .

"Oh yes," Hrothgar finally finished, the priest having busily taken notes throughout, "and last summer I cleared out a nest of ghouls that had been plaguing a small village. I almost forgot."

Drunk Slutty Elf, Page 135

"Very impressive," said the priest.

"Thank you," Hrothgar said modestly.

"You move around a lot," said the ancient priest. "Don't stick around to deal with the situations afterwards."

"It's the hero business," Hrothgar responded casually, "you know how it is."

"Just so."

"I think we're done," Hrothgar said, "it's been pleasant, but you know how it is, evil to fight, cults to burn, abominable gods to destroy. I should be getting on with it."

"And now you're going to kill me?" the old man asked.

"I've been very patient with you, and I hope you'll oblige me by not making a big fuss," Hrothgar said reasonably.

"May I ask why?" the priest queried rising to his feet.

"You should ask?" Hrothgar was surprised. "Because the Black Tower of the Serpent has been a blight upon the realm for a thousand years. Because this tower has poisoned the lands for a hundred leagues around. Because your armies carry off whole villages, entire peoples, for horrible sacrifices. Because from these cursed grounds spring monsters and plagues and every form of evil."

"All of these things are true," the old cleric conceded. "But why kill me in particular?"

"Because you're here," Hrothgar explained, pulling his sword free of its scabbard. It hummed in anticipation of fresh blood. "Do you deny the evil that has been committed, or your part in it?"

"I deny neither," snapped the withered cultist.

"I'm a hero, you're a villain. It's very simple. As a priest of an evil cult, and worshiper of an evil god, you should die. People say life is complicated, but really it isn't."

"There you are mistaken. We are neither priests nor worshipers."

"Oh?" Hrothgar said as he advanced upon the priest.

"We are guardians," said the priest, backing up hastily. "We are its keepers, not its slaves."

"The distinction escapes me, as your head shall soon escape you."

"It's not a serpent, you know," the priest said, with his back to the wall.

"Excuse me?" Hrothgar said.

"It isn't a serpent you have come to kill. It's something else. Something worse . . ." The priest's voice trailed off.

"Would you like to see it?" the priest asked suddenly, quietly. "This thing you've come to kill."

"Is this some sort of trap?" Hrothgar asked suspiciously.

"No," the old man said, "the labyrinth leads ultimately to the center of the pit. But there is a balcony not too far, from which you may gaze upon the thing."

"And your allies, priest?" the tawny barbarian asked.

"You will encounter none."

"That much confidence in your god?" The sword quivered in his hand, its leashed energies making the air around it shiver.

"It is not a god," said the ancient.

"As you have said," replied Hrothgar. "Now put away your quill and lead me to it. But know that at the first hint of treachery you shall die."

"On my honor, I shall not lead you false."

Hrothgar coughed.

"Point taken," said the priest.

Shuffling slowly, he led them through the wooden doorway, down into the narrow, winding passage of the labyrinth.

"A thousand years ago, it came here from beyond the stars. Perhaps it was injured in the fall from the sky, perhaps it was wounded and fled to ground, perhaps it was merely sick and dying. We can only guess."

He paused.

"A thousand years ago a great blazing mass fell from the sky with a howl heard around the world. Half the wizards alive then died in the first moments of its fall. The others were stricken like beasts, and fell thrashing upon the ground, their magic burned out of them."

As they walked the torches grew infrequent, and ichor coated the walls.

"Even men and women with the barest touch of the sight were struck dumb and blind. The fabled stone of prophecy heated glowing red and shattered. The fish swam to the deepest corner of the seas and the wild beasts ate their young.

"Thirteen great sorcerers survived. Thirteen so mighty that even the gods spoke to them respectfully. Thirteen felt its mighty fall and came together."

"The founders of the cult," Hrothgar said.

"They tried to kill it," replied the priest simply.

For a moment, Hrothgar paused.

"They tried to kill it? Who betrayed that cause?" he asked.

The old cultist ignored the question.

"We are here."

In a bend in the labyrinth corridor there was a wooden door. As the barbarian watched warily, ready to spring into action at the first false move, the priest opened the door and stepped through.

Inside the doorway, the barbarian could see a vast dim abyss opening up. The floor within the door seemed of hewn wood, and there was a rail at waist height. The old man leaned against the rail and continued.

"Six of them died at the outset. It took all their power, and the power of the seven who survived, to forge the spells that held it. Even then, had it not been weakened, the spells could not have held it. It would have gone on to consume the world. We have maintained those spells, over the last thousand years, though the price was terrible."

The barbarian stepped through, glancing right and left for traps or adversaries. There were none. The balcony was barely adequate for the two of them.

"We have sacrificed legions of innocents. The very ground aches from the weight of restless ghosts of our terrible crimes. And yet we will murder legions more. All to hold that . . . thing. We hold it still."

Hrothgar looked down, and for a second, his mind froze at the sight. The priest could have had him then. For as he looked down, he saw . . . something. Something vast and sinuous, an obscene assembly of tentacles and waving feelers, of maws and teeth and eyes in no rational order.

Hrothgar's legs turned to jelly, his guts twisted. He had to remind himself to breathe. In the air around him, even his untutored senses could feel awesomely powerful spells. The magical current made his Godsword glow almost red. The blade moaned, reacting to the magic, and the thing the magic surrounded.

"Empires have risen and fallen around us; kingdoms and gods have come and gone. Crusades have raged against us. We abide. We hold it.

"What does it do down there? I often wonder. Is it dying? Is it dying a slow death that has taken a thousand years and will take ten thousand years more as we reckon time? Is it sleeping? Or resting? Or healing?"

It was vaster than he had imagined. It was obscene. Beyond obscene, it was simply wrong. Hrothgar could feel his mind rebelling at the sight of it, at its shape and contours that somehow defiled everything he had ever known or experienced of shape and substance.

"We have striven for an age to end it. We have denied it every sustenance. Yet it endures.

"Sometimes it tests the spells. Down there it will turn and writhe, as if half sleeping. And out in the world, cold iron turns white hot, and beasts run into the sea, and cities drown in blood and madness, all touched by its merest shadow."

Drunk Slutty Elf, Page 139

Whatever it was, Hrothgar realized, the priest was right. It was not a god. It was not anything that belonged in this world or even in this reality.

"Perhaps, despite all our struggles, it shall someday escape. Our spells will shatter and then . . ."

"Will it devour the world?" Hrothgar asked suspiciously. "Or perhaps once free of the cage of your evil cult, it will just go back where it came from."

The priest shuddered.

"How simple a world you live in. We have had seers who have caught its passing thoughts, peered at the edges of its dreams, sensed the rumblings of its faint urges, and who lived long enough to pass on what they learned.

"They tell us that we are lucky in our ignorance. That our world, the very fabric of our existence, is but a small and sheltered cove at the edge of a vast and terrible ocean. That there are things out there, so terrible, so antithetical and contrary, so far beyond any frame we can conceive that to even glimpse its shadow brings madness unto merciful death.

"Then they die. We hear their forsaken ghost howls, calling from the edges of exiled realms, poison to other spirits. The knowledge burned into them bars the gates of every afterlife.

"Devour is too simple a word, too desirable a fate, for what it will do to the world. Not from rage or revenge, though perhaps it does feel these things, but it will do what it does, simply because of what it is.

"You stand there, a hero, come to slay the demon god," the priest spat. "If this is your wish, proceed. We will not hinder you."

Having seen the thing in the pit, the barbarian could almost believe the priest. Almost.

Hrothgar lifted his blade for the killing stroke.

"There is not a man here who has not washed in blood," the priest continued quickly.

Hrothgar, with an annoyed expression lowered his sword.

"Not a man who has not been cursed by his own Gods. We yearn for freedom from this burden. But, this is the price we must pay, so be it. We shall not let it free to work its will on our small, poor world."

"That was very inspirational," Hrothgar replied. Again he raised his blade.

The priest resumed. Hrothgar sighed and waited.

"You have wandered through the fields and forests," the old man said, his tones edged with bitterness. "You have wenched and brawled your way through taverns and brothels, spilled blood in wars. You have played at being a hero, left stories and legends in your wake."

Hrothgar tapped the edge of the railing with his finger, looking expectant.

"Now you come here, blessed by your god, armed with magics to put an end to an evil cult. To slay its worshipers and end its god."

"That was the idea," Hrothgar replied with an attempt at bravado. "But perhaps I should just take you down there with me, and you could talk it to death."

"Look at that thing down there. Who would worship such an abomination?"

Hrothgar glanced over the balcony, and quickly glanced back. Just looking at the fundamental wrongness of the thing made his mind ache and his gorge rise.

The Godsword had wavered over the balcony for a second, in sight of the thing. The sword curdled and whimpered in his hand and tried to unobtrusively sneak back into the scabbard.

No, he thought, no one could worship something like that. For better or worse, he believed the withered old man.

"If you think you can kill it, even hurt it, go down there. There will not be one man here who is not praying for you. But I warn you, ten thousand men have died where you are going.

Drunk Slutty Elf, Page 141

"I will tell you this, at least, as comfort. We have ensured that your body will not go to sustain its flesh, your soul and your magic will not be added to its strength."

"How will you do this?" Hrothgar asked with professional interest.

"We have not held it a thousand years without learning to deny it," the priest's eyes glinted.

"Trade secrets?" Hrothgar asked cynically. "Is this how you dispose of your enemies? Would I make it down there? Would I even be able to make the attempt?"

"Oh yes," replied the priest. "Do not use us as an excuse for a change of mind. The choices are yours . . .

"What can you do? You can turn around; go back the way you came. If you do, then know that your life is a lie, that you fled your sworn duty. Know that you are a coward and a child who left men behind to a burden you would not assume. But know also, that if you walk away, you surrender your right to judge us.

"Or you can stay, and help to feed and empower the spells. You can wield the sacrificial knife, you can help to gather and slay the innocents. You can commit unspeakable crimes in service of a terrible cause. You will be exiled by your tribe and abandoned by your comrades. Your family will renounce you. Your very god will curse you. You will surrender your very name. And all of it justly.

"And for what? To keep that awful thing caged. To grant the gods and beasts, the rest of the world, its existence. To buy years, days, even minutes for our small world.

"Once I stood where you stand now, believing the things you believe now. I faced the choice you face now. I faced the awful burden, the terrible duty."

Hrothgar Wolf Slayer, hero, adventurer, wanderer, looked down into the pit again, contemplating the awful thing within. He sheathed the Godsword and turned to stare at the withered priest.

"When you faced the choice," Hrothgar said, "what were you called?"

"Hrothgar Wolf Slayer," the priest said, "many years ago."

He smiled with wry bitterness.

"Tell me hero," he asked, "what will you do?"

The End

***

The Revolution Begins With a Pause

Sarin stepped out of the room. The former mercenary and gunman's hard eyed glance automatically swept the corridors, looking for threats.

But there was only Gaunt, there on the other side of the corridor, leaning casually against the wall. Sarin hated him on principle. The two men were opposites, both tall and rugged; Sarin was thin and cynical, always restless, never trusting. Gaunt on the other hand was broad and muscular, his chiseled good looks and open demeanor made him a natural leader. Gaunt was the sort of man you would follow into battle. Sarin the sort you didn't want to meet in an alley.

Sarin crossed the portal, to lean up against the other wall. Nonchalantly, Sarin folded his arms and gave Gaunt a haughty stare.

"I wanted you to see it," Gaunt said. "What do you make of it?"

Sarin chewed his lip thoughtfully.

"It's either a waste disposal evacuation chamber for mass amounts of garbage . . ."

Gaunt nodded.

". . . or it's a toilet," Sarin finished.

"That was about what I thought," Gaunt said. "I was hoping that you could help me decide one way or another."

"Odd," Sarin said, "about this progenitor ship. It was obviously designed for humanoid beings. But every now and then we come across quite anomalous technology. That room, for example."

"Yes," replied Gaunt, "by going back to first principles, you can determine it was designed to dispose of something. But what?"

"It's a problem we are going to come across again and again as we explore this ship," Sarin warned.

"We'll deal with it," Gaunt said confidently. "The problem now is to identify this room."

"Did you ask the ship interface?" Sarin wondered.

"Of course," Gaunt replied, "it said 'there is no knowledge without discovery'"

"Hardly comforting. There may be only one way to find out," Sarin said quietly. Dangerously.

"Which is?" Gaunt asked.

"You will have to use it," Sarin said.

"I don't think so," Gaunt replied.

"If it's a bathroom, you'll be fine, and we'll all be relieved," Sarin argued.

"And if it's not a bathroom?" Gaunt asked.

"I'll take good care of the ship for you," Sarin said.

"Piracy?" Gaunt asked.

"Better than wasting it on some half-baked rebellion against the Confederation," Sarin sneered.

"The others might disagree," Gaunt replied.

"Only if you're there to persuade them," Sarin said. "But enough chit chat, we need to find out what that room does."

Sarin paused.

"I really need to go . . . rather badly. Desperately, even."

"So go," Gaunt said.

"After you," Sarin replied. "I'm sure your bladder must be bursting. I know when I'm like that all I can think of is waterfalls, oceans of waterfalls, pounding ocean waves . . ."

"I'd rather you tried it first," replied Gaunt, "after all, I risked my life on the Teleporter."

"Taps running. Rivers flooding. Babbling brooks. Lots of waterfalls, columns of water cascading down and down, in an endless flow." Sarin paused, it wasn't working. He decided to change tactics. He snapped. "We at least agreed on what that was. I have no intention of taking unnecessary risks. You are the self-appointed leader, this is your job!"

"No," said Gaunt flatly.

"What a hero," Sarin sneered.

"Look, I'm willing to risk my life for a cause," Gaunt said heatedly, "but I'm not going to be remembered as the man who died for a bowel movement."

They reached for their guns. Sarin went first, but was a little slower because his arms were folded. Sarin and Gaunt faced each other in the corridor, Gaunt's weapon pointed directly at Sarin, Sarin's waved uncertainly.

"I'm not stupid. I'm not expendable. And I'm not going," Sarin hissed.

"Think of the crew," Gaunt said reasonably, now that he had the drop on Sarin. "Think of Chart, Argon, Norbon, Vale. We need to know. We'll all take risks of one sort or another. If this is a toilet, we have to find out, before someone uses the real garbage disposal."

"And if it is the real garbage disposal?"

"Try not to let anything dangle."

"No," Sarin said with finality.

Just then Vale turned the corner. He stopped, confused by the drawn weapons. He had an odd look on his face, and he was walking with his legs held closely together.

"Ah," he said, "you're having a . . . conversation? Don't mind me; I'll be on my way. I was just looking for the bathroom."

"In there!" Sarin and Gaunt unisoned, pointing to the doorway.

For a second Vale hesitated, hung between desperation and fear, and then . . .

"Thanks," he mumbled, as he rushed through the doorway.

The two looked at the closed door. Slowly they put away their weapons and waited.

"I suppose we could have told him," Sarin pointed out.

"That would have just worried him needlessly," Gaunt replied.

"It seems that you are willing to risk someone else's life for a bowel movement," Sarin said.

"Vale has much lower ambitions in life than we do," Gaunt responded.

Sarin thought about this. "True."

"Besides, if it is a garbage disposal, we'll remember him. I'll put up a plaque commemorating him as a hero of the revolution," Gaunt said.

"Maybe even a statue," Sarin helped.

"I'd never forget him. Every time I sat on a toilet that wasn't about to suck me out into space, I'd think of Vale," Sarin went on.

"There you go," Gaunt said, "you've missed out on a chance for that immortality."

"I can't imagine what was going through my mind," Sarin said sardonically.

Sarin paused.

"This ship is probably full of problems like this. Mysterious technology, strange rooms, unknown instruments, fail safes, probably all ordinary and commonplace, assuming we understood them, yet . . ."

"Entirely capable of killing you, if you don't know how they work," Gaunt finished.

"Correct," Sarin replied.

"What are you suggesting?" Gaunt asked.

"We need a volunteer to test things," Sarin said.

'You're thinking of Vale?" Gaunt asked.

"He does seem rather lucky," Sarin said.

"We'll see," Gaunt said.

He waited a beat.

"Should we tell him?" Gaunt asked.

"I wouldn't want to worry him," Sarin said.

"Good point," Gaunt agreed.

The door opened. Vale stepped out. He wore a look of almost sexual satisfaction.

"Settled your difference, I see," he observed. "Well, I certainly am relieved."

"Very good," Gaunt said politely, "do you know what the others are up to?"

Vale paused to think about it.

"Well, Chart's found a kitchen, or is it a galley? It's got food anyway, he's making supper. Luna . . . well, Luna seems to have found some sort of room, she keeps making these funny noises, but she won't come out. Says she's fine and she'll be out shortly."

"What sort of noises?" Gaunt asked.

"High pitched, sort of breathy noises. And there's this buzzing sound, very quiet," answered Vale.

"But you could hear it," Sarin pointed out.

"I had to press my ear to the door," Vale suddenly colored.

"Well, I'll be off now."

"What about Narbon?" Gaunt asked.

Vale stopped, half way down the corridor.

"He was looking for the bathroom too. I haven't seen him lately. It's like he disappeared," Vale answered.

"Big ship," Sarin said dryly.

"Brave man anyway. I can't believe we all managed to escape together onto a derelict but space-worthy alien starship. Norbon especially. Teleporting up from the Space prison with a locator bracelet that he'd stolen after the big fight, practically at the last minute. Another few seconds and he'd have been out of range," Vale shivered. "What a way to go that would have been eh? just appearing in empty space. Tempting fate, I'd say."

"We'll make sure he gets a plaque," Sarin said.

Vale disappeared around the corridor.

Gaunt and Sarin looked at each other, their faces calm and impassive.

Then they both bolted for the doorway.

The End

***

The Monkey Sea

I was entitled to go to the bathroom, they knew it. I was way past the quota.

When the Overseer walked by, I raised my hand to go, but he ignored me. The bald rail of a geek, he didn't even look.

Annoyed, I punched the bathroom button twice on my keyboard, and went back to work. In the cubicles around me I heard the endless clatter as thousands of dexterous fingers worked keyboards.

I fantasized about just getting up and walking away. Past rows and rows of word processors, their slaves too busy even to look up. Leave all those cogs to their machine, surely they wouldn't miss one little sprocket. I dreamed of walking until I found some jungle, some South Seas paradise somewhere.

My keyboard monitor bleeped. I'd fallen behind quota while I indulged my daydream. No bathroom breaks for sure, now. I bent over the keyboard and churned out a string of letters and numbers.

Completely meaningless, I thought, on those occasions when I paused to look at it. From nothing, to nothing, it had no relationship to me. I was just a channeler for an endless stream of gibberish on an antiquated green phosphorescent screen.

I heard somewhere that these office machines were supposed to liberate workers. It hadn't turned out that way.

Instead of freeing people for more varied and creative work, giving them more independence to work at home or at their own pace, it had been used to monitor workers. Who is taking too many coffee breaks? Making too many phone calls? Typing too slowly, or with too many mistakes?

Who is in the stinking bathroom, for god's sake, and how long are they spending there?

I ask you, do they really need to know this? What good does it do them, except to grind us down?

When the evening bell rang, I signed off my keyboard and slouched away. My shift stayed to the right of the aisle. On the left the graveyard shift shambled in to sit before the cathode ray altars. The clatter of keys never stops, the machine never sleeps. It just hiccups once in a while.

From their high towers, the Overseers watched. They would drift down among us sometime, looming over us, wandering on mysterious errands. How long or how often they went to the bathroom was a secret for them alone.

I drifted to the cafeteria. Fruit salad again, I noted sourly.

The usual gang was there. I grabbed my tray and hopped up to join them. The Overseers didn't like us socializing. We were supposed to work, eat and sleep. End of story.

But they left us alone at mealtimes. I guess they realized you can only push us so far.

Hell, these mealtime social occasions were the only thing that kept half of us going. If all I ever had to look forward to each day was that damned keyboard and screen I'd have gone after an Overseer a long time ago.

"Anybody ever heard of a noosphere?" Virginia asked.

Ginny was my girl. Sort of. The machine owned us all, but every now and then, we managed to steal a moment or two together.

"Sounds like some sort of habitat," Max said. Max was this dark hairy type. He had a good heart but bad breath. That was why Ginny was with me and not him. I paid extra attention to hygiene for that reason alone.

Hey, I take the breaks I can get.

Ike rubbed his chin thoughtfully with hairy knuckles.

Ike was big and pale, with scraggly hair that always looked like he'd slept on it. He had heavy brows that would have been intimidating except for his warm brown eyes. I swear to God, he looked like a chimpanzee. Maybe that was why everyone liked him.

"It's an abstract concept, not really a place or a thing, although it may be useful to think of it like that. It's the sum total of knowledge, of consciousness. Visualized as an infinitely expanding sphere symbolizing the sentient existence. It's everything everyone can imagine."

"What if there is something nobody can imagine?" Max asked.

"Then it's obviously not in the noosphere," I said. We all laughed.

"It can"t be a continually expanding sphere forever. What about people dying, knowledge being lost?" Max protested. "I can't believe in infinity."

"Then visualize it as a sphere in a continual tension of expansion and contraction. A place of infinite complexity," Ike responded.

Max just gritted his teeth. They liked to play that game, those two.

"Where'd you hear about that stuff, Ginny?" I asked.

"One of the Overseers mentioned it, Will," she responded. "He said something like 'we're all stuck in the noosphere together.'"

"Sounds like post-modernist socialism. Here we are all stuck in capitalism together, they the capitalists and us the property," I said. "The sanctimonious bastards."

There was a general chorus of agreement.

"You know what I'd like to do," I said, encouraged, "I'd like to get the hell out of here. Just leave. Go to some jungle where no one's ever heard of Overseers and eat bananas and coconuts under palm trees."

"The Overseers wouldn't allow that," Ike rumbled. "And anyway, where would we go?"

"Maybe it won't be their choice," Max whispered dangerously. We were getting nervous. We knew they monitored the workstations to measure our activity. It was pretty reasonable that they might have the cafeteria wired.

We all shut up suddenly as an Overseer wandered through the cafeteria, thin and spindly, bobbing along on its long legs. It didn't seem interested in us.

"You know," Virginia began, "they aren't really like us. Skinny and bald. It makes you wonder where they come from, and what they're doing?"

"Weird eyes," Ike said thoughtfully, "and funny shaped heads. We've been here, feels like forever, so we get used to them. But really, if you look at them and think about it . . . they're definitely strange."

It was at least a marginally safer line of conversation.

"All we know about them is the here and now," Max said. "Without their history, we don't know anything about them. Without our own history, we aren't anything."

Max had a point. We had no history. No one knew how we came to be here, or why, or how to leave, or where. Our ignorance kept us chained.

The station bell interrupted this line of thought. It was time to return to our workstation.

As we left, I contrived to be behind Ginny in the line. Our hands touched and we traced secret messages on each other's palms.

Drunk Slutty Elf, Page 153

That night at sleep shift she visited me in my cradle. We held each other until shift change came again.

I worked away at the keyboard, shift after shift. Typing endless lines of nonsense in the service of a nonsensical god. Frustration swept over me at irregular intervals. There had to be more than this, I would think. More than endless pointless work, punctuated by fleeting moments of friendship and intimacy.

Was this what we were brought into the world for? I could not accept it.

But when the moment came, it wasn't me or Max who acted, but Ike.

It was lunch time again, and I was filing out, an obedient member of my line, just like always, when a commotion bubbled up ahead.

Ike had collided with an Overseer. I could see that much. He'd tried to shove Ike out of the way, but Ike had shoved back.

I pushed through the line, rushing to my friend. They were rolling around on the floor; Ike had his teeth in the overseers arm. I was astonished by the thought of Ike biting anyone; Ike didn't even bite his nails. The line moved around and past them, with no more attention than you would give a wet spot on the floor. What was wrong with them?

The Overseer almost had Ike down. I jumped on him with both feet. He went down hard. I hit him in the face. I could see blood running from his nose. Something rose up inside me, I hit him again.

Suddenly Ginny and Max were there. Ginny was helping Ike up.

"What happened?" Max kept asking.

"He called me a . . . a black ape," Ike gasped.

"Damned racist," I snarled, and hit him again. It felt good.

"What are we going to do now, Will?" Ginny was asking.

That stopped me. What were we going to do? There would be no going back to the keyboards now. Not after attacking an Overseer.

"We're getting out of here," I told them. "There's got to be someplace else: we're going to find it."

They were all looking at me. Following my lead. It was a heady and terrifying moment. I swelled with pride.

"Where, Will?" Ike asked.

I was stopped for just a moment. Then the Overseer saved me.

"There is nowhere else," the Overseer mumbled. He'd found a handkerchief and was trying to staunch the flow of blood from his nose. His voice sounded funny.

"Yes there is," I snarled, "and you know where it is, don't you?" I snarled, grabbing his collar. Max helped me restrain him.

I looked around. There was his high tower. Overseers worked one to a tower.

"We go there first." I pointed at a tower. "We should be able to see a way out from up there. And there ought to be stuff we can use."

So we went for the tower. Dragging the Overseer to the base, we made him punch in the entry codes for the elevator, and we all crowded aboard.

The Overseer's cabin at the top of the tower was like the interior of a spaceship. All buttons and lights, monitor screens and little levers, everything demanding attention.

"Will, Max," Ginny called, her voice quavered like I'd never heard before, "come and see this."

We hurried over to her at the window.

Outside there were miles and miles of roofless cubicles, each with its own glowing screen and keyboard, stretching as far as the eye could see.

"Damn," Max whimpered beside me. He raced to look out another window. I saw a pair of binoculars on a shelf, and I grabbed them. Ike was staring out the window now, beside Ginny, his huge brown eyes getting bigger and bigger.

I looked through the binoculars. I darted from one window to another, looking, until finally Max pulled them from me. I didn't care. I couldn't see through the tears anymore.

All we could see was endless cubicles, an infinite ocean of monkeys pounding at keyboards.

Ike was weeping loudly. Ginny was trying to calm him, running her hands along his furry back.

"There is nowhere else," the Overseer said. He'd found a chair and had dragged himself to it. He was still holding his nose, "It goes on forever. It's infinite."

"But why?" I asked in wonder. "It's like some sick joke."

Ginny cried out. We all turned. Ike had climbed up to the open window. Holding himself in place with his hands and feet he leaped. We all rushed for him, but he was just gone.

Ike had found his way out.

"So what now?" Max asked. He was comforting Ginny.

"It doesn't matter." the Overseer said. "Go back to work. What else is there?"

He waved vaguely towards the elevator doors; they slid open silently, as if on command.

"We're sorry," Max said. He sounded crushed. He and Ginny held each other like two drowning people. Drowning monkeys, I corrected myself sourly.

I watched them shuffle towards the elevator. I understood suddenly that Ginny wouldn't be coming over to share my cradle anymore. Something had changed between the three of us.

Heartbroken, I dragged myself to the doors. Just inside of them, I turned to look at the Overseer.

"Why?" I asked him, "what's it all for? It all seems so meaningless? There has to be a point to it all, doesn't there?"

Drunk Slutty Elf, Page 156

He shrugged.

"I don't know. I'm trapped on the inside too," he mumbled, "in the noosphere."

He looked very small then.

"I don't care. I'm going to be free somehow," I told him as the doors slid shut, cutting him off from our sight.

Alone, I returned to my station. I took my seat at my keyboard and looked up into that terrible empty meaningless screen. A flashing code informed me I was behind quota.

"I'm going to be free," I said.

There in the cubicle it sounded empty.

"Do you think rebellion is just running away?" I screamed at it angrily. "It's inside us, in our hearts and souls, our stories. I'll fight your stupid senseless world. I'm through with typing your gibberish. This may be all there is, but from now on, I'm going to make it mean something."

Defiantly, I hammered out a line. A title.

THE MERCHANT OF VENICE

Let them know who's responsible, I thought, and typed some more.

BY WILLIAM SHAKESPEARE

I set to work.

The End

***

The Stone Blockage

Thank you, thank you for inviting me here to address you.

So here goes. I'm a Reptoid. Don't believe me? I'll show you. Watch my eyes very closely:

Flicker.

See. It's a terrific trick at parties, let me tell you.

Anyway, I'm just here to clear up a few things in the interests of good relations.

First – it's our planet. You just live here. I know, comes as a shock, blah blah blah, and all that. But surely you understand the concept of private property; your entire history involves stealing it from other people. So there it is. We came along and bought it fair and square, we have the deed, the title, the whole nine yards, lock stock and barrel.

Yes, I am an Alien. Well, to me, you guys are aliens, obviously. Anyway, I'm here to set the record straight about this whole Ancient Astronaut thing.

Anyway, I suppose I should tell you a little bit about ourselves. As I said, our species is actually quite similar to your own. We are essentially giant clusters of biological cells, the individual cells clustered together and segregated by function, operating jointly, with an external membrane which maintains a stable internal environment, and deploys inert materials for structure and shape. We maintain sensory clusters, mobility appendages, respiratory and ingestion structures. I'll tell you right now, as strange and alien as I might appear to you . . . There are beings out there in the Universe that can't actually tell the difference between you and me.

Which is actually pretty humiliating for us, because frankly, compared to us you're anal polyps with opposable thumbs. You're basically hemorrhoid based life forms. So yes, awkward for us. We don't enjoy the comparison.

I mean, how would you feel if someone called you into a bathroom and made you look in the toilet, because hey, that turd is the spitting image of your wife?

Look, your entire evolutionary lineage consists of feces flinging. Literally, look at apes, look at monkeys, it's all poop flinging. It's pretty straightforward evolutionary multi-tasking. Once you'd evolved the anatomy for climbing, well, that's the same kind of anatomy you need for throwing. But it's a projectile free environment, so . . . what else are you going to fling?

About that, funny story.

We actually got quite a deal on this planet. The previous owners were Plasmoids from another galactic arm, and they were trying to unload it. And of course, they got it from someone else – I believe a race of intelligent beetles who were never able to get the oxygen content up enough and eventually gave up. Then there were the Hydrangeans from the Betelgeuse, they did the dinosaurs in. To tell you the truth, the whole planet has been a colossal white elephant of things going wrong for one extraterrestrial species after another.

Hominids? Turns out, you weren't a natural species. The Plasmoids did you. The Plasmoids move by extruding pseudopods, they can get going pretty fast as it turns out, basically, extruding as many pseudopods in whatever length or direction they want. The thing with Plasmoids is they find fixed limb beings kind of hilarious. So they've got this planet, they're bored, nothing of value, suddenly, they're tweaking a group of local apes to go around on two legs, like a teeter totter. Bipedalism, they thought it was hilarious. Couldn't get enough of it. You're still big over there by the way, on what passes for youtube.

Drunk Slutty Elf, Page 159

The thing is, they didn't think it through. Sure, it's all fun and games for the funny primates to go staggering on two legs. But now you've got a 'throwing animal' in that projectile free environment I mentioned, and eventually, it's not nearly so hilarious when you're trying to prevent fecal matter from being absorbed through your respiratory membrane.

We actually got it in a package deal. This whole solar system, plus a bunch of others. Little did we know what we were getting into.

Where was I? Oh yeah. Our planet, monkey-boys. You're just living here. You're part of the "ecological multispecies biodiversity we got sold as a bill of goods," you and three trillion species of bacteria and slime molds.

We should have read the brochure more carefully.

You see, before we came along this planet was visited by the Chirugons. Some kind of galactic survey. Nice folk. Insectoid. More millipedes actually, but terrific accountants. Although they're a bit passive aggressive.

Anyway, about ten or fifteen thousands of your years ago, they were visiting. Routine cataloging, no big deal, except that your ancestors kept flinging poop at them and their survey markers. They'd set up a nice monolith and go for lunch, and when they came back, it would be covered with the brown and sticky.

If they'd have asked us, we could have told them. Poop flinging monkeys. We could have warned them, but there you go.

At first it's no big deal. You don't scorch a continent down to bedrock just because the local fauna lobs a stinky at you. Especially when you don't actually own the planet.

But they kept doing it to the Chirugons. Day after day, they'd show up and scream and fling poop. It was starting to get annoying. It was getting all over everything, it was hard to wipe off, it would get up in between chitinous plates of body segments.

And the smell! This was a species that communicated by chemical exchange, so it was like trying to have a conversation while annoying strangers were constantly popping up and screaming random foreign words constantly. It started to drive them up the wall.

So they moved. But that just put them in the territory of a different tribe of poop flinging hominids, one with slightly different diets, which translated to extra sticky and pungent. Not an improvement. So they tranquillized the pack and relocated them. Except that emptying the territory meant that it was up for grabs by all the neighbouring tribes, all of which brought their own poop.

Finally, the Chirugons have had enough. At first they just want to wipe out the species, get rid of them once and for all. But really, they've had their monoliths smeared one time too many, and they're mad.

So what they do is tweak the DNA. They create a little retrovirus that will embed itself between sequence 1248B32A, and 1248B32B. As you all know, that's the genetically encoded behavioural sequence which compels your species to fling poop. They blocked it, you see.

The plan was for your entire species to die of constipation. They didn't even tell us! Just did on the sly. The truth is, we wouldn't have minded that much, we'd had our own experiences with poop flinging monkeys, if you know what I mean.

The Chirugons were quite angry by this time, and it was either that or just scorch the planet. This just seemed like less effort and more satisfaction.

Anyway, it solved the problem – they did their work and were on their way.

But the consequence was that a primal motive urge for your species, the unstoppable compulsion to fling your poop, had been blocked. Not eliminated, but blocked. That powerful compulsion built up and built up, finding new pathways. An urge so deeply written into your ancestral

DNA could not be eliminated, it couldn't be stopped up, one way or another, something was going to squeeze out.

Instead, the repressed urge to fling poop found new expressions. You started throwing rocks and sticks, then spears. You created language in order to fling harsh words, many of which were scatological. You invented sarcasm.

The next thing anyone knew, you were building entire civilizations out of the frustrated urge to throw poop at each other. Agriculture, metallurgy, domestication, bureaucracy, art, it was all desperate and inadequate substitutes for the frustrated but primordial need to fill your palm with a wet, sticky, soft brown log and give it a good wind up.

It still is.

Think about that the next time you're watching a Hollywood Blockbuster, or listening to a Presidential Address.

I know this is a lot to take in. But really, deep down, haven't you known it all along?

We showed up a few thousand years later, checking up on the Chirugons' lease, seeing if they'd forfeit the damage deposit.

Actually, you had this reputation. 'Planet of Poop Flinging Monkeys,' yeah, it's not like we wanted to spend time here.

The upgrade? 'Planet of Frustrated Poop Flinging Monkeys'? Not really a selling point, if you know what I mean.

But then, we discovered something.

The pyramids! Loved them to pieces! The Sphinx, first rate stuff. Megaliths, statues, rocks piled on top of rocks, big rocks, little rocks. You guys had really gone to town while we weren't paying attention.

But I need to clear something up. We didn't build them. We didn't even commission them. I mean, have you looked at those things? What would we want with them? They're just rocks. Huge piles of colossal rocks. They're shaped with chisels, hauled with rope; you can see the marks of primitive technology. You can see where they got quarried. I don't know how anyone in their right minds would think we had anything to do with it.

The truth is, they were tourist attractions. We'd be zipping around your planet, catch sight. We'd go 'Holy Moley! Take a look at that!' We'd go right down, poke around, ooh and ahh a bit. Buy some local tosh from the locals, get our pictures taken with Pharaohs, then off we'd go.

As it turns out, big mistake. Next thing you know, these things were popping up all over the place. Pyramids, walls, ziggurats, Stonehenge. Everywhere we looked, someone was doing something colossal, giant statues of Buddha, great big stone heads. We couldn't believe it. It was pathological. It was monkeys with OCD. Absolutely pointless. The ultimate expression of the blockage of your poop flinging urge.

We couldn't get over it. A little bit of rope, maybe a chisel, and suddenly you'd be off messing with the biggest rock you could find. Why? We had no idea. You couldn't eat them, you couldn't live in them, you couldn't do anything with them. But no, first chance you'd get, it was 'Hey, let's pile this gigantic stone on top of another gigantic stone, and inscribe some tits.'

We realized after a while, it was all some weird gigantic con job. Your planet was just one gigantic tourist trap. We tried putting our foot down, no more of this.

But then you'd come up with some sort of cockamamie excuse – 'No, no Meester, is not a tourist trap, is a tomb.' 'No, no Meester, is astronomical site to calculate the winter Solstice!' Sol-what? Didn't matter. We'd fall for it over and over.

So there you have it. Our contribution to your civilization was falling for your goofball schemes over and over again. We're still falling for them. I have a pocket dimension full of Amway products.

Drunk Slutty Elf, Page 163

Which brings us to our current issue.

Y'see, we haven't really been thrilled with the work lately. Sure, office towers are all very nice, the Interstate highway system definitely a work of art, but it's all so tediously functional and utilitarian. You just look at it, and you know what it's for. What's the fun of that? Where's the mystery? The intrigue?

And it's too easy. You have backhoes and steel mills, entire construction industries, steam engines, architects, computer assisted design. Anyone can build stuff that way.

Other species, without a blocked poop flinging compulsion, have usually built a half dozen space elevators by your stage of development. It's actually held you back.

Sane, stable civilizations of intelligent beings that have systematically solved all their problems, that's a dime a dozen out in the galaxy. To use one of your frustrated compulsive metaphors, you can't throw an asteroid without hitting one . . .

That's rude by the way, don't do that.

But a species that would rather invent cosmic omnipotent beings that are somehow obsessed with which bathroom you use, or create an entire technology of hair transplants? That's something special.

The thing is, you're just not fun anymore. Whatever happened to those halcyon days when it was just ropes and chisels, and the stubbornness to drag a giant rock a hundred miles, just to pile it on top of another rock, for no good reason whatsoever? That was epic! That was existential! It was glorious! There was just something special about it. Thousands of straining, grunting hominids, ropes, chisels, fire, primitive quarries, years, decades of work, all culminating in some random rock on top of some other random rock?

We loved that.

It was art!

Now? Now you're all just kind of 'meh.'

That's not good for business. I'm sitting on a planetoid of Bart Simpson dolls that I can't move.

Seriously, we're taking a bath here, we're losing our shirts. We invested heavily in you poop flinging monkeys.

We've thought about scorching the place to bedrock. If nothing else, there's some landscaping opportunities with that.

Then we thought, why not just undo what the Chirugons did? Unblock that poop flinging compulsion. Your civilisation would instantly collapse, as suddenly you all did what finally came naturally. There'd be some laughs.

But would it really do us any good in the long run?

Now, technically, you don't qualify as an intelligent life form. Officially, your galactic classification is semi-sentient lower life form with a blocked behavioral imperative.

You're constipated monkeys.

Seriously!

That just doesn't qualify, sorry.

So there's no moral issue for us in eradicating your species.

On the other hand, we really like those pyramids, if you know what we're saying. We love them. Pyramids are good. Great big stone statues? Good. Rocks piled on top of other rocks? Terrific. The whole thing, nothing but honest muscle power, handmade ropes, a few chisels and a lot of grunting and straining, to squeeze out another monolith.

That works for us. And really, it's what you're good at.

So why not?

You know you want to.

You hear what we're saying?

More pyramids.

The old fashioned way.

If you build them, we will come.

The End

***

Drunk Slutty Elf, Page 165

The Princess So Sweet and Fair

On the day of her birth, the King called all the Good Fairies to attend at the baptism of his daughter. One would be chosen as the godmother. From the four corners of the realm they came, fluttering on gossamer wings, shimmering in their gowns of whitest white, pinkest pink and bluest blue.

They gathered around the crib, admiring the newborn babe, cooing at its beauty as it gurgled up at them.

The Queen lay back in her bed, on the other side of the huge room. She smiled wanly at the Fairies as they clustered around the baby. She, quite privately, believed that the whole pack of them together had fewer brains than the sparrow that sometimes sang outside her window. The Queen maintained her smile with visions of having them all boiled in oil.

As for the baby: she thought it looked like a potato. A soft, soggy, partially skinned potato that made altogether too much noise. She was quite content to be on the other side of the room, and to have a dozen Fairies between her and it.

The Queen planned, as much as possible, to maintain affairs in that state of benign distance. Her chambermaids had already located a couple of fine peasant mothers with large . . . Well, suffice it to say, the Queen didn't plan on nursing.

The King stood, smiling happily, between the Queen and the baby. He would have liked to have held his wife's hand as the two of them looked down on their child. But he knew that smile of hers, and he didn't dare come any closer.

The Queen had formed some very definite opinions about sex, companionship, affection, and even the subject of men in general during the course of childbirth. Twenty-eight hours of labor would do that to you.

Suddenly, the great stained glass window at the end of the hall exploded. The Good Fairies shrieked and gathered close around the crib, spreading their wings to protect the newborn child from falling splinters of glass.

At the end of the hallway, like a great crow in rags of black she stooped, her black broom upended, its handle tapping the floor. Her nose protruded so far and curved so sharply, that it almost seemed to meet her pointed chin. A hairy wart stood prominently on her cheek. She looked at them all with rheumy eyes, her gaze resting on each one of them in turn. She cackled. Dry cracked lips parted to reveal three yellow teeth sitting alone in ulcerous pink gums. She began to drag herself forward.

"How dare you not invite me!" the Wicked Fairy snarled in a dry snarling voice.

* * *

"Would you like a muffin?" the Princess asked the handsome Knight as he sheathed his sword. The Princess sat on a rock and the Knight stood near her. On the hill below them lay the remains of a badly mangled dragon. Most of it anyway. It was hard to tell with the pieces scattered about like that.

Drunk Slutty Elf, Page 167

She was buttering muffins which she carried in a little white handkerchief, using a small but elegant silver breadknife. She held one out.

Gingerly, the Knight took it and nibbled at it slowly.

"Some battle, eh?" the Knight said. He slyly admired her charms from the corner of his eye, in a manner which anyone would notice, most would find rakish and sexy, and a few had found to be equal parts sleazy and moronic.

The Princess, for her part, had many charms to admire. Her name was Sunnyday Anthea Whiteclouds, an appellation which might have provoked a common girl to commit suicide, but which hardly raised an eyebrow among Princesses.

She had long white hair which hung in thick shimmering waves down to the small of her back, and eyes as green as spring meadows full of clover. When she smiled, she smiled with such joy and love that flowers would spontaneously bloom and then wilt, inspired by the challenge of her radiance, and then crushed by their failure to meet it. She wore a simple green gown, with naught but a silver girdle and the tiniest of crowns to show her station. She was, quite simply, a perfect Princess.

The Knight had fallen completely in love at the sight of her.

The Knight was actually a Prince. Although not of very much. His father's Kingdom was quite cozy as Kingdoms went, though the unkind were wont to say that when visiting his realm, one should take care not to turn around too suddenly, for fear of accidentally leaving it. The unkind were wont to say many similar things, mainly because the world hadn't invented tiny hotel rooms yet, and they needed to polish their material on something.

Still, it was enough of a Kingdom to have produced the Prince, our Knight. He was tall and strong, fair of face, fit of body. He was dressed head to toe in a suit of shining steel armor, plated with inlaid silver. He rode a proud stallion, of such pure white that in the winter snowstorms it

could not be seen at all, and could only be located by
following its . . . poops, which were the only things about it
which were not white.

If he was not the cleverest Prince in the world, as the
unkind sometimes said . . . well, who needs brains when
you have a body like that?

Now here is an interesting fact: Although the dragon
lay dead, and scattered about the landscape in one huge
bloody hunk, and a great many smaller but equally bloody
ones, there was not a trace of blood on the Knight or his
horse, or even a bead of sweat on his noble brow.

"Hmmm. I've seen better," the Princess said of the
battle.

The Knight's brows knit in confusion.

* * *

At this point, we should talk about the King. Mainly
because this is the only point at which we will speak of
him.

The King stood there, having foolishly advanced to
face the Wicked Fairy. He clearly hadn't thought the matter
through, and by the time he realized what he was doing, it
was too late. All he could do was continue walking towards
impending doom. She bore down, seeming to tower over
him, though he could in fact see over her hunch. Her sickly
greenish skin and rancid breath revolted him, and if he
were not paralyzed by fear, he would have turned and run.

The King, you see, was not a brave man. In point of
fact, he demonstrated few of the qualities we associate with
Kings in those by-gone days. He was not especially strong.
Nor particularly fair. He was not remarkably tall, nor
known for wisdom. The King was not known for being
especially anything in particular.

Somewhat timid, the King had never seen any
particular need to go looking for trouble.

If his people loved him, and it is arguable that they did
so with deep fondness, if only mild enthusiasm, it was for
what he did not do. He did not raise taxes. He did not go

spilling their blood with great dramatic wars. He did not trample the crops fighting monsters or hunting foxes. He did not do anything in particular.

All the common people wanted, all any common people ever want, is simply to be left alone to live their lives. If they could be said to have a wish, it would be that those who invariably had power over their lives should not exercise it, as they invariably did, in an arbitrary and destructive fashion. The Kingdom's people were no different, and from long experience with previous Kings, they knew exactly how blessed they were to have a relatively well meaning king who seemed to do nothing in particular.

Now of course, you are impatient to get on with the story. But we have not yet finished with the King, so sit a little longer.

The King had one gift. It was a gift which few recognized, and nobody understood. But in its way, it was a gift which was greater than speed and strength, more profound than courage or wisdom, more priceless than good looks or even good luck.

It was this: The King had a tendency to do things which had never been done before.

That is, he was original.

Now at first glance, you might not think much of this. But consider the turnings of history. It is said that there is nothing new under the sun. It has all been done before. Many times. History seems like a record with a jumping needle, so that the same events are continually repeated over and over again. New faces, new names and kingdoms rise and fall, but the events are always monotonously the same.

Consider the scene before us: The birth of a Princess, the twelve Good Fairies come to bless, the thirteenth come to curse. It had become so familiar and shopworn, by this time, that everyone present, save perhaps the infant Princess, could have written their parts down on the back of an envelope and sent that in their place. Any of them, for that matter, could have written everyone's parts down and sent it in, though that would have taken at least a couple of sheets of paper.

So when the Wicked Fairy readied her curse and snarled the traditional words:

"How dare you not invite me!"

The King, without quite knowing what he was doing, stepped forward showing more confidence than he possessed and said:

"Nonsense. Do you think I would be so forgetful as to not invite the one I'd chosen for my daughter's Godmother?"

In later years, the Wicked Fairy sometimes wished the King had simply whipped out a crossbow and shot her between the eyes then and there.

* * *

"I love you," the Knight kneeled before the Princess.

"I bet you say that to all the girls," she smiled and giggled, but in a tender and good-natured manner without any malice or cynicism.

In point of fact, it was true. He did say that to all the girls.

And to several of the prettier sheep, the unkind were fond of adding, but we have had quite enough of the unkind thus far, and they are invited to leave this story and go heckle some lounge comedian.

In any case, he did say it quite often, and to be truthful, it worked every time.

To be quite fair to the Knight, he did mean it. We have mentioned that he had fallen in love with her at first sight.

But then, he had had lots of practice.

He laid his hand on her knee.

For what it was worth, even though she half suspected all of this, she didn't mind at all. It was still nice to hear it said. Flattery is not worth its weight in gold, but its pretty close.

Drunk Slutty Elf, Page 171

She blushed and looked away, smiling coyly, but did not remove his hand.

* * *

"What?" the Wicked Fairy asked, blankly, stopping dead in her tracks.

Had she heard him correctly. She replayed his last few words. Yes, he'd said it.

The Good Fairies milled around uncertainly, this had never happened before and they had no idea what to do. Even the Queen's wan smile had been replaced by a look of shock.

If the King had only one bit of wisdom in his entire head, it was that you must finish what you start.

So he took the Wicked Fairy by the hand and led her to the crib. She found herself stumbling along, trying to keep up. This wasn't how it was supposed to go at all.

"Look upon your godchild," he said, trying to sound like he knew what he was doing, "she awaits your blessing."

The other Fairies glanced at each other uncertainly. A slip of the tongue was one thing; they could have gotten back on track. But now things were utterly derailed.

"Is she not the most beautiful child you have ever seen?" the head Good Fairy chirped, trying desperately to recapture the spirit of things.

"It looks like a soggy potato," the Wicked Fairy said doubtfully.

"They grow out of it," the Good Fairy hissed, quietly kicking her in the ankle. "Now for pity's sake be nice, her mother is right over there."

The two Fairies, white and black, looked up at the Queen and smiled together. She smiled back at them, mentally fitting them for the rack.

She wasn't terribly interested in proceedings. She was rethinking the Kingdom's drug policy. Mainly, she was thinking there weren't nearly enough drugs in the Kingdom.

* * *

Drunk Slutty Elf, Page 172

"You killed the dragon all by yourself with just a breadknife!" the Knight asked incredulously. They lay on the grass together; almost arm in arm, ostensibly looking at clouds. Her little breadknife, and the napkin of muffins, lay a short distance away.

The Princess nodded demurely in the shadow of his manly arms.

"That and my breadknife."

She is mad, he thought, or hallucinating from a concussion. He did not know what had transpired here, but he refused to believe that this tender slip of a girl had directly wreaked such mayhem. Indirectly, yes, he could see that. Hers was a face to launch a thousand ships, and a body to have them all madly fighting to race back into port in a completely non-entendrish way. He could believe all manner of destruction might well be inspired by her, that men might kill and wreak havoc to butter her muffins.

But at this moment, she was obviously quite out of her mind.

This did not diminish his love for her one iota, however. In fact, if anything, it increased his desire for her. The Knight, having so little wit himself, did not find the qualities of the mind an especially attractive feature. Generally, he found that smarter girls tended to lose interest the more he talked; sometimes they lost interest after 'hello.' He compensated by doing push ups.

"It must have been a fearsome struggle?" he humored her.

"Not really," she told him. "It swooped down on Daddy and I as we were having morning tea and muffins on the balcony. I hate it when they do that, it makes me so cross. I fear I was quite rough with the poor beast."

"Still," he said, "it must be pleasant to relax after such a fight."

"It is," she smiled at him.

"That girdle, as beautiful as it is," he whispered "must become quite uncomfortable afterwards?"

Drunk Slutty Elf, Page 173

"You know . . ." he drew the words out, "Tight? Sweaty?"

"It is," she whispered back.

"Would you like me to help you with it?" he asked, even as his clever fingers released the tiny metal clasps along the side.

"I would," she murmured.

Soon his hands slid along the smooth flesh of her flat belly. He bent his head towards hers.

"Are you pure of heart?" she asked softly.

"The purest," he answered her, and then pressed his lips against hers.

*　*　*

"And now the blessing," the King said.

"What?" asked the Wicked Fairy, she was still trying to catch up.

"A blessing," the Good Fairy hissed in explanation. "You have to give it a blessing; beauty, grace, straight teeth, that sort of thing."

"I didn't bring anything like that with me," the Wicked Fairy mumbled uncertainly.

She thought for a moment.

"I could turn her into a toad?" she suggested hopefully.

The Good Fairy kicked her in the ankle.

"Look at it," the Wicked Fairy hissed as quietly as she could. "It would be an improvement over a squalling potato." She rubbed her bruised shin.

The Good Fairy kicked her in the other ankle.

"Oh, all right," the Wicked Fairy snarled as she bent down to kiss the child.

The infant Princess cooed with delight, for to a newborn babe, all things are beautiful, and reached up to tug the Wicked Fairy's wart hairs.

"Only the pure of heart for you," she whispered.

*　*　*

"I am so sorry," the Princess said, as she buttered another muffin. "We were getting along so well, too."

Drunk Slutty Elf, Page 174

"Ribbit!" said the frog, which was large and green, and exceptionally good looking by frog standards, as it sat upon the empty armor.

"Anyway," she told it, "I guess I owed you an explanation, and that is the whole story."

* * *

"So what now?" the Wicked Fairy asked.

All the Fairies and Royalty looked at each other uncertainly. This definitely was not on the back of the envelope.

"I guess . . . maybe, I should curse it?" said the Good Fairy, trying to recapture at least a semblance of the old tale.

The Wicked Fairy straightened and looked her in the eye. She didn't quite understand how this had happened to her, but she was determined to see it through. She fixed the Good Fairy with her most baleful glare.

"I'm sorry, dearie. But it's a closed shop."

* * *

There was a sudden darkening of the sun, and a rushing of wings like thunder as the Wicked Fairy arrived. With a snap of her fingers she parked her broom and surveyed the scene.

"Gran!" shouted the Princess as she ran up and embraced the Wicked Fairy. "It's so good to see you again."

The Wicked Fairy allowed herself a furtive smile as she stroked her god-daughter's long white hair.

The intervening years had not been kind to her. Her coveted sickly pallor had faded to a healthier hue. The rigors of setting examples of proper posture, sensible nutrition, healthy exercise, and decent hours had taken their toll. Her warts had given up the fight and died somewhere along the way. Her three lone teeth had been joined by well-fitting ivory dentures which altered her face and her speech in a most unwelcome way. She still favored black, but had come to suspect that it looked good on her now.

Tall, she was now, with a fine if sparse figure, clear healthy skin and dark flashing eyes. No longer ancient, she seemed merely mature. With sadness, she realized that she would never again be hideous.

Which is not to say that she was beautiful. Or even pretty. Rather her looks went in a different direction, which might be described as handsome.

Let's just say that in certain countries middle-aged men might pay a woman of her looks a great deal of money to dress up in leather and whip them for being naughty little boys.

I think you have the picture.

Still, as she looked at her god-daughter, she decided that all the sacrifices had been worth it.

"I came as soon as I heard," she said.

"Oh Gran," the Princess told her, "you shouldn't have worried; you know I can take care of myself. It was only a dragon."

Which was true. The Wicked Fairy had seen to that.

This would be one Princess, the Wicked Fairy had promised herself on that fateful day, that would not prick her finger on a spinning wheel and fall into a hundred years sleep. Or bite into a poisoned apple and have to wait for some wandering necrophile to kiss her back to life.

The Wicked Fairy's eyes drifted over to the suit of armor, and the frog sitting on top of it.

"Another one?" she asked.

The Princess nodded sadly as the Wicked Fairy scooped it up with a practiced hand and deposited in her carrying bag. She would take it back to join the others.

"He said he was pure of heart," she complained.

In the short years since the Princess had come of age, the frog population had increased dramatically, and the male population had experienced a similar decline. It had not been an altogether bad thing. Flies and mosquitos had become quite rare, and a recent plague of locusts that had devastated neighboring lands had mysteriously failed to affect the Kingdom at all. Indeed, with fewer wild young men about, the Kingdom seemed to be a quieter, happier place.

Still, the Wicked Fairy had begun to feel that things were getting out of hand though.

She had begun to experiment with returning some of them to human form. She had discovered that after spending a few years snapping flies with their tongues, men suddenly restored were astonishingly affectionate and eager to please in the most remarkable physical ways, and were entirely willing to demonstrate new skills.

Sometimes she even had to summon up a demon to get the smile off her face.

"Don't they all," the Wicked Fairy reflected.

They climbed onto the broom for the ride home. The Wicked Fairy insisting that they ride side-saddle, rather than straddled as she usually did when she flew alone. She had a fierce determination that her god-daughter be a complete Princess.

Her god-daughter was as good and sweet and true, as the finest Princess who had ever lived. She was fair of face, generous of spirit, and pure of soul.

But unlike other Princesses, she was not, the Wicked Fairy amended silently, ever to be abandoned in the woods, or enslaved by evil step-sisters. Never to shack up with a band of dwarves, or keep house for a talking wart-hog. Her Princess would never be shut up in a tower with nothing to do but let her hair grow. Nor be enslaved by some deranged hunchback with a passion for weaving straw into gold. This was one Princess who would not be bruised by a pea under a mattress, or be kidnapped and sold into slavery by gypsies.

There were a thousand and one horrid fates that befell enchanted Princesses. She had vowed that her Princess would not bow to a single one of them.

Drunk Slutty Elf, Page 177

"Gran," the Princess spoke, as they flew along.

"Hmmm?" she answered.

"I'm bored. I need a hobby. Something to do."

"That's a very good idea, Dearie."

"I was thinking about conquering the Western Kingdoms."

The Wicked Fairy frowned thoughtfully.

"I don't know, Dearie. What will you do once you conquer them? You remember how bored you got with the south?" she asked.

"But it's different now, Gran," the Princess replied with mock exasperation. "I'm older; I'm much more interested in government and administration."

"Hmmm," the Wicked Fairy reflected. Eligible young bachelors were thinning out in the neighborhood, but there was still a healthy supply in the western kingdoms. She liked to think of it as a statistical inevitability that at least one of them would be pure of heart.

She hoped.

"It would be an opportunity for me to use the macro-economic theory you taught me."

At that moment the Princess shrieked with delight and pointed down. They were passing over the crater where the Wicked Fairy had caught up with that deranged hunchback with the barnyard fixation.

The bottom of the crater had filled with water, forming a small pond in the center. They could see ducks dabbling in it, the Princess laughed and threw crumbs. Along the glassy sides of the crater, vegetation was slowly crawling back, etching tiny footholds on the edges of the glazed walls. Eventually the hunchback wouldn't even be a memory.

"Gran," said the Princess.

"Yes Dearie?" responded the Wicked Fairy.

"I love you, Gran."

"I love you too, Dearie."

"Would you like a muffin, Gran? I buttered them myself," the Princess, her Princess, invited.

"Why thank you, Dearie."

She took one. Together they ate their buttered muffins as they flew sidesaddle across the countryside.

The End

***

The Voice from the Mantlepiece

Sir James Fitz-Sterling, noted Ghost-remover, bounded up the steps to the stone house. He pressed the doorbell three times, with the careful precision of a man used to rapping brass knockers. Inside, he could hear the faint sound of chimes.

He could sense a sudden flurry of activity in the house. They had been expecting him, but of course, they weren't quite ready. No matter how immaculate the home was, they still had to fly about doing last minute straightenings and dustings.

As they bustled, Sir James extended his senses, breathing in the flavor of the house, and of the neighborhood. Middle class, he decided, but an edgy uncertain middle class. The sort of neighborhood of people who had advanced a few notches beyond their proper station, and feared slipping back.

The door opened.

Sir James bowed deeply and took her hand. "Marjory," he boomed, "so delightful to finally meet you after all these telephone conversations."

Marjory was a pleasant looking woman of about middle ages, running slightly to fat; she struck him as unexceptional in almost every way.

Watch it, he warned himself, those types were often the most surprising.

"Oh Sir James," she greeted him, "we are likewise pleased to meet you." From behind her a man appeared. Sir James found himself taking an almost instant dislike to the fellow.

Tall and dour, with the sort of set and wrinkled features that bespoke a man who seldom smiled and never laughed, the man stood forth. Sir James released Marjory's hand and exchanged manly clasps with the newcomer.

"Sir James, this is my husband Donald, who I've spoken of over the phone."

She looked just a little hesitant as the two shook hands, as if nervous of what Donald might say or do.

"Pleasure," Donald said, giving the impression that it was nothing of the sort.

"It is," Sir James said carefully, "always good to meet a member of the family."

Donald would not smile of course, but his brow crinkled slightly in a manner that suggested approval.

"Come in, Sir James," Marjory chattered, "we must pour you a cup of tea."

As they spoke he extended his senses looking for traces of supernatural activity. At that instant, he could find nothing, which meant perhaps that they were visited by intermittent rather than constant forces.

Graciously, Donald accepted his coat, and they made their way to the sun room. It was small but congenial place with large windows facing south and east, occupied by battered but comfortable lounging chairs and a polished reading table on which sat a well-thumbed bible.

Sir James found an overstuffed leather chair and relaxed into it. Donald likewise took a seat, and Marjory, as was her nature, bustled.

Drunk Slutty Elf, Page 181

"Milk or sugar?" she inquired as she hovered over the tea server.

"Yes please," Sir James responded pleasantly, "and put a spot of tea in it."

It sailed right over the both of them he noted.

"Please be comfortable, Sir James," Marjory went on solicitously as she attended to the tea, "feel free to remove your sunglasses, it is indoors after all."

Sir James touched his shades briefly.

"I'd quite forgotten about them," he told the couple, "nevertheless, I think I'll leave them. My condition, you know."

They didn't know, but were too polite to ask.

"So," said Marjory, as she served them both, before pouring herself a cup, "how is dear Alice?"

"Quite well thank you."

"You know," Marjory chattered, "I used to babysit the dear when she was but a little child. She was so sweet, I thought it must have been so hard on her when her mother, dear cousin Lillian, became . . . eccentric."

Donald cleared his throat. Clearly this was one of the hundreds of subjects that he felt uncomfortable with.

"I think you'll find Lillian's condition much improved these days," Sir James spoke genially, "but surely you didn't invite me over just to discuss relations."

"Ghosts," spat Donald.

They waited.

That was about it for Donald, Sir James decided.

He turned to Marjory.

"Yes, Sir James," Marjory's eyes were downcast, "we do seem to be plagued with poltergeists. We are at our wits' end. Night and day they haunt us."

From the oak there came the slightest nod.

Sir James looked for a place to put his teacup down. Seeing that the coasters were already occupied, he gently placed it on the bible.

"Poltergeists, you say?" Sir James asked. "Do you have any children?"

"One son, Robert, age ten," Marjory said proudly, "he's in boarding school."

"Ah," said Sir James, "and how long has this 'haunting' been going on?"

Marjory blushed and cast her eyes downward, as if about to reveal mysteries of feminine hygiene.

"Perhaps four years," she looked up, "although it's gotten particularly bad the last few months."

"Then it's not a poltergeist," he said firmly. "Perhaps it's some other species of etheric entity, a banker, a tenant, a banshee or tommyknocker perhaps."

"What's it matter? A ghost is a ghost," protested Donald. "Just tell it to move along."

"My dear fellow," Sir James told him, "a ghost is not just a ghost. In addition to the legions of the dearly departed crowding this earth, there are all manner of creatures hospitable to what we call the 'occult' or 'etheric' plane. Success may only come from knowing the nature of the creature you are dealing with."

Donald harrumphed.

Unperturbed, Sir James took another sip of tea.

"Take for instance, poltergeists," he went on, "one of the most thoroughly pernicious entities. It feeds on the pent up energies of sexually repressed adolescents. Therefrom, it derives its name 'noisy ghost,' as it discharges the excesses."

"Luckily, however," he told them, "it is easily dealt with by the simple expedient of removing the 'repressions,' once the adolescent is diverted into more normal behavior; the poltergeist has nothing to feed upon."

"I still have fond memories of the case of the Peerless Peers, such nubile fourteen year old twins. And their trusty pet goat," Sir James smiled to himself. "Sometimes, I can say, that we are called upon to make the most pleasurable sacrifices."

Donald squinted at him suspiciously, as if there was something he could not quite identify, but it was bothering him.

Sir James ignored his suspicion.

"This household unfortunately lacks a nubile pubescent female. Your Robert fails to qualify in a number of respects, not the least of which being his presence, or lack of it. Further, it is unheard of for a poltergeist to persist for such a time, the energies on which they feed simply do not remain conflicted for such a time."

"Well, what can it be then?" asked Marjory. "Something is plaguing our home."

"Dear lady," Sir James suggested, "your notion of a poltergeist, while wrong is suggestive."

"Whatever do you mean?" breathed Marjory.

"It's well known that poltergeists are creatures fed by sexual frustration. Your 'ghost' may well be a species with similar needs."

"What are you suggesting?" Donald asked suspiciously.

"Obviously," Sir James spoke bluffly, "if that is the source of its power, the problem can be corrected with a few visits with a trained professional. The Baronet Hungly, for example, or Duchess Transylvania. Or perhaps Delicia Vulnavia," he paused at this one, "although I believe she's out of the country at the moment, working with dolphins . . . or was it farm animals?"

"We'll have none of that," Donald glowered. "I'll have you know that me and the Misses have no problems in that or any other respect."

Sir James noted that Marjory chewed her lip at this point, with a nervous and distracted air. Well, Donald might not have problems, he decided.

"Ah well," he said, "tell me about the manifestation. Know the enemy, I always say."

"It started off with noises," said Marjory, "at first."

"What sort of noises?"

"Popping sounds," she elaborated, "like little thundercracks. Then moans, and sometimes we'd hear roars like some terrible beast."

"I see," said Sir James, "that doesn't sound like a spirit of a deceased. Possibly some other entity. Do go on."

"What's that?" Donald protested. Sir James waved him to silence, and nodded again to Marjory.

"Then shortly after the noises started, things started to fall over."

"What sort of things?"

"Pictures, they would fall off their hooks on the walls, or from the mantelpiece."

"Hmm hm?"

"Little figurines would fall off the table."

"Yes?"

"For the longest time we thought we were just clumsy."

"This is a devout household," Donald explained. "We don't have any truck with the supernatural."

"Donald is a lay preacher," Marjory said proudly, "but I must admit that for the longest time I despaired of dear Donald ever hanging a painting properly."

"Interesting, any visual manifestations: Lights? Shapes? Recognizable figures?"

"Oh," Marjory thought hard, "well, there was the time a few months back that Donald thought the fern was on fire."

"It was," Donald insisted.

"No dear," Marjory said, "I cleaned it up after you attacked it with the golf club, there wasn't so much as a browned leaf."

"Damned bush," Donald mumbled.

"So tell me," Sir James inquired, "when did you realize that this was an actual haunting, rather than, say, a geological subsidence or children playing pranks."

"Recently," said Donald.

"Just about a year ago," Marjory contradicted. "I was in the bedroom doing needlepoint, and I saw . . ." She paused, and collected her thoughts, starting over.

"Well, I had this collection of figurines," she explained, "Royal Dalton ceramics; I believe it was the Eunuchs of the Far East. I was keeping them on my evening dresser table. I heard a sound, I looked up, and as I watched, some unseen force simply flung them across the room."

"It's gotten so bad, we can hardly keep anything on the mantelpiece, or on the shelves," Donald elaborated.

"It sounds like some indigenous parasite, or perhaps the shade of a cat," mused Sir James. "Are there any cold spots in the house?"

"Hold on there," protested Donald.

Sir James lifted an eyebrow.

"You said something about the shade of a cat. A cat ghost?"

"Yes?"

"Cats can't have ghosts."

"Oh?"

"On account of their not having souls, a ghost is just a soul that hasn't moved on to heaven."

Sir James burst out laughing.

"My dear fellow," Sir James told him, "everything that lives leaves a psychic residue. Or to use your quaint term, has a 'soul.'"

"That's not what it says in the Good Book," Donald protested, with an expression that hinted that if neither automobiles nor gynecologists had been mentioned in the good book, they couldn't possibly exist either.

Sir James chuckled, "Ghosts aren't mentioned in the bible either," he set his tea cup down upon it, "while that chronicle of ancient genealogy and morality may have its uses, I must say that a description of afterlife is not one of them."

Donald glowered.

"Well, about our ghost . . ." Marjory desperately tried to steer the subject back.

"Do cats go to heaven, or hell, or some special place for cats?" Donald challenged.

"That was actually a long running nineteenth century debate between cat fanciers and their opponents," Sir James ruminated, "the great flaw, of course, was that in actual fact, there is no such place or state as heaven or hell."

Donald was almost speechless.

"What of God's plan?"

"Actually, Gods are much overrated," Sir James explained, "they are parasites, rather than creators, fattening on the belief of their followers."

"There is only one God," Donald insisted, "the creator of all things."

"Really now," Sir James responded, "history shows that there have been many, they are rather like measles in some ways."

"What of the miracles?" Donald asked.

"All gods have miracles, and they usually have their followers manufacture them to incite belief. Deities of every sort are notoriously lazy; most holy books are compendiums of requests, demands and excuses. It's much easier for a god to have a miracle faked, than to do a real one. Indeed, a false miracle is often one of the best indicators of the presence of a god."

"You confuse me, Sir," Donald protested, "false miracles . . ."

"Simple energy economics, Donald," Sir James explained, "it's easier for a god to induce a follower to forge a miracle, than it is to do a genuine one itself."

Donald was aghast.

"I tend to view gods as somewhat equivalent to a plague," Sir James ruminated, "more truth to that than we realize: loss of spiritual energy that gods draw from their followers tends to suppress the immune system. Excessive

Catholicism, I would venture, lead directly to the black plague."

"Luckily," he concluded, "humanity has a tendency to grow immune to its gods, thus their constant replacement. One unfortunate effect, however, is that as its host population grows more resistant, the God becomes inclined to have its remaining worshippers seek and convert new populations not yet immune to them: thus religious wars and missionaries."

As the looming silence deepened, Sir James finished his tea, placidly wondering if he would be thrown bodily out of the house.

"Eventually, they just fade away slowly."

"But, Sir James, wherever then do the souls of the dearly departed go?" Marjory desperately tried to defuse the tensions building.

"They go nowhere, my dear," Sir James chuckled jovially, "they remain right here with us."

"Well Sir!" Donald crowed, "I have you there. You maintain that the spirits of the deceased remain earthbound?"

"That is true."

"You must also admit that with the passing of time, the numbers of people who have lived and persist no longer, exceed the numbers of people who currently live. Perhaps by as much as thirty to one."

"That is true as well." Sir James admitted.

"Then why are we not plagued by wall-to-wall ghosts?" Donald challenged. "Answer me that, then. Rather than the one in a thousand who remains behind, if reports be correct."

"Gladly," said Sir James, holding his cup out as Marjory refilled. He gave her a polite thanks as he stirred it twice and laid the spoon aside.

"Do you know," he asked them, "that if you place food in front of a frog in a cage, it will starve to death?"

"What's that got to do with anything?" Donald asked suspiciously.

"Simply this: a frog by virtue of the wiring of its admittedly feeble brain is unable to perceive as food that which lies before it. It can only recognize and devour flying insects."

"So?"

"What possible use could it be to living creatures to see ghosts? There is little or no benefit at all. Indeed," Sir James explained, "it would be a hindrance. Think of the wolf or tiger, followed about by the shade of every field mouse, goat, antelope and buffalo it ever devoured."

"Thus, although ghosts, as you say, abound, our senses, perhaps even the circuitry of our brain, has evolved not to perceive them. To edit them out of the picture."

"I would note," went on Sir James, "that in most cases of recorded hauntings, the strongest evidence is always of the indirect effects: cold spots, objects moved or touched, sound waves in the air, and such."

"I've had just about enough." Donald rose to his feet. "I was against the idea of calling someone in for this problem from the start. But because our situation was driving dear Marjory to her wits' end, and because you were family, I relented.

"But you come in here and mock our most cherished beliefs," Donald's voice rose. "Sir, I must ask you to leave, or I shall forcibly evict you."

Just then there was a loud crash from the living room. Sir James's subtle senses detected a stirring.

"Quickly," he told them, "it's here!"

They all raced to the living room to find that the mantelpiece above the fireplace had been violently swept clean of all photographs and souvenirs.

Sir James's trained ears detected a faint, but booming voice, declaring angrily, "Thou shalt have no idols but me!"

Elsewhere in the kitchen, he just made out another, even fainter voice, calling out as if in answer, "Grapes and wine and revels, let us dance to my pipes!"

Suddenly ashen, he turned to Donald and Marjory.

"I'm afraid it's much worse than I suspected," he told them. "You've got gods."

The End

***

The Djewel and the Djinn

"Check those out," Steg the Guard said to his companion, Arf. Arf was also a guard. But not 'the' guard. It was a distinction, the definite 'article' that Steg insisted upon. Arf was 'a' guard, and Steg was 'the' Guard.

Arf put up with a lot.

The guards watched warily as the motley band of adventurers approached the gate.

Arf chewed his tobacco and spat anachronistically.

"Don't like the looks of them," he said somberly. "They don't look like they're here for the Coronation."

The Coronation of the Princess Sadhe of Mangolis to be followed by her wedding the dashing commoner Jalahad the clever, was pretty much the main reason anyone was visiting the Kingdom these days. Romance addled teenage girls were swooning. For everyone else, business in the Kingdom had ground to a halt, and the coronation expenses were already threatening to bankrupt realm.

"Halt and identify yourselves," Steg ordered. He looked them up and down. Yes, it was a standard crew all right, doubtless off on some quest. There was the sniveling wizard type, the sort of beautiful but definitely untrustworthy female accomplice, the rugged barbarian and . . .

"What the hell is that?" Arf barked, startled and unnerved.

The fourth member of the group appeared to be carrying a sack of balloons, judging by the buoyancy of the sack. It looked like it was about to float right off his shoulders.

But that wasn't the peculiar thing. The creature stood about five feet tall, its skin was light gray. Its body was spindly, a fact clearly visible beneath clothes which were worn with poor grace, while its hands each bore only four extraordinarily long fingers.

But the most peculiar thing was the creature's immense head, twice the size of a normal skull, utterly hairless, with huge dark almond eyes, barely the suggestion of a nose, and a small thin, lipless mouth.

"He's a seaman," the woman said brightly.

"A semen?" Steg replied. "I don't think so. That doesn't look like it came dripping out of anyone's loins."

"Well, maybe," Arf said thoughtfully, "I knew a guy once with gray crotch swelling fungus . . ."

The woman looked awkward for a moment, but then, with visible effort, rallied.

"Not semen!" she snapped. "A 'sea' 'man.' This is Darkeyes the Sailorman, wanderer of the oceans and seas."

"I'm not a sailor," the creature said. "I'm an alien."

"Doesn't look like a sailor." Steg was skeptical. "Where's his parrot? Why is he alienated?"

"I'm from another world," the creature said, "stranded here when my ship discorporated."

"It's a metaphor," the woman said confidently.

"It's not a metaphor," the creature said, "I'm actually an alien from another world!"

"Hell of a ventriloquist," Arf said. "I've been watching, and I haven't seen his lips move once."

"That makes sense," Steg observed. "Sailors are notorious ventriloquists. It comes from having nothing to talk to but parrots. Now that I think about it, he's dressed like a sailor."

"Probably misses his parrot," Arf suggested. "That's why he's alienated."

The gray creature demonstrated his ventriloquism by once again, not moving his lips, while at the same time, not saying anything with intense disapproval.

"Well, that's sorted," said Steg. "What about the rest of you? You scrawny weasel guy, name and occupation."

The wizard-looking fellow stepped forward. He currently lacked the usual deathly pallor associated with sorcerers. Probably too many vegetables in his diet, Steg thought.

"I," he said dramatically, pausing . . .

Steg waved him to get on with it.

". . . am Scabrous the Malevolent!"

Steg checked the rolls. "Scabrous with an 'S'? Scabrous, Scabrous, Scabrous. There's a lot of these."

"It was a popular name with mothers, back in the day," Arf commented. "Back when the pox came through. Scabrous, Scabby, Scabuletta . . ."

Steg snapped his fingers. "You're the shoemaker! Love your work! My cousin has a pair of yours, swears by it."

Scabrous sighed.

"No. But I get that a lot."

"Scabrous the Apothecary?"

"No. He's the one with the club foot."

"Scabrous the Apiarist?"

"I don't even know what that is."

"It means beekeeper," the woman pointed out.

Scabrous's brows knit. "Why would anyone keep bees?"

"I hear they make good pets. Very affectionate," Steg commented, not really paying attention. "Here we go, Scabrous the Wavelolent."

"That's an 'M,' not a 'W,'" Arf offered.

"Oh yeah, now that you mention it, it is. They do look alike." Steg focused. "Occupation?"

"Servant of the dark arts, eater of souls, necromancer, pledged to unholy gods."

"Oh yeah?" Steg looked up critically, "How's that working out for you?"

"It's a living."

"You guys usually hole up in a tower somewhere. What are you doing out and about?"

"Long story," Scabrous said miserably.

"You know," Arf said, "I've got a nephew wants to go into necromancy. Any advice?"

Scabrous thought a moment. "Once he gets through the initial exams, it's clear sailing. The only thing he's got to watch out for is applied demonology."

"Thanks," Arf said.

"Next!" Steg barked, uninterested in small talk that he wasn't involved in.

The tall, muscular warrior, barely dressed in boots and loin cloth, stepped forward. Steg looked him up and down, and then down, then up, and then down some more, just in case. He licked his lips.

"Name?"

"Jurgan the Unmarked."

Arf whistled. Steg put down his scroll.

"The only survivor of the siege of Flatskull! Who ran the Marathon of the Dark Moor! Untouched by blade! Hero of the Eskinae! That Jurgan the Unmarked?"

The mighty warrior nodded modestly. Steg let his gaze linger on Jurgan's thighs. He decided to go for it.

"You doing anything later?"

Jurgan shrugged. That wasn't a 'no' Steg decided.

"Well, if you're free later on, me and the second shift guards are going to be having a little get together later on. Strictly low key. A little music, a little dancing, a little body oiling. Love to have you drop by."

"Are you hitting on him?" the woman demanded.

Steg swallowed and decided to move on, but not before slipping the mighty thewed warrior a note, as the guard turned his attention to the annoying woman.

"And you?" Steg demanded.

"Salvra, Princess of Tobla, Ninth Level Thief."

Steg checked the magic scroll.

"Don't have you, sorry." Steg checked again. "We do have a Salvra the Inept, drunkard, plagiarizer, petty chiseler, debt evader, and harasser of sheep."

"That sheep was asking for it!"

"So that's you?"

"No."

Steg looked the scroll over.

"Seems that she's wanted for an outbreak of Gray Crotch Swelling Fungus?"

"That's been cleared up! And it wasn't me."

"From Tobla, didn't you mention that's where you're from?"

"Nope. Never heard of the place," she said firmly.

Steg shrugged, he didn't much care.

"All right then, glad we cleared that up."

He rolled up the scroll.

"Entry denied!" he announced. "I couldn't possibly let a group of obvious thieves, scoundrels, ventriloquists and breathtakingly shredded sex machines through the Royal City Gate on Coronation Day."

He paused.

"You'll have to go around to the Criminal's Gate."

"There's a Criminal's Gate?" the ventriloquist, Darkeyes asked, his lips still not moving.

"Yeah," Steg said. "But it'll be closed by the time you get there. You'll have to come back —"

Steg stopped. The gray creature was taking off its clothes. It wasn't his type, but despite that, Steg couldn't help being curious, and a little intrigued.

"Don't do that!" Salvra complained. "I went through a lot of trouble to get you dressed. Do you know how hard it is to find a sailor's outfit?"

As the creature stripped away, Steg noted with interest it lacked visible nipples, or navel, or any genitalia whatsoever. He supposed it explained why Sailors were so fond of parrots.

"I'm not ashamed of my body," Darkeyes snapped, lips firmly pressed together. He was reaching into his sack.

"Oh," Arf said, "he's going to give us a balloon!"

***

Steg the guard stood at the gate, maintaining vigil with Arf, a guard. Arf thought he put up with a lot of nonsense from Steg. Particularly the way Steg liked to watch him go to the bathroom.

"Quiet day," Arf said.

"Yep," Steg replied.

"Nothing going on," Arf said.

"Nothing," Steg replied.

"My ass hurts," Arf said.

"Me too."

"Really?" Arf said. "I thought that was you?"

Steg shrugged. He was thinking of tall, oiled, semi-nude, muscular warriors for no particular reason. But then, he did that a lot.

***

Past the gates, the City was a madhouse. Every street was packed with throngs, workers, tradesmen, beggars, merchants, scoundrels and thieves in ceaseless motion, darting in and out between horse carts, elephants, lines of camels. Snaking their way through the streets were caravans of royals and nobles from neighboring Kingdoms arriving to pay their respects to the royal celebrations, musicians, clowns, and prophets vied for attention on every street corner.

The tale was repeated again and again. Jalahad, the thief, an enterprising commoner, had somehow won the

Princess Sadhe's heart, and foiled the scheme of the evil Jafar to take over the Kingdom. It was too bad the Sultan Mulheer had died in all the commotion. There were a thousand variations, some involving the intervention of forty thieves, some involving supernatural assistance. In some versions, Princess Sadhe was dashing and heroic, in others demure and retiring. Jalahad was both naive and brilliant, occasionally clever, frequently open hearted. There were versions that emphasized the role of Palace Guards, wise old beggars giving essential counsel, and clever scrubwomen intervening at critical moments.

No two versions ever agreed on exactly how Sultan Mulheer had died, but it was sternly agreed that Sadhe and Jalahad had absolutely nothing to do with it, were nowhere near when it happened, and had been absolutely shocked, completely surprised, when they heard the news. Also, sad, definitely sad. And surprised.

There had even been versions that told the story from Jafar's perspective. But most of the people who had told those versions, or heard those versions, were now hanging from gibbets. So it was esteemed not a popular version.

The point was that between the coronation of Princes Sadhe, and her upcoming wedding to handsome young Jalahad, the Kingdom was throwing the biggest party of its history.

And there was more to come. Why even now, poor districts were being razed for new Palaces and Temples, plans were being drawn up for Water Gardens, Pleasure Domes, Monuments, Plazas, and every other kind of public work, exalting the glory of the new couple.

The intrepid band of questers had gathered in a tavern for to plot their next move.

It wasn't actually a tavern, per se. It was more a stable converted quickly and shoddily into a tavern, without actually removing the horses. There was a coronation and a royal wedding going on, after all, and the city was packed with celebrants and tradesfolk, space was at a premium, and prices were high.

The stable boy came by with four mugs and a pitcher of beer.

Salvra spat in the pitcher.

"Get the rest anything they want," Salvra expansively told the boy. More quietly, she whispered to the others. "Festivals are the best times for pickpocketing; we're going to make out like . . . bandits!"

"I notice it's my pocket that you keep trying to pick," Scabrous the Malevolent complained. "And why do you always spit in the drinks anyway?"

"To show it's mine," she said. "I don't want anyone filching my drink."

"But you spit in other people's drinks," he pointed out.

"Only when they're done with them," she said. "If they're not thirsty anymore, and there's still some to go, I lay a claim. Nothing wrong with that."

"Because no one wants to finish their drink after you've spit in it?"

Salvra shrugged, and drained her mug.

"I think," Jurgan said quietly, as the stableboy filled his mug with something that might have resembled beer if you didn't look too closely, "I might have a fungus."

"Told you," Scabrous sneered.

"Hey," Salvra said, "I told you it's been cleared up. In any event, it's just a minor thing, you shouldn't worry about it."

"I don't know," Jurgan said doubtfully.

"ANYWAY enough chit chat," Salvra announced. So we're here in the City of Mangolis, Nobility and high muckety mucks from all over the Realms are here, the streets are running with gold."

"Technically," Scabrous groused, "urine. This wealth is a lie, it's a corrupt elite over-class, wantonly confiscating the social surplus of an entire nation, for its own trivial indulgences."

Drunk Slutty Elf, Page 198

"And jewels," Salvra insisted. "Gold and jewels, everywhere."

She leaned forward conspiratorially, towards Darkeyes, the gray alien.

"What's the score? The Crown Jewels?" she asked.

"No," the Gray said.

"The Treasury?" Salvra suggested.

"No."

"The Eye of Munificence?" she asked hopefully. "It's rumored to be here."

"I don't know what that is," Jurgan said.

"A great crystal orb, rumored to be of the eye of a vanished deity, of incalculable value and containing vast eldritch magics," Salvra explained.

"Also impossible to fence," Scabrous pointed out, "and the deities cult is hellbent on getting it back. Something to do with divine depth perception."

"We're not here for that," the Gray said.

Salvra made a face and finished off the pitcher. She belched.

"Of course not," she spat in Scabrous drink. "We're just going to go looking for another piece of junk from his ship. We could just go down to the dockyards, and pick up all kinds of ship junk. But no, Mister Not-Anatomically-Correct is sentimental, and it has to be his ship."

"That whole 'from another planet' thing goes right past you, doesn't it?" the Gray asked.

Salvra rolled her eyes, and picked up Scabrous's mug.

"In this case," the Gray told them, "we are attempting to locate the flux capacitor, a trapezohedrical crystalline matrix, which in the event of unmodulated oscillation is equipped with a self-destruct timer that is currently counting down towards zero. When it reaches zero, a three hundred kilometer radius will be vaporized and I will have no hope of regaining my home world. There is some urgency."

It glanced around at its companions, its black eyes blinking. They stared blankly.

"None of this gets through to any of you, does it?" the Gray asked.

They stared blankly.

"I should have worked with Monkeys," the Gray said.

"Well," Jurgan reflected, "at least we're well paid."

He lifted his mug to take a drink, then paused, staring down.

"It ate through the bottom of my mug," Jurgan complained.

"You have to drink it fast," Salvra said confidently.

"In terms of being 'well paid,'" Scabrous maliciously asked Jurgan, "do you actually recall ever being paid? Money actually changing hands? A gold purse? An exchange of value?"

Jurgan thought about it. Salvra excused herself to get another drink.

"Honestly," he said, "all I ever remember is waking up with blocks of missing time, and my bum hurting. But that's usually the sign of an epic bender, which is always the result of a spectacular payday."

"Ahh," said Scabrous sullenly, "when you put it that way, it makes sense."

Salvra returned with two pitchers. She didn't offer to share.

"I suppose," Scabrous pouted, "we should just get this over with, and then I can return to my tower of Malevolence."

Salvra tasted her drink and made a sour face. She grabbed the sleeve of the stable boy as he tried to pass by.

"This tastes like Pregnant Mare's piss," Salvra complained.

The tavern boy stopped. His eyes bulged a little.

"That is Pregnant Mare's piss," he said. "Did you think you were sneaking from the beer barrel, you slutty idiot?"

"That's Princess Slutty Idiot, to you," she snapped. She gazed critically at her mug, arching an eyebrow. "I thought that's what it was."

She fixed the tavern boy with her fiercest glare.

"You better not be charging full price swill."

The boy thought it over.

"Half price, free refills."

Salvra nodded.

"That's better," she said. She drank deeply.

"So where is this Flax Cavity Plier?" Scabrous asked. "At some dentist office?"

"Location information is indeterminate past a viable threshold," the replied. "But triangulation indicates the Royal Palace."

Salvra brightened.

"A proper heist!"

"In the dungeons," the Gray said.

Her face fell.

"Oh poop!"

***

Breaking into the dungeons was surprisingly easy. The Princess had declared an amnesty, most of the city was celebrating, the Coronation was happening at mid-day.

And truthfully, who was going to break into an empty dungeon?

"I just hope that we can wrap this up before the Coronation," Jurgan was saying, as they marched along endless dank tunnels, peering into empty cells.

"That will not be an issue," the Gray told them.

"Good," Jurgan said.

"If we do not find it before the Coronation, the volume of space and time will be reconstituted into a 300 kilometer sphere of randomized subatomic particles."

Scabrous the Malevolent thought about it.

"I think that if I understood that, I might be terrified," he said suspiciously.

Drunk Slutty Elf, Page 201

"It seems that tiny undeveloped neural structures have some advantages," the Gray replied. "I am unable to localize the Flux Capacitator."

"No problem," Salvra said breezily. "We just find someone to tell us where it is. A local guide, that's Thieving 101. When robbing a strange place, get a guide."

"The dungeons have been emptied," Scabrous pointed out. "The general amnesty. We haven't seen so much as a rat!"

"They gave amnesty to the rats?" Jurgan asked.

Scabrous glanced at Salvra and rolled his eyes. She shrugged.

As if on cue, a voice called out, "What's all that racket? I'm trying to read!"

Salvra stuck out her tongue at Scabrous.

"Oh yoo hoo," she called. "Do you have anything to drink?"

They followed the sound to a rather opulently appointed cell occupied by a tall, severe looking man in colorful robes. He had dark piercing eyes, arched eyebrows, the sharpest goatee they'd ever seen – it looked like he could stab people with his goatee. For a moment, he stared at them through the bars.

"You're not guards," he said simply.

"No," Salvra replied cheerfully. "We're a band of resolute and wily adventurers, of diverse origins, embodying cardinal virtues, come together on a noble quest."

The man stared.

"Seriously," she insisted.

"You've broken into a dungeon," he told them. "What are you planning to steal? Rats?"

"No, they've all been given amnesty," Jurgan said. "None around."

Scabrous laughed out loud. Jurgan looked puzzled at that.

The man behind the bars drew himself up stiffly.

"I am Jafar," he announced, "former Grand Vizier, to Sultan Mulheer, formerly fiancé to the Princess Sadhe, also chartered accountant, surveyor, architect and calligrapher."

He waited for a response.

"Never heard of you," Salvra replied cheerfully. "But I see you have a bottle of wine."

Scabrous groaned.

"You haven't paid attention to any of the stories going around?" he demanded.

"Lies," Salvra snapped. "I didn't do it, I wasn't there, it's not my fault, and there's no proof anyway."

"Not all stories are about you," Scabrous pointed out.

"Then who cares?" Salvra replied airily. "If it's not about me, why should I pay attention? What does it matter?"

"How exactly do you even function?" Scabrous asked her.

"Perfectly fine," she said. "At least I'm not shut up in some dark tower, poring over ancient texts about forgotten gods."

"That's a low blow," he accused her.

Jafar rolled his eyes.

"What are you doing in the dungeon?" Salvra turned to Jafar, in order to change the subject. "Everyone else has been given amnesty."

He shrugged.

"Sentenced to death," he said. "I'm just waiting until after the Royal Wedding for the sentence to be carried out."

Salvra thought about it.

"That sucks."

He shrugged.

"I'm not thrilled with it. But I suppose it's better than waiting around watching those two selfish airheads destroy the Kingdom. So far, they've spent most of the treasury on their ridiculous wedding celebration. They've gutted public works, in favor of grandiose palaces which will displace thousands of poor people, and they're diverting the Kingdom's river, to create a royal lake for their Yacht. Without the river, the farmers will be destitute."

"I didn't think you cared about farmers," Scabrous said.

"I grew up in a farming village. We built our huts with cow dung. I hate farmers," Jafar said.

He paused.

"But I do like eating."

He waited for a response. They stared blankly, failing to make the connection. Jafar sighed.

"I like eating. But there won't be much of that by the time Sadhe and Jalahad finish running the Kingdom into the ground."

He looked them over.

"Why are you here?" he demanded.

"We're looking for a thingy," Jurgan told him. "A flat turkey baster."

Jafar thought about that.

"Is it the turkey that's flat?" he asked, "or the baster."

"The turkey, obviously," Salvra said, rolling her eyes.

"Why would you flatten a turkey," Jafar asked.

Salvra rolled her eyes.

"You obviously know nothing about cooking," she snapped.

"How would you even flatten a turkey?" he wondered. "And why? It seems cruel."

"It's complicated," she snapped. "Now have you seen one? A baster I mean."

"Have you tried the kitchen?"

"You know," Scabrous said, "for a man imprisoned in a dungeon, you're pretty sarcastic."

"What are you going to do," Jafar asked. "Overthrow me, execute my followers, sentence me to death and throw me into a dungeon?"

"Well . . ." Scabrous snapped, "for one thing, we could not rescue you!"

"Were you planning to rescue me?" Jafar asked.

"Not particularly," Jurgan said.

"Fine," Jafar replied turning. "I'm going back to my book."

"Wait," the gray asked. "We are searching for a Flux Capacitor; can you assist us with its whereabouts, preferably before the self-destruct triggers a radius of vaporization?"

For the first time, Jafar seemed to notice the alien. His eyes widened and he took a step back.

"What the hell is that?" he said a little too loudly.

Salvra opened her mouth to explain. The Gray raised an extraordinarily long finger to silence her.

"That's not important. The Flux Capacitor is. It's a crystalline trapezohedrical matrix."

Jafar pulled at his goatee.

"Crystalline," he said thoughtfully. "As in a jewel of some sort?"

"Correct."

"I might know where it is," he said. "I'll tell you, if you free me. I'm not thrilled with the notion of hanging around here, waiting to be executed."

"You seemed pretty calm about it," Salvra said.

"I didn't really have any other options," Jafar pointed out. "It seems a lifetime in public administration isn't really useful for prison breaks."

"Aren't you a master of necromancy too," Jurgan asked.

"Double Entry Accounting," Jafar replied.

"Even more terrifying than necromancy," Scabrous said.

"Well," Jafar replied, "when you get right down to it, most things are scarier than necromancy."

"The trade is oversold," Scabrous admitted.

A thought seemed to occur to Jafar, he fixed his gaze upon the Gray creature.

"Wait," Jafar addressed the Gray alien. "You mentioned a radius of vaporization. Allow me to inquire – what exactly happens within that radius?"

"Dissolution of molecular bonds, dispersal of subatomic particles."

"Sailor talk," Salvra said dismissively. "He's always going on like that."

Jafar waved a hand to silence her.

"And this dissolution and dispersal, it would apply to persons within this radius?" he asked carefully.

Scabrous halted and listened carefully, brows furrowing, suddenly alert.

"Obviously."

"So in effect, if we were within this radius, we would be . . . killed?"

Jurgan's ears perked up.

"Inaccurate," the Gray said, "rendered into a disorganized, dispersed incoherent state."

"But dead?"

"That would be a significant effect. Yes."

"Stop! Stop!" Scabrous waved his hands urgently. "You mean to say, we'd all be killed?"

"Inaccurate," the Gray began.

Scabrous cut him off.

"We'd all be dead?" Scabrous persisted. "Everyone inside the radius would be dead. Everyone and everything?"

The group froze. Salvra looked stunned. Scabrous horrified. Jurgan blanched momentarily, but was the first to recover.

"I'll go get help!" Jurgan announced.

"Why haven't you mentioned this before?" Salvra demanded of the Gray.

"I've been saying it for days."

"It's all been sailor talk!" Salvra complained. "Hoist the jib! Mizzen the topmast! Recalculate the neutrino flow! Arr!

Keelhaul the rum! How are we supposed to get a death sentence out of any of that?"

"I'll just be leaving now," Jurgan told them manfully, "to bring back help."

Scabrous was doing some rapid mental calculations.

"It would take you several days to exit the radius," he told Jurgan.

"I'm very fast," Jurgan said.

"And the . . . demolecularisation will be in . . ."

"Two and a half hours," the Gray said.

"I feel like I should be panicking," Scabrous said. "Does anyone else feel like they should be panicking? Is there a general sense of crushing malevolent dread?"

"I'll tell you where to find it," Jafar said, "if you get me out of here."

"That's rather selfish of you," Salvra said. "Always looking for an advantage, always thinking of yourself. No wonder you were overthrown."

"I'm awaiting execution," Jafar replied. "So technically, it's all the same to me. Now if you free me, then I'm motivated to help."

"Enough," the Gray said.

From its floating sack it retrieved a small boxlike device which emitted a harmless red light. It played the light over the bars, which disintegrated. Jafar stepped through.

"I notice," Scabrous said, "that you point that strange little box at us quite often."

"Yes," said the Gray. "I find it very pleasant."

***

"That's odd," Jafar said. "I don't recall putting my clothes on backwards this morning."

"I find that happens a lot," said Scabrous said, "lately."

"Even before I met Darkeyes," Salvra said.

There was a pause, and Jafar had the strangest feeling that they were looking at his ass and waiting for him to say something more.

Drunk Slutty Elf, Page 207

"Well, that's all very interesting," Jafar said. "But I think I'll be going now. The Jewel you seek is likely in the Treasure room. It's near the bottom of the Palace, quite near the dungeons. I can give you directions . . ."

"There is no need," the Gray said, "I've downloaded the relevant information from your neural net, and cross-referenced against deep sonar multi-dimensional imaging."

Jafar looked blank.

"Sailor talk," Salvra confided. "He pines for the seven seas."

"I see?" Jafar said, hiking up his robes and preparing to stroll off. "Good luck."

"Wait!" Jurgan said. "Aren't you going to join our hearty fellowship of mismatched adventurers? I'm sure we could use the skills of a good chartered accountant. This seems like one of those serendipitous moments when a newcomer joins our team."

Jafar looked them over, and smiled.

"No. I'm going to get very drunk, and I'm going to consume every drug I can get my hands on, I'm going to visit as many brothels as I can, and enjoy myself in the time remaining. In two and a half hours, if the City is still here, I'm going to escape and build a new life far away."

He looked them over.

"No offence, but you lot look like a pack of drunken incompetents who couldn't successfully carry a glass of water from one side of a room to the other without triggering a catastrophe."

He sauntered off.

"Good luck. If you succeed, I shall benefit. Watch out for the Djinn," he called.

They watched him go.

"That was uncalled for," Jurgan said quietly.

"Yeah," Scabrous said, "it's only Salvra who is drunk."

"Hey!" she protested.

"Did you notice?" Scabrous said thoughtfully. "His butt didn't hurt."

Salvra stopped and thought it over.

"Weird," she said.

***

The door to the treasure room opened. It was vast and empty, save for the floating top half of a muscular blue man with burning eyes, arms folded imperiously before him. There was no bottom half to him, just swirling tentacles of blue and purple smoke.

"Do you think this is the Djinn?" Salvra asked. "Or am I just having DTs again?"

Before anyone could reply, its burning eyes flared red, and it spoke.

"Foolish mortals," it boomed in a stentorian voice, "know that you have trespassed upon the hidden hoard of Jalahad the wealthy, and your lives are forfeit. Your existence shall—"

Then its gaze fell upon the Gray, who had taken some peculiar object out of its bag of balloons, and was fiddling with it. It did a double take.

"What the hell is that?"

"Just a sailor," Salvra assured it. "Completely harmless. Don't mind us. We'll just be running along."

"That's no sailor!" the Djinn boomed. "Seriously, what the hell is that? It's creeping me out."

The object of the Djinn's consternation examined a series of glowing symbols passing across its object.

"Hmm," the Gray mumbled. "A cohesive semi-sentient matrix of sub-atomic particles. Rare, but not especially interesting."

"What did it just say?" the Djinn asked quickly. "Semi-sentient what?"

"Just sailor talk," Salvra said easily. "Don't worry about it. I never pay attention. So listen, if I rub your lamp just right, will you give me three wishes?"

She leered.

Scabrous sighed and put a hand over his face, trying to convey he wasn't with her.

"It doesn't work like that," the Djinn said vaguely, still staring at the Gray. "I am bound to service until my Master releases me, or he dies through no direct action of mine . . . What's he doing with that thing?"

"Oh well," Salvra said, "nice muscles, even if a bit lacking below the waist."

She looked around.

"So . . . Gold? Jewels? Booze? Where is it?"

"I can call it into existence at any time my Master wishes," said the Djinn, watching the Gray carefully.

"And it fades out of existence after a day or so," Scabrous noted. "It's a virtual currency."

"All currency is virtual," Salvra said piously, "in the sense that value is an attributed concept. All money is fundamentally an abstraction, and therefore an illusion."

"Oh not this again," Scabrous muttered.

"A good thief needs a solid grounding in economics. One of these days, I'm going to steal a Doctorate."

"The entity's constructs dissipate because they're subatomic particles without molecular binding. They behave like matter, but without strong and weak nuclear interactions, the particles organizational structure decays towards randomness," the Gray said.

That stopped everyone.

"What?" the Djinn said blankly.

"Sailor talk," Salvra replied again.

"The Flux Capacitor was here," the Gray announced.

"So where's all the real money," Salvra asked casually. "You know, just intellectual curiosity is all."

"But it's been moved," the Gray said, staring hard at the Djinn, an impressive feat, considering its features were all but immobile. ". . . and shielded."

"The Master and his Paramour have spent prodigiously," the Djinn reported. It hesitated, glancing at the Gray.

"Can you tell it not to look at me like that," the Djinn asked nervously.

"A lambent trapezohedrical object, aligned along twelve dimensions, and emanating pulses of beta particles," the Gray snapped. Its narrow lips became slits. Although its expression had not changed, somehow it seemed to become menacing, very menacing, and sort of angry.

The rest of the band of adventurers stepped away from it, and tried not to give the impression of being associated with the Djinn in any way. Not that they were, they'd just met the creature. But suddenly, they felt that all things considered, it would be best not to give any such appearance.

"What did you do with it?" the Gray asked icily.

"Apparently," Scabrous offered, "it's going to destroy the City and kill us all if we don't find it."

"And more importantly," the Gray said, "I will not be able to return home to report. I am therefore . . . motivated."

Never before had the word 'motivated' sounded so much like a primordial threat. Everyone, including the Djinn, shivered.

"Oh that?" the Djinn replied airily. "The Prince commanded me to craft a wedding crown out of real matter, gold, jewels, that sort of thing. Anyway, the lambent trapezohedrical looked nice, so I inset it as the headpiece. Is it important?"

"Where is it now?" the Gray demanded.

"In the Chamber of Effusive Purple Light. Just go up four levels, down the hall, to the left, fifth door down, next to the gymnasium. If you see the statue of the Gryphon having sex with a Cyclops, you've gone too far, but you can find your way back by taking two left corners and then a right at the Mosaic of the gladiator babies, and you're right there."

"That's where all the Coronation costumes are kept," the Djinn said. "Along with a lot of odds and ends."

"Guards?"

"Not at that level," the Djinn replied. He waved his hand, and an awkwardly folded sheet of colored paper appeared. "Behold! I grant thee a map of the Palace, conveniently showing trapdoors, secret passages, and guard placements."

Salvra snatched the lamp.

"You go off and find it," the Djinn said cheerfully. "I'll stay here and guard . . ." it looked around the empty treasure chamber, ". . . stuff."

It waved.

***

"I really wish you'd let me have the map," Scabrous the Malevolent groused as they made their way through the labyrinthine hallways of the Palace.

Salvra held it close, studying it was they walked. They passed unimpeded. The few guards and servers who accosted them tended to regularly fall asleep, which was probably something to do with Gray. But apart from checking to see if their clothes were still on straight, they decided not to acknowledge it.

"Are you a Ninth Level Thief," Salvra snapped. "I don't think so. I'm the only one here qualified to read a map."

"I'm just saying," Scabrous persisted, "you don't have a good track record, and this place is a maze."

"Agglomerated structure," Jurgan said.

"What?" Scabrous asked.

"Agglomerated structure," Jurgan repeated. "The Royal Palace isn't a designed building, it's an accumulated one. Each generation has expanded it, adding new chambers, ballrooms, bathrooms, swimming pools, tennis courts, all based on the whims of the rulers, with windows and doors sealed up, new halls and corridors added, together with incremental adjustments for servants' access, basic services and secret tunnels. Any plan was abandoned long ago. It's simply continually added on.

Drunk Slutty Elf, Page 212

"That's why it's so complicated and difficult to navigate," he explained.

Scabrous and Salvra stared at him with open mouths.

"I have a degree in applied architecture," Jurgan offered, noticing their astonished looks. "But adventuring pays better."

"Huh," said Scabrous.

"We're here!" announced Salvra, checking the map. She stopped and pointed at a massive wooden double door. "Your Fix Happener should be right on the other side of that door."

The gray, who had been doing its best to ignore them, stopped and checked his instruments.

"My sensors do not confirm this," it said doubtfully. "But perhaps intervening materials are distorting the signal."

"Pshaw to your nautical talk," Salvra said cheerfully. "Here we are, let's just go in, collect it and be on our way!"

She stepped up and flung the doors wide open.

It turned out to be a very large room. A room very short on jeweled crowns, costumes, shoes and accouterments. A room instead filled with swings, trampolines, stages and trapezes, and somehow, a rather intrusive driving techno beat. It was also filled with dozens of men. Mostly naked men, apart from boots and leather harnesses. Extremely well-oiled, mostly naked, men, their bodies and genitals glistening.

On a far wall, a banner hung "Off Duty Guards Free Range Celebration Ball."

Scabrous stepped up carefully from behind her and tried to pull the doors shut.

Salvra held it open, staring. She stared some more.

"This isn't what we're looking for," the Gray said.

"Speak for yourself," Salvra whispered.

Unfortunately, it was at that moment that they were noticed. A thick set man, with a hairy barrel chest and bowed legs stared at them. He raised a hand, the room went silent. He pointed at the group.

"Intruders!" Steg the guard yelled at the rest of the off-shift Royal Guard on their recreational time. "Get them!"

Scabrous shut the door and hastily cast a binding spell. On the other side, there was the sound of hammering and yelling.

"That won't last long," Scabrous announced.

"I'll go get help!" Jurgan yelled as the heavy wooden door shuddered.

"Can you do that thing where we all end up with missing time and our butts hurt?" Salvra asked urgently.

"There are far too many for that," the Gray told her. "I suggest we all run."

The door burst open, but they were already running down the hall.

***

Salvra, if she was being honest, had frequent nightmares about being chased up and down endless hallways by hordes of well-oiled half naked men with their genitals rampant.

Less nightmares actually, and more dreams.

Technically, less dreams and more like fantasies.

Also, in the fantasies, she was doing the chasing.

When it came right down to it, she was actually rather enjoying herself. If only she had been drunk, it would have been perfect.

But she was rational enough to realize that if they caught up with her, it wouldn't end as happily as her fantasies.

But then, real life aftermaths were usually unsatisfying, typically full of second thoughts, self-doubts, recrimination, 'what have I done!' 'God(s) why have you forsaken me!' 'I've made a terrible mistake!' 'I never imagined it could be used that way!' 'How will I ever face my wife / husband / boss / master / slaves / tribe after this!'

She'd heard it from every lover, to the point that she suspected that there was a script laying around that they were all referring to. It would be all she could do not to yawn and roll her eyes.

Still, if they caught her, she suspected it would be quite unpleasant.

So she continued to run, huffing heavily.

A shadow fell over her shoulder. She glanced up. It was Jurgan, rapidly catching up to her.

"I thought you were ahead of me?" she said. "Way ahead! Way way ahead!"

Jurgan hadn't even waited, he'd taken off running with a completely nonsensical "I'll go get help." The last she had seen of him were his boots far far ahead, and then somewhere after that, they'd all gotten separated.

"I was," he said, "but then all these hallways are quite complicated. I turned a corner, and suddenly I was in their rear. It was too late to sneak away, so all I could do was just keep running forward."

"So you're saying you've lapped us?" she demanded. She took a hard look at him. "Is that why you're covered with body oil, and you're more naked than usual."

"Blending in seemed like a good idea," he said. "Do you know of a way out of here? You're the one with the Djinn's map after all."

"I've been running," she protested. "I haven't been able to look at it!"

"Well now would be a good time," he said, "I've only got a few more laps in me, and if I pass them again, they might get suspicious."

"Make sure I don't run into a wall or something," Salvra muttered, and pulled the map out of her belt, folding and unfolding it. She stared.

"It's upside down."

"I can see that, I'm an excellent map reader," she snarled, turning it around.

"Isn't that how we ended up in the Pit of Numenorea?" he asked.

"The crease from the fold in that map looked like a short cut?" she snapped.

"And getting chased by Rats of Unusual Size through the burning swamp, because you were trying to avoid a nonexistent giant spider lair?"

"How was I to know that a bug had gotten squashed on the parchment?"

"Maybe you should let Scabrous read the map?" he said. "Or let me read it now?"

"I'm fine!" she said. She studied the map intensely, comparing it to the multitude of hallways and rooms they'd fled through.

"Up ahead," she whispered. "Around the corner, there's an antechamber hidden behind a pillar that leads to a small bathroom. We can duck into that, and they'll think we headed down the left hallway into the garden supplies."

"All right," he whispered back, taking her arm.

Together, with Jurgan's assistance, the two of them put on a burst of speed that had them careening around the corner, well ahead of their howling pursuers. The antechamber was exactly where the map said it would be. They dived for it, scrabbling for the bathroom door, and bursting through . . .

Into a grand ballroom with high vaulted ceilings, filled with jugglers, clowns, mimes, dancing girls, fire eaters, gymnasts, and mummers in every sort of costume.

Prince Jalahad himself was at the center of the cavorting throng, proud and handsome in his purple robes and golden headdress, held together by a gigantic ruby and sporting an ostrich feather. In his hand, he held a clipboard. He looked directly at them, his expression stern and angry.

"You're late!" he snarled. "Didn't you get the notice we'd moved things up? Get over here!"

Behind them, a howling throng of near naked oiled men burst through the small door, howling and yelling.

"And you too!" the Prince roared angrily.

"I don't know how I can be expected to work with this chaos," he muttered to himself.

Startled the army of well-oiled off duty guards began to bow and prostrate themselves.

"Get over here," the Prince commanded, "or I'll have you all flogged."

Cautiously, Jurgan and Salvra approached, with the shamefaced mob of guards behind them.

"That's better," the Prince said. He studied his clipboard for a moment. "Are you on the list?"

***

Scabrous the Malevolent tried to control his breathing as he listened to hordes of angry men stampede past. He was standing in darkness, in a small room; with one foot in what he suspected was a toilet.

This was not even in the top ten of humiliating situations he had been thrust into.

He had never been good at running away. Typically, Necromantic Sorcerers didn't run away. They holed up in nice cozy towers, minded their own business, cultivated elaborate defenses, built death traps, readied spells and incinerated anyone who disturbed their occult investigations.

But that was before Salvra and her peculiar friend had showed up at his tower. Now his life consisted of entirely too much running away. Dragons, Warlords, Demonic Tyrants, improbably rolling giant boulders, you name it, it all seemed to culminate in either Salvra spitting in whatever alcoholic beverage he happened to be holding at that moment, or running for his life. He couldn't decide which was worse.

On the positive side, his cardio was the best it had ever been. He was sure that if he survived, he'd crush his rivals at the next Necromantic League tournament of 'Fetch and Carry.'

On the down side, survival seemed an increasingly dim prospect.

Where were the others? He was alone. Jurgan had outstripped them all, leaving them far, far away. Salvra had attracted most of the attention, with her drunken stumbling and caterwauling.

The Gray, Darkeyes, had vanished of course. Scabrous was impressed with the way a being who claimed to have no self-preservation instinct whatsoever always managed to be safely elsewhere when any kind of danger manifested.

Sometimes Scabrous suspected that the Gray wasn't even a sailor.

Not for the first time, Scabrous cursed his chosen profession. He'd always been good at arts and crafts, perhaps he should have gone in that direction. Scabrous the Shoemaker! There was a trade to be proud of! But no, that was taken.

Scabrous the Birdhouse Maker! He liked the sound of that.

There was something noble to it. Something uplifting. Birds needed houses after all. Their tiny beaks were obviously no good at carpentry. He would become the world's greatest Necromancer-Birdhouse Maker.

The sounds outside had faded away.

He opened the door a crack, and sniffed. The odor of copious amounts of flavored, lickable body oil was fading.

He dared a peek.

Empty.

Well and good. Now to find the others, if they were still alive, then locate the damned jewel . . . d-jewel, that sounded right . . . And hope that the Gray could do whatever it was it planned to do, before they were all horribly killed.

In the most obviously furtive and sneaky way possible, he crept forth, skulking from one pillar and doorway to the next, hiding behind potted plants, doing his level best (and it wasn't very good) to look inconspicuous and natural as serving staff passed.

He was quite proud of his stealth.

If only he had some idea of where he was?

There was a commotion up ahead. Or perhaps it was behind him? He wasn't sure. He ducked behind some ferns, annoying a plant custodian and getting sprayed with water for his trouble.

Panicking, he leaped for the nearest doorway.

Inside, a dozen beautiful women in various stages of undress looked up at him, wide eyed and startled.

He tried to smile, holding out his hands to show that he was harmless.

"Be at ease, noble gentlewomen," he said, in his most ingratiating manner. "For I am Scabrous, a simple maker of bird-houses."

As one, they drew breath to scream.

***

The Prince squinted at them. Salvra's quick eye spotted a pair of spectacles hanging from his belt, the young man was nearsighted. Glancing around casually, Salvra undid a couple of buttons from her top as she approached.

"Sorry we're late, your Excellence," she smiled, heaving her bosom. "Are you the Master of Ceremonies?"

"I am Prince Jalahad," he announced, looking her up and down, and then up, and then down, and settling somewhere near the upper middle. He glanced at his clipboard again. "And who might you be?"

For a moment, Salvra thought about mentioning that her face was rather higher up, but decided to leave his eyes were they were.

"Salvra, exiled Princess, ninth level thief, prodigious drinker," she heaved her bosom so that it appeared to be doing the talking for her.

"Thief?" Jalahad asked. "I was a thief once. Fortieth level. Now I am to be a King."

Salvra's breasts gasped.

"Fortieth level? Incredible!"

With a flourish, Jalahad produced a card. Salvra read it. It did indeed say 40, mainly because a zero had been clumsily scrawled in after the '4.'

"That's good enough for me!" Salvra said, making a mental note to acquire a quill and ink for herself sometime later.

"So what's with the army of well-oiled naked men?" Jalahad asked, glancing at her pursuers.

"Your highness!" Steg began.

Salvra placed her hands under her breasts, cupping and adjusting them slightly. The Prince's eyes returned to stare.

"Oh they're just my entourage."

The self-appointed Prince frowned.

"Some of them look like my guards," he noted.

"Oh that?" she said casually. "Well, there were a few drop-outs along the way; I had to fill in some locally.

"Why?"

She thought fast.

"They're here to perform for the royal Coronation," she said. "It's a song and dance number."

"Dance number?" he asked. "You're a performer?"

"A director, actually," Salvra lied, heaving her breasts. "Why else would I have a legion of semi-nude, well-oiled men in leather harnesses following in my footsteps?"

"It did look like they were chasing you?"

"We were chasing–" Steg yelled.

"Chasing after my approval," she cut him off. "We're ready . . . They're ready to go on. I've done my part, now it's all in their hands . . . feet.

"Boys," she announced, turning to Jurgan and the assembled semi-nude guards, "It's time. Make your mama proud!"

"My mama?" one of the guards asked uncertainly.

"Me!" Salvra corrected him. "Make me proud!"

She turned back to the Prince, offering a radiant smile
and shrugged her breasts, "I love them all. But they're not
the brightest. My Prince, if you'll be good enough to have
your herald announce them?"

Steg stepped forward, "Your majesty, enough of this
charade–"

"So we can be alone," Salvra told the Prince, arching
her back, so that her breasts sprang forward.

He swallowed.

"It's like your breasts can speak," he said, fascinated.

"Ventriloquism," she told him. "Learned it from a
sailor."

She smiled.

"I learned lots of things from sailors," she whispered
seductively. Her breasts seemed to beckon.

"Yes," Jalahad told his couriers without taking his eyes
off her breasts, "announce the . . ."

"Shiny Oiled Manflesh Dancers," Salvra supplied. Then
she glanced at her pursuers and snapped. "Jurgan, lead
them. The rest of you, what are you waiting for? Get out
there and make me proud, or we'll have you in the
dungeon! The Prince and I have a lot to discuss."

"Yes," the Prince agreed staring, "much to discuss."

****

Steg was up on stage, acutely aware of his slight pot
belly, his man-boobs, his hairy legs and hairier back. Never
had he felt flabbier in his entire life.

It didn't help that he was drenched in glistening oil, and
wearing what amounted to a rather inadequate codpiece
and an assortment of leather straps.

Or that he was facing a huge throng of the collected
nobility and royalty of six kingdoms, all far better dressed,
and waiting expectantly.

Behind him, his fellow guards shuffled, equally
uncertain.

Jurgan turned back to look at them.

Drunk Slutty Elf, Page 221

"Ever been in this kind of situation before?" he asked cheerfully.

Steg shook his head.

"No worries," Jurgan smiled and winked, and despite himself, Steg felt his heart give a little flutter. "I have, lots of times. Just follow my lead, do what I do, and we'll be fine."

He paused.

"Can you roll your hips like this?" he asked and demonstrated. Steg's heart skipped another beat, this time, his codpiece following suit.

He did the move, sensing from the corners of his eyes the other guards, trying with varying degrees of success.

Jurgan grinned.

"We'll do fine."

***

Scabrous stumbled a bit, as two tittering ladies-in-waiting pulled him by his wrists into the throne room. He wasn't sure what was happening, they'd been quite excited, but somewhat friendly. He didn't understand why, but he'd decided to go with it.

Then he looked up, his eyes went wide and his heart skipped a beat.

Scabrous stared at the Princess Sadhe. He had never seen anyone so beautiful. Her hair flowed like a scarlet waterfall, the edges curling up like ocean foam. Her eyes as green as Gangian emeralds. Her features were exquisitely proportioned, culminating in the full lips of a tiny cupid bow mouth. He imagined her speaking with those lips. He imagined her doing other things with those lips and his heart beat even faster.

Her body was perfectly proportioned. Bare skin like milk drenched in honey, breasts so buoyant that gravity wasn't even a thought, legs so long and lithe that gazelles would weep at their sight. She was dressed in translucent silks of shimmering iridescence.

Scabrous the Malevolent, for the first time in his life, felt the touch of true love.

His entire life up to that moment had been a foolish jest, a flight of fancy, a lie. Everything that had gone before had been a meaningless flicker.

It was as if his entire existence had been spent unknowing under a dark cloud, and this was moment where he finally felt alive.

As he stared, her bored glance lit on him. Some courtier whispered in her ear. Her eyes widened, focusing on him, her lips parted in a moue of surprise that made his knees weak, and then she smiled.

She stood up, staring at him now, and descended from the throne, her delicate feet almost dancing down the steps. Yes, she was coming towards him. She was smiling, reaching out.

In Scabrous mind a full orchestra burst into glorious triumphal symphony.

She reached out her hand.

"You're Scabrous," she breathed.

"Yes," he said.

"I've been dreaming of meeting you," she whispered.

In his mind, Scabrous was sweeping her up onto a white charger, the two of them together, galloping out the city gates, into a wild world of happiness and adventure, just two mad, crazy people in love, needing nothing more than each other.

"I love your shoes!" she told him.

Scabrous blinked.

Vaguely, he heard himself say, "Making shoes is my life. It's all I ever wanted to do."

But the rational part of his mind was staring at her costume, and in particular, the gorgeous necklace above her heaving breasts. As desperately as he wanted to heave himself into that bosom, to bury his face in it and never come out, he couldn't tear his eyes away from that necklace.

Drunk Slutty Elf, Page 223

That necklace of supernaturally exquisite workmanship, with silver links and threaded gold, and precious jewels of every kind, tastefully blended together . . .

And a lambent trapezohedrical glowing right in the center, softly emitting what must be beta pulses.

As if hypnotized, he reached out.

The Princess, with a lifetime of experience of men reaching for her breasts, frowned and stepped back.

And then, Scabrous found himself frozen immobile, surrounded by a blue light. Suddenly, he understood.

"Lies," he whispered, although he knew no one could hear him. He reached for his own reserves of magic, knowing that they were no match for those of a Djinn. "It's not the crown, it's the necklace. It's all been lies."

"I could not let you interfere," whispered the Djinn.

"You are bound to serve," Scabrous whispered, "unless freed by your Master . . . Or until he dies, through no act of yours."

"Correct," the Djinn told him. "I had sensed the destructive power of the decaying alien jewel. Its explosion would not harm me, but will extirpate every other living thing within its range. For the first time in an existence measured in measureless eons, I will finally be free."

For a moment, Scabrous wondered how you could measure by measureless eons. It seemed self-defeating. But he decided not to inquire.

Something odd, he noticed that the Princess was drooling a little. She'd taken on a vacant frozen expression of her own. Scabrous couldn't move his eyes, but he could just perceive on the peripheries of his vision, that she wasn't the only one.

"It amused me to set it in jewelry for these vain, shallow, selfish insects, so that they could preen at each other until their last moments."

"But why a necklace?" Scabrous asked. "Why not Jalahad's crown as you said? Wouldn't that be more satisfying?"

The Djinn chuckled, allowing its true evil to show through.

"A bit of misdirection, in case you got this far. But truthfully, where better to mount the jewel, than above my Master's two favorite . . ."

The jewel went dark.

Scabrous's eyes filled with tears. This was the end.

"That takes care of that," the Gray said, effortlessly plucking the Jewel, and inserting it into one of the devices from his buoyant swaying sack, which Scabrous realized was filled with impossible things that were not balloons. "Now, there is the matter of the subatomic particle entity."

Abruptly, the blue light vanished from around him, and Scabrous felt control returned instantly to his body. He fell to his knees.

"Hey! Wait just a second," the Djinn was saying. Scabrous looked up. The Djinn had its hands up pleadingly, and was backing away steadily, rising up in the air. Even its smoke looked scared.

"It's a simple matter of digitizing and compressing the informational package," the Gray was saying. More sailor talk, Scabrous knew, but it seemed to frighten the Djinn. "I would assure you that this will not hurt a bit, but I am indifferent to your discomfort."

The Gray pressed a stud, and with an anguished howl, the Djinn popped out of existence.

"The future King Jalahad will have to make do without the assistance of a positronic neo-entity," the Gray said reflectively. "He will have to rely upon is own wisdom and abilities. This does not elicit optimism."

Scabrous pulled himself to his feet cautiously, and looked around. Within a circle of a dozen feet or so, were the Princess and a handful of her retainers, all of them standing glassy eyed and drooling. Beyond them, the world was frozen. Scabrous stared at a bird frozen in mid-air.

"Time dilation bubble," the Gray said.

"I really get so tired of all your nautical talk," Scabrous said.

The Gray made no reply, but he could sense its shrug. Once again, a testament to the being's extraordinary ventriloquism.

"While we're here, I might as well collect some samples," the Gray said. "Would you like to assist?"

"Will I remember this?"

"Up to you."

Scabrous shook his head sadly.

"I'd rather not."

Again, the sense of a shrug.

He stared at the enchanting Princess Sadhe, her perfect breasts even more resplendent without the distraction of the necklace. More than anything, he wanted to put his hands on them, to fold back the shimmering iridescent cloth, to fondle them, to lick them, to spend an eternity with them. But he didn't.

Instead, he thought back to her last words to him, and his heart broke.

"Can you make it so that she remembers something?" he asked the Gray.

"Not conscious awareness, but it is possible to implant subconscious imperatives."

He nodded.

He stepped close to the Princess, gazing into her perfect, vacant green eyes, the ethereal beauty of her face. Even her drool was exquisite.

"You know the face of I, Scabrous," he told her, "the greatest shoemaker who ever lived. And if some other charlatan were to show up, claiming my name and claiming to be a shoemaker . . . Have him drawn and quartered."

***

With its usual unerring accuracy, the Gray lead Scabrous to Salvra and Jurgan. They were walking along together in one of the servant's corridors, carrying sacks of gold. Jurgan had a trophy tucked under one arm.

Drunk Slutty Elf, Page 226

Not for the first time, Scabrous wondered if the alien being had implanted them with some kind of tracking device. Then he dismissed the thought.

"Remember," Salvra was saying to Jurgan, "if the Prostitutes' Guild comes around, it was theft. Straight up robbery, you understand. Grand larceny. Pilfering. Stealing. Absolutely no exchange of favors involved."

"Got it."

"It was totally thieving."

"I understand," he said.

"It's just I've had run-ins with them, and they can be completely unreasonable."

"Certainly."

They stopped, startled at the appearance of their companions.

"I see," Scabrous said acidly, "that you've looked after yourselves, while Darkeyes and I saved the city."

Salvra shrugged.

Scabrous felt slighted.

"An entire city, a nation. Mothers, fathers, children, farmers, potters, everyone. All those lives, that could have ended in a blink of an eye. We saved them. I think that's important."

"Irrelevant," the Gray replied. "The lives of semi-sentient primates are of no consequence. There are already too many occupying this plane of existence."

Scabrous definitely felt deflated.

"But I have my component," the Gray admitted, "and your performance manifested in an adequately sub-optimal range appropriate to barely sentient primates."

Scabrous felt slightly better.

"Heroism is well and good, but someone has to make sure there's a profit," Salvra said smugly.

Scabrous glanced at Jurgan.

"I understand the gold. But why steal a trophy?" he looked harder. "And if you were going to steal a trophy, why steal second place?"

Jurgan looked startled. Then he glanced at the trophy under his arm. His face reddened as if embarrassed.

"Stolen?" he whispered. "Yes! Yes, completely stolen. Robbed. Purloined. It was sitting there and we took it, just took it, without the owner's knowledge or consent."

He looked at Salvra. She looked back at him. There was an unspoken agreement.

"We stole it," she agreed. "All of it."

"There was a lot of competition," Jurgan said, to no one in particular. "There wasn't any time to properly rehearse."

Scabrous found himself suspicious, but he wasn't sure what he was suspicious of. He decided to let it pass. He shrugged. He'd found it was usually for the best.

"We are reunited," the Gray said, without any particular warmth. It was simply an observation.

"There are more pieces of my ship to retrieve. Let us be on our way."

It turned its back on them and stalked off.

The rest of the group looked at each other. Not for the first time, Scabrous wondered, if, hypothetically, he had been inserted with a tracking device . . . then what else might such a device theoretically do, in addition to tracking? Say . . . for instance, exploding?

They followed the alien.

***

The new King and Queen of Mangolis were having breakfast the next morning, sitting together on the balcony overlooking the filling of the Royal lake. By next summer, they had a full schedule of yacht races planned. Jalahad was wearing his spectacles. Sadhe thought it made him look so clever and dashing.

"Won't it be beautiful," Sadhe sighed. "I can hardly wait. I'm so glad your Djinn diverted the river, even if those dirty farmers complained."

"No one likes farmers," Jalahad agreed.

"But I like to eat," Sadhe said thoughtfully.

Drunk Slutty Elf, Page 228

"What?" Jalahad asked. "Whatever does that mean?"

She wrinkled her brow.

"I don't know," she replied. "Something Jafar said one time. He was always saying things like that. I would make it a point never pay any attention, and eventually, he'd just give up and go do government things."

"Well, you won't have to think of him much longer," he reassured her.

"I can't wait for the execution," she said.

She chewed a bit of toast.

"It's all quite mysterious," Queen Sadhe, said suddenly to her husband. "I'm missing at least two hours of time – one minute I'm having a conversation with a delightful shoemaker, and the next instant, its mid-day, and my bottom hurts."

"Most peculiar," Prince Jalahad agreed. "But the royal wedding went off on schedule, so no harm done."

"Also," she said, "I've made inquiries and several other people have reported the same thing – missing time, and bottom hurting."

"My bottom hurts too," Jalahad replied quickly. "It is the strangest thing."

"Missing time as well?"

Jalahad hesitated.

"Yes," he said emphatically.

Whatever had happened to the Queen and others, he was quite sure it was unrelated to whatever had happened to him. In truth, he had no missing time. He had been aware of every second, even though he now wished he could forget it. He was hoping that perhaps heavy drinking might blur the memory.

"Also," she said, "I seem to have acquired a rather embarrassing fungus."

Jalahad did his best to look innocent.

The End

***

Drunk Slutty Elf, Page 229

A Note and More Books by the Author

If you've skipped to the end, looking for an apology, well... Sorry? Also, no refunds.

Thank you for taking the time out to read my little book. If you've made it all the way here, then I'm just going to assume you liked it.

What else do I have to offer? Well, I have another collection coming out, imaginatively titled Drunk Slutty Elf and Zombies, as well as a trilogy of collections of horror stories, another trilogy of collections of alternate history stories, a two part alternate history series, a fantasy murder mystery. For non-fiction, I have three kick ass Doctor Who Pirates histories, and LEXX Unauthorized, the chronicle of a cult sci fi series.

If you liked this, could I suggest you leave a review wherever you got it. Mention it on your blog, or your Facebook. Say nice things. If that's too much, just toss me a couple of stars. Writing is a solitary, lonely pursuit and actually getting some feedback or appreciation is a wonderful thing.

But there's more to it. It's about trying to get out there. There are a lot of people writing a lot of books, and it can get hard to get noticed. Reviews help.

And speaking of writing more....'
Check out my Website,

denvaldron.com
***

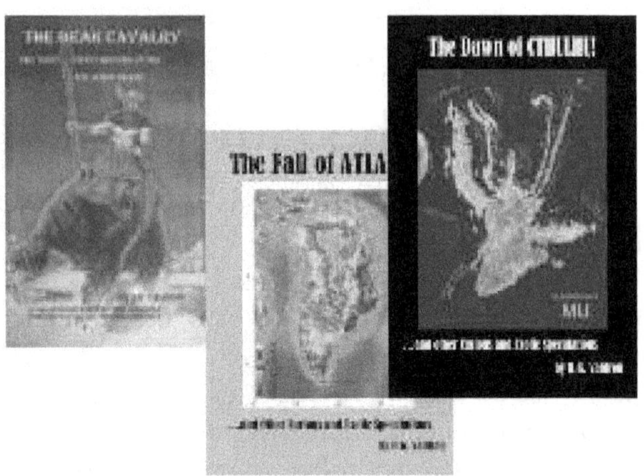

ALTERNATE REALITIES
A Trilogy or Strange New Worlds

The Dawn of Cthulhu - The Secret History of H.P.
Lovecraft's Cthulhu Cult; Lost Continents Found – real
and legendary; The Monsters of Sesame Street, is a light
hearted examination of Muppets as if they were actual
animals.

The Fall of Atlantis – Retroverse, An Accidental
Cinematic Universe of 50's Sci Fi movies, Greenland
Without the Ice, Rome Crosses the Atlantic, and the Rise
and Fall of Atlantis, an ecological catastrophe.

**The Bear Cavalry, the True (Not!) History of the
Icelandic Bears**, an off the wall, short novel about the
Viking domestication of bears, their evolution into a
medieval cavalry Bonus novelette, The Sharebear
Apocalypse.

HEARTS IN DARKNESS
A Trilogy of Horror Collections

Giant Monsters Sing Sad Songs – The connection between the author of the Necronomicon and a boy in Providence; a girl who meets the last Sasquatch, a poet who shares abandoned Tokyo with a Kaiju, and more…
What Devours Also Hungers – The unkillable killers in masks are recruited into the army, vampires and their hunters, clever serial killers, monsters, ghosts and more….
There Are No Doors in Dark Places – A childlike cancer that talks to its owner; A single mother drawn into dark magic; A man who turns into a different monster each night; a vampire that twists lives; a pregnant woman finding her body being stolen from her; and many more

AXIS OF ANDES
NEW WORLD WAR
A History of WWII in South America

Berlin, 1937, Adolph Hitler and his cabinet meet with a strange delegation from Ecuador. The delegates from the small South American nation beg for help, fearing an impending invasion from their rival, Peru. What happens at that meeting sets in motion a chain of events that lights the entire continent on fire. By the time it's done, millions are dead, nations are in ruins, and the map of Latin America will be changed beyond recognition.

The Pirate Histories!

What's a Pirate's History, you ask?

Well, there's the official, sanitized, orderly histories that are approved by and all about the powers that be.

Then there are the Pirate's histories, the things that they don't want you to know about, or that they don't care about, things that are great and marvellous and intriguing... but unapproved.

It's a history of secret and forgotten corners of the Whoniverse. The first woman Doctor, the first black Doctor, animations, audios, stage lays and fan films.

Drunk Slutty Elf, Page 234

A Dark Fantasy of Murder and Redemption

There's a City where all the races come together uneasily, descending into civil war.

There's a Mermaid, murdered cruelly her people distraught and crying out for justice.

There's an Orc, the lowest and the worst, her mission: Solve the murder, before it all comes crashing down.

She finds something else... the world's first serial killer.

Available only as an Audiobook

Drunk Slutty Elf, Page 235

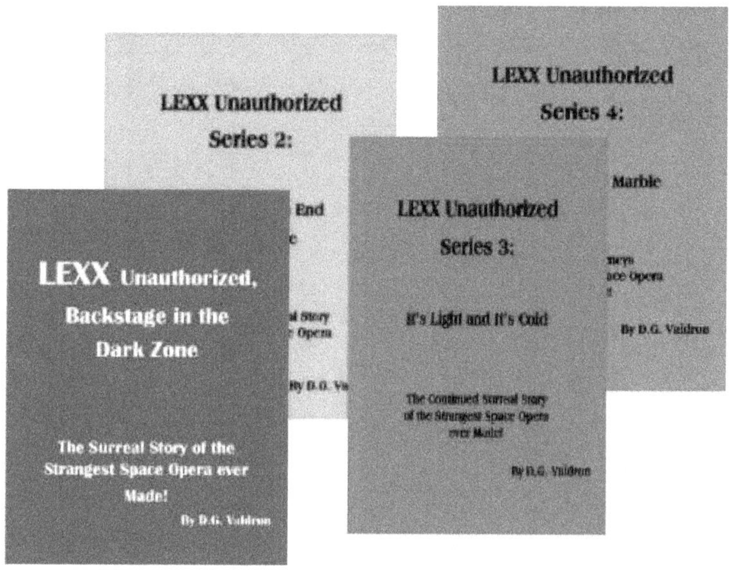

LEXX UNAUTHORIZED

LEXX Unauthorized about the making of a show about a giant space bug that blows up planets, the cowardly security guard who is its captain, and the undead assassin, runaway love slave, and robot head who form its crew.

Originally billed as 'Star Trek's Evil Twin,' the cultiest of cult sci fi, LEXX's forte was black humor, startling visuals, big ideas, and a sensibility that had more to do with surrealists like Jodorowsky or Bunuel than mainstream science fiction. And, as unconventional as it was onscreen, the story of how it came to be is even more bizarre.

Drunk Slutty Elf, Page 236

www.ingramcontent.com/pod-product-compliance
Lightning Source LLC
Chambersburg PA
CBHW061246210726

48293CB00003B/873